HOTEL MACABRE
VOL. 2

EDITED BY

JOE MYNHARDT

PUBLISHED BY CRYSTAL LAKE PUBLISHING
WHERE STORIES COME ALIVE!

Crystal Lake Publishing
www.CrystalLakePub.com

Follow us on Amazon:

WELCOME
TO ANOTHER

CRYSTAL LAKE PUBLISHING
CREATION

TABLE OF CONTENTS

"There must be something in books, things we can't imagine, to make a woman stay in a burning house."
—Fahrenheit 451, Ray Bradbury

INTRODUCTION

STORIES ARE ONE of the oldest gifts we share with one another. Especially the scary ones.

Long before books or screens, before ink or paper, humans gathered around fires to trade tales of wonder, fear, courage, and hope. No matter the century or the medium, storytelling remains the pulse of who we are, how we learn, how we connect, and how we discover ourselves in worlds both familiar and fantastical. Whether whispered, written, performed, or illustrated, stories help us make sense of the shadows and the light. It prepares us for even the most bizarre of situations.

Today, we're fortunate to live in an age where stories arrive in countless forms. Books invite us to vanish into other worlds for hours. Films cast their own spell through light, movement, and sound. Comic books blend art and narrative into something vibrant and visual, yet leaving lots of space for the reader's imagination. Poetry captures entire universes in a handful of lines, while live readings remind us that stories are meant to be heard as much as read, especially in the hands of a skilled performer. Each format unlocks a different door in the imagination, and each offers a new way for creators to reach readers, listeners, and dreamers of every kind. Dreamers who might one day go on to become creators themselves.

Anthologies like this one celebrate that rich diversity. Within these pages, you'll find authors whose voices span decades and genres, alongside rising talents whose words may become your new obsessions. This collection is both a showcase and an invitation. A chance to spend some time with storytellers you love and to take a chance on voices you've never heard before. These are the seeds of new nightmares, new journeys, and new inspirations.

JOE MYNHARDT

So open the doors of *Hotel Macabre Vol. 2*. Step inside. Wander its halls. Get lost a little—on purpose. Because inside these pages, you'll find creators at their boldest, stories at their most haunting, and a reminder of why we fell in love with stories in the first place.

Joe Mynhardt
19 November 2025

Joe Mynhardt stands as a paragon in the horror literary world, a Bram Stoker Award-winning South African publisher, editor, author, story coach, public speaker, and mentor with over a decade of experience. As the founder and CEO of Crystal Lake, Joe has transformed a humble 2012 startup into a multifaceted Intellectual Property powerhouse.

With a track record of working with and publishing works by luminaries such as Clive Barker, Stephen King, Charlaine Harris, Ramsey Campbell, John Connolly, Jack Ketchum, Jonathan Maberry, Christopher Golden, Graham Masterton, Damien Angelica Walters, Adam Nevill, Lisa Morton, Elizabeth Massie, Joe R. Lansdale, Edward Lee, Paul Tremblay, and Wes Craven, Joe is the quintessential mentor for aspiring authors. His deep industry insights and extensive network place him in a unique position to guide both new and seasoned writers in the genre.

Joe is also the author of the Shadows & Ink series, a guide to horror writing and publishing.

AH, MR. FARLES-CHORT, GREAT TO HAVE YOU BACK, AS YOU RECALL, I'M YOUR HOST, JASPER BARK. I HOPE YOU'LL ENJOY YOUR STAY AS MUCH AS LAST TIME.
I HAD A TERRIBLE TIME LAST TIME! EVEN WORSE THAN READING ONE OF YOUR BOOKS! I'VE VISITED FOUR TIMES AND IT'S ALWAYS LOUSY!
BUT I CAN'T UNDERSTAND WHY, YOU SAID ON TRIPADVISOR: "THE PLACE WAS SPOTLESS, THE STAFF HELPFUL AND THE FOOD DELICIOUS"
YET YOU GAVE US NO STARS.
OF COURSE I DID. JUST LIKE YOUR STORIES, HOTEL MACABRE IS FAMED FOR THE HIDEOUS FATES OF ITS GUESTS. ALL EXCEPT ME!
I WAS NEVER HAUNTED, NEVER MURDERED THERE WASN'T EVEN A RAIN OF FROGS! WHAT KIND OF SERVICE DO YOU CALL THAT?

ONE WORTH A LITTLE MORE THAN NO STARS! SPEAKING OF STARS, MAYBE THE FAULT ISN'T IN OUR STARS. MAYBE IT'S IN YOURS.
LUCKILY, WE HAVE AN IN-HOUSE ASTROLOGER, FOR MATTERS SUCH AS THIS.
MADAME LABAVSKY, THIS IS OUR GUEST, MR. FARLES-CHORT. HE NEEDS TO KNOW WHY HE'S NEVER HAD A BAD STAY WITH US.
KLONK!
I SEE STARS!
ACCORDING TO YOUR STAR CHART, YOU'RE BORN UNDER A PARTICULARLY LUCKY CONFIGURATION...
...NOTHING BAD WILL EVER HAPPEN TO YOU.
DAMMIT!!!
THERE'S ANOTHER ASTROLOGICAL EVENT I'VE BEEN MEANING TO DISCUSS WITH YOU FOR AGES NOW.
A GIANT METEORITE IS ABOUT TO HIT THE HOTEL!
NOW YOU THINK TO TELL ME!?!
TO BE CONTINUED ON THE LAST PAGE...

DON'T CRY FOR THE DEAD

Graham Masterton
& Karolina Mogielska

'TRAGIC,' SAID ROBERT'S SERGEANT, wiping his nose on a crumpled tissue. 'Poor young lad falling down the well like that, just because somebody couldn't be arsed to put a decent lid on it.'

Robert leaned reluctantly over the side of the well, looking down at the glittering black surface of the water ten metres below, as if he were peering into a freshly-dug grave. When he thought that nobody could see him, he spat down the well to rid himself of the horrible bitter taste in his mouth. Then he turned around and walked through the long grass to the black vinyl body bag in which they had zipped up the farmer's son after they had retrieved him from the well. They had found him jammed upside-down with his head under the water, so it had taken two firemen over three hours to extricate him.

What a shitty fate, Robert thought to himself as the bag was opened. *If he hadn't fallen headfirst, he might well have survived.*

As soon as the vinyl was peeled back and the boy's pale young face appeared, Robert regretted that he had asked to see him. The boy's eyes were plum-coloured and puffy, his lips tinged pale blue, and his hair was still bedraggled. On the right side of his head Robert noticed a deep Y-shaped laceration where he must have hit it on the bricks as he fell, with a dribble of blood that had been smudged by the cold well water.

The boy's elderly next-door neighbour was standing a little way away, his hands clasped as if he were silently praying. He had told Robert that the young lad's name was Grześ, short for Grzegorz.

Minutes. Seconds. Your whole fucking life is decided in the blink of an eye. One minute you're young and happy and don't have a care in the world. The next it's all gone, thrown away, and you're left with nothing but darkness, forever.

'Okay,' said Robert, nodding to the paramedics that they could zip up the body bag again. 'Damn! Fuck! I'll never understand those fucking peasants! As if it was too much like hard work to put a decent solid cover on their well.'

Robert gave the broken lid an angry kick. It was made of rotten wood with oilcloth stretched over it, and when he kicked it, it folded in half, the way it must have folded when young Grześ climbed onto it, like a trapdoor. A trapdoor down to hell, and the end of his life.

If only his father and mother had cared half as much for their family and the upkeep of their rundown farm as they cared for their home-distilled vodka, that small boy would be running through the meadows now with a slice of bread rather than lying dead in a stifling vinyl body bag. It was still the middle of the summer holidays and all his friends would be wearing T-shirts and swimming trunks, but within a few days, after his postmortem, Grześ would be wearing a short funeral jacket and holding a rosary in his hands. His chilly, lifeless hands.

Robert's heart was boiling with rage against the poor boy's parents, the drunken country bumpkins for whom their child's life seemed to be no more valuable than that of a pig or a rabbit. He couldn't count how many times he had been called out to local farms, because a child had been impaled on the merciless reel fingers of a combine harvester, or even disembowelled by the rasp bars which separated the grain from the chaff? How many times had he attended accidents in which children had been playing on top of high stacks of hay, only to fall onto the concrete barn floor below, fracturing their skulls or their spines? Or stood by watching paramedics tearfully giving up trying to resuscitate a small toddler who had choked on an unripe plum?

His pensive mood was interrupted by the appearance of an iridescent green fly which was already showing an interest in the interior of the body bag. For Robert, it was surprising that these creatures were sniffing around a dead human body even before it cooled, as if they were tiny vultures of the insect world. *I bet if they were bigger, they would devour you as soon as you breathed your last breath.*

DON'T CRY FOR THE DEAD

With a feeling of bitter satisfaction, he mashed another fat fly which had just landed on the lid of the well, and then another. Then he flicked their bodies down into the dark unforgiving hole in which Grześ had died.

There, you greedy bastards. See how you *like dying.*

Robert had to duck down when he entered the orange brick house; the door frame was at least two centimetres too low for a man of his height.

He was struck first of all by the pungent smells of cigarette smoke and alcohol and burned sausage and body odour, and by the sound of somebody noisily banging the cupboard doors in the kitchen.

The mother of the drowned boy was sitting on an old wooden bed with a frayed straw mattress, groggy from tranquilisers, her eyes unfocussed. She was 48 years old, with short blonde messy hair, but she was so tanned and wrinkled from working outdoors on the farm that she could have been mistaken for ten years older.

Over the bedhead hung a gigantic reproduction of Mary the Mother of God, holding a flowery heart in her hands. It was difficult to see the Virgin's face, because an elaborate spiderweb hung over one corner of the picture-frame, thick with dust, as if it hadn't been cleaned since it had first been nailed up there.

Robert sat down on the bed next to Grezś's mother. 'I hate to tell you this, Mrs Krystyna,' he said softly, 'but I have to ask you some questions. If and when you're ready, of course.'

In reality he felt no sympathy for this woman at all. The only person for whom he felt any sorrow was little Grześ. But it was professional procedure to be gentle.

She didn't answer. She didn't even turn her head to look at him. She continued to stare at the battered wooden wardrobe on the other side of the room as if she expected its doors to fly open and Grezś to come jumping out, shouting, 'Fooled you!'

'Mrs Krystyna?' Robert repeated. 'Mrs Krystyna?'

Her husband Romek came out of the kitchen with his mouth full, holding a half-eaten sausage and mushroom *kanapka*. He was stocky, unshaven, wearing filthy blue dungarees. With his snub nose and tiny eyes, Robert thought that he looked like an XL bully dog standing on its hind legs.

'Oh, come off it, officer. Can't you see that my wife's in shock?' he blurted out, trying to play the hero.

You want to be a hero? Too late, you rotten psubrat. Where were you when your son was drowning four metres underground in ice-cold well water?

'Krysia, you must eat,' said her friend Marianna, setting down a plate of steaming potatoes with a fried egg on top. 'You can't give Grześ his life back, no matter what you do.'

She picked up a spoon, scooped up a potato and held it in front of Krystyna's mouth as if she were feeding a child. At the same time, she glanced at the photograph of the delicately smiling little boy, hanging on the wall behind her in a gilded frame. Although she used to like little Gzreś, this photograph made her feel unaccountably anxious. He appeared to be sneering at her, rather than smiling, now that he was dead. She felt that he could see something in the kitchen behind her that didn't belong in our world, and that was why he was sneering. After all, he no longer belonged to our world, either, and maybe that was what enabled him to see it.

And maybe it wasn't a *something* that he could see, but a *someone*.

Marianna's eyes were red like Krysia's from lack of sleep. Since little Grześ had passed away, she had come every day to take care of her neighbour, because Romek made his living by working on their farm, and it was impossible for him to take any time off. They had two hectares of wheat and ten hectares of potatoes, as well as ten cows, fifty hens, and at least as many ducks, two geese, and a goat. They also owned a whole garden of apple, plum, and hazelnut trees, and blackcurrant bushes.

Apart from the fact that he needed to keep on working, Romek was a simple peasant who expected his life to be hard, because it always had been, right from the days when he had come home straight from school and had to dig up carrots until it grew dark. He was not the kind of man who was suited to give solace to his grieving wife.

Okay, we've lost Grześ, but we can have another child. All it takes is a man and a woman, right?

DON'T CRY FOR THE DEAD

Of course the death of his son was a sad event, but as the people in their village often used to say: *That's life. What can we do about it? All we can do is go on living.* Or—as it was written on little Grześ' gravestone—*God's will.*

'Krysia, for Christ's sake, you must eat something! Do you think Grześ would want you to starve yourself because of him?'

Marianna was a patient woman, but she was growing tired of this never-ending mourning. She dropped the spoon back on the plate and sat back in exasperation. Krysia didn't even seem to hear her, but was staring with that unfocussed look at the world outside the window. It was beginning to rain, and it made a prickling sound against the glass.

How many times did I ask Romek to make a decent lid for the well? I could have made one myself. I should have warned Grześ that it wasn't safe. Was he suffering much? I bet he was. I bet he was wondering why his mother didn't come to rescue him when he was lying upside- down in the dark abyss of that well. Was he frightened? He must have been terrified. I bet his little heart was thudding in his chest like a sparrow trying to tear itself away from a cat's claws, still having those dying sparkles of hope for surviving. Did he know that he was dying? Was he aware that he would not be sitting with us for supper this evening, nor any other evening, ever again? He never could have realised that he would be lying instead in the hospital mortuary waiting for a postmortem, and that the headline in the local paper this week would be Ten-year-old Boy Drowns in Well, *and that boy would be him.*

Tears began to slide down her cheeks. *How did that happen? I only sent him to close the chicken coop. Why did he go to the well? If only I had gone to take care of the hens myself. If only.*

She was shaken out of her reverie by Marianna, who was gripping her shoulders and shouting at her.

'Krystyna! You need to stop thinking about Grześ! Nothing is going to bring him back! You have to worry about yourself now! If you go on grieving like this, it will only make you ill!'

Krystyna said nothing, although she lifted her hand to acknowledge what Marianna had said to her.

'Let me make us some camomile tea,' said Marianna. 'That will make you feel calmer.' But as soon as she had gone through to the kitchen to put on the kettle, Krystyna returned to her grim thoughts about Grześ.

You should have lived, my darling boy. You should have been here now. Only a few seconds decided your fate. If only you could come back. If only I could turn back the clock. If only merciful God could stave off that bad luck. My little son, please, come back. I'm begging you, with all my heart and soul! I cannot live without you. Come back!

After Sunday Mass, Romek was the last member of the congregation to leave the tiny church, Mother of God Queen of the World. As he came out onto the porch he paused; it was raining, and it was then that he felt a light touch on his shoulder.

It was Jurek the organist, Marianna's husband, breathless and bald with half-glasses perched on the very tip of his nose.

'Romek? I'm sorry to be personal, but my Marianna's very concerned about your wife. We really think that you should have a word with her.'

'What's this all about, Jurek? You of all people know that we lost our son. That's not something you can get over in five minutes.'

'Of course, Romek, surely. But Krystyna's mourning has been going on for nearly three months now. And it's still so intensive. Marianna says she's crying every time she goes round to help her, and she's crying whenever I meet her, too. In fact, she's flooded with tears no matter where she is. In the street, in a shop, even when she's driving your cows into the meadow. She's not in church today, is she? I'm sure she doesn't come to Mass any more because she's always sobbing out loud. And I dread to think what she's like at home, behind closed doors.'

Jurek bit his lip. He was clearly embarrassed, but Romek guessed that he had been instructed by Marianna to talk to him about Krystyna's never-ending grief.

'Please, Romek, she can't go on like this. Talk to her before she ends up with a serious mental illness. Or take her to see Doctor Nowicki. Mourning like this can only lead to something bad.'

'Something bad? You don't think that Grześ dying and my wife being in such a miserable state about it, that isn't bad enough already?'

'There are things in this world much worse than death, Romek.'

'Oi, Mister Busybody, you listen to me. I thank you for taking an interest, but it's been hard enough without anybody giving us advice that we didn't ask for.'

'But there is evil all around us, Romek! Evil that only waits to be woken up! God is not always watching over us, especially when we turn our hearts away from Him. And Krysia's endless mourning is such a manifestation of turning her back on God. God is there to comfort her, but she's rejecting His comfort.'

'Oh, get real.'

'Romek, please listen to me. I've been playing the organ at this church for nearly twenty years, and I've seen the way that God works, over and over again. He's like a father, protective but not always tolerant. Grześ passed away because it was God's plan. We have no way of understanding it, of course, but it was His plan.'

'He fell down the fucking well, Jurek. That's all.'

'Yes. And I know that as parents we should be the ones who are buried by our children, rather than vice versa, but for some reason God called your son. Maybe little Grześ was more needed in heaven, rather than here, who knows? He was the sweetest of boys, after all. Or maybe God was teaching you a lesson.'

'Excuse me?' snapped Romek. 'God was teaching *me* a lesson? I hope I misheard you then! I think you'd better shut your trap before I get really angry!'

'*Romek—*!' Jurek began, but Romek roughly pushed past him and stalked off between the gravestones, in the rain. Soon he disappeared behind the trees, following the wild path that led through the meadows to his house.

The organist stood watching him until he was out of sight. He felt bruised, as if he had been in a stupid meaningless scuffle, and lost it. Turning around, he went back into the church to extinguish the candles that were still burning after Mass. As he approached the altar, however, he heard the softest of whistles, and a sudden chilly breeze blew through the church. All the candles were snuffed out by themselves, and ribbons of smoke coiled up past the stained-glass window.

Jurek shivered. *Something is coming. Something like a storm. Something more terrible than a storm. I can sense it.*

He raised his eyes to the figure of Jesus hanging on the giant wooden cross.

'Merciful God,' he whispered. 'Whatever it is, please protect us.'

'I don't think those gravediggers made a proper job of Grześ' grave,' said Romek, rubbing his filthy hands together under the kitchen tap. 'When I went to the cemetery this morning, I saw that there's a small hole by one side of it. It's not the work of a mole or a dog or anything like that.'

Krystyna was lying on the bed in her clothes, staring at the plain wall. *It was my little Grzesio who helped me to whitewash these walls. Winter will be here before we know it, and my poor little Grzesio is lying in his grave now, cold and lonely.*

'Krystyna, are you listening to me?' said Romek, coming out of the kitchen. He visited the cemetery as seldom as he could, but in the weeks after the funeral Krystyna had been spending all day beside Grześ's grave, sobbing, and eventually he had insisted that she should stay at home, and that he would keep the grass cut and the candles lit. Still, he didn't know which was worse—her crying in the cemetery from morning till night, or her crying at home.

It was late morning in early September. The sun had been shining, but now a storm cloud rolled over it and the world suddenly became dark.

Krysia was sitting at home alone drinking her fifth coffee, which she had topped up with vodka to numb the constant pain which was still tearing her apart. She was about to fill up her cup once more when she heard a faint knocking at the heavy oak front door.

It was so faint that she was not at all sure that she had heard it at all, especially since the vodka had made her feel dazed and slightly unreal, and so she sat and waited to hear it repeated.

If anyone was knocking, they didn't knock a second time, but then a whisper touched her ears as softly as a late-summer breeze. '*Mummy?*'

No, she thought. *It's the vodka. It's only my imagination.*

But then she heard the whisper again. '*Mummy?*' and she shivered in the same way she used to shiver on summer days when she climbed out of the chilly farm pond. The pond where she used to take Grześ, when they played together.

She stood up and pushed back her chair. The vodka and the Relanium tranquiliser she was taking made her feel that she was viewing the world through thick window glass.

'*Mummy?*' the whispering persisted. '*Mummy?*'

It sounded so much like her little Greszio, but even though she was drugged and half-drunk, her common sense told her that it was impossible. She made her way unsteadily to the front door and opened it. When she saw who was standing on the porch, though, her knees almost gave way under her.

There was her beloved son, his face pale and blueish, his suit muddy, his eyes puffy and plum-coloured.

'*Mummy,*' he said. '*I can't get to sleep.*' His voice had a strange vibrancy to it, as if he were talking through a harmonica.

'Grześ? Is that really you? It's really you! How is that possible?'

'*Mamusiu nie mogę spać. I can't get to sleep, Mummy. I'm so tired.*'

Krysia stumbled onto the porch, wrapped her arms around him and lifted him off his feet. He was stone cold and his suit was damp. He smelled like chicken that had gone bad, but he was Grześ, he was really Grześ, and he had come back to her.

She carried him into the cottage. His arms and legs hung down stiffly and his head tilted back, his eyes staring at her without blinking. She laid him down on her bed and tucked him up in the thick patchwork quilt.

'There, my darling,' she told him. 'Now you can sleep. And when you have slept, we can change you and wash you and you can start to live your life all over again.'

When she went to close the front door, she heard a deep baleful growl somewhere in the distance. The sun had reappeared from behind the clouds, but a storm was coming.

'Romek! Romek! Grześ is alive! Grześ is alive!'

Krystyna was running through the fields, flinging her arms about like a lunatic. Three of her neighbours were digging up potatoes, and they stood up and looked at her with pity.

'She's drunk again, isn't she?' said one of them, leaning on her rusty hoe and shaking her head. 'She's been mourning so much it's driven her stark raving mad.'

Krystyna found Romek in the next field, trying to get his tractor to start.

'Romek! Grześ is alive! He's come back!'

'What?' said Romek. He dropped his spanner onto the ground, took hold of her shoulders and shook her. 'What are you blathering about? What's it all about this time? For Christ's sake, you're pissed again, aren't you?'

'He's alive! He came back! He came back!' Krystyna repeated in a frenzy. 'It was a mistake, him being dead! He's still alive! The doctors made a mistake!'

'Krysia, we buried Grzesio over three months ago! Calm down before people start saying that you've gone crazy!'

Two of Romek's young farmhands were standing not far away, ankle deep in beetroot leaves, and they were staring at Krystyna with their mouths open.

'Come back home and see for yourself!' Krystyna insisted, tugging at his sleeve. 'He came back, I swear to you!'

Romek looked over at the two young farmhands and shrugged. He wanted to avoid making a fool of Krystyna in front of them, and so he followed her reluctantly back across the fields, giving a half-hearted wave to the potato-diggers as he passed them by. He could see by the expressions on their faces what they were thinking.

When they entered the house, they were met by an overwhelming silence, as if they were deaf. It was the same silence that haunts every house where a child's laughter could be heard in the days before they died. Specks of dust were dancing in the rays of the late summer sun that shone through the sheer lace curtains. Krystyna's coffee cup lay on its side in its saucer, next to the half-empty vodka bottle. On the bed, the patchwork quilt was still folded over in a triangle, the way it had been before Krystyna had wrapped up Grześ and told him to sleep.

'He's alive. He came to the door. He told me that he couldn't sleep.'

'Krysia, Grzesio isn't here. He's dead.'

At the same time as he was trying to talk some sense into her, Romek was glancing around the house, as if he had the tiniest hope in the back of his mind that by means of some miracle, Grzesio really *was* still alive. He even went into the kitchen and opened the larder to take a look inside.

'You have to go to the doctor, Krysia. We can't go on like this any longer.'

DON'T CRY FOR THE DEAD

Krystyna sat down on the bed and started to sob, and Romek stood beside her, at a complete loss to know what to do. It was no good shouting at her for mourning their son, but it was no good hugging her, either. She was inconsolable.

Because he was focussed on Krysia and exhausted by all the weeks of her mourning, he failed to notice three muddy footprints on the wooden floor. They led from the side of the bed to the rickety stairs that went up to their attic.

He did hear the storm growling, though, and he knew that he would be spending the rest of the day ploughing the beet field in the pouring rain, only to return to more tears.

'Romek, are you going to the cemetery today?' asked Krysia, putting down her cup of strong coffee. It was six o'clock the next morning but her eyes were already red and her eyelashes were sparkling with tears.

Romek put down his fork. 'Krysia, please. Don't even start.'

'I wanted you to take this rosary and lay it on his grave.'

Romek pushed away his breakfast plate with its half-finished scrambled eggs and stood up.

'I won't have time to go today, Krysia. I may not go there ever again, if you're going to carry on like this.'

With that, he zipped up his anorak and left the house without another word. As he went out through the garden gate, he saw Marianna coming through the trees to see Krystyna. She called out to him, but he ignored her and carried on walking. Because he didn't stop to find out what she wanted, she couldn't tell him what Jurek had seen that morning on his way to the church. It looked as if someone or something had been digging up Grześ's grave again.

When he returned home that evening, Romek was pleasantly surprised to find that the house was quiet and warm and that there was an appetising smell of roasting chicken. Krystyna was in the small side room where Grześ used to sleep, and she was changing the bedding. As she folded the sheets, she was humming a strange melody that he had never heard her humming before.

He went to the bedroom door, and she turned and smiled at him. He could see that she was no longer crying, although her eyes were still red, as if she hadn't slept. He decided not to ask her how she was feeling or what peculiar song she was singing. If she had accepted the loss of Grześ at last and serenity had returned to their house, then it was worth the price of his silence.

In the days that followed that evening, she no longer wept and moaned, but her behaviour became increasingly odd, as if she had accepted Grześ' death by believing that he was still amongst the living. Romek could only hope that she had stopped drinking in secret. Every evening at suppertime, she prepared much more food than usual, and afterwards he would find most of it in the waste bin. He hated to see good food being thrown away, but he still said nothing about it. The serenity that had returned to their house was more than worth it.

He didn't even react when Krystyna returned from the local fair and he caught her hiding children's clothes in the back of their wardrobe—two T-shirts and a pair of shorts. And he pretended to be asleep when he heard her at night singing strange songs and lullabies in Grześ room, or reading fairy tales out loud. Some of the stories were scary, and some of them seemed to make no sense at all. He wasn't a book lover, but he remembered some of the stories from his childhood, like *Hansel and Gretel* and *Little Red Riding Hood*, and from what he could hear, Krystyna was distorting each of those stories to make them even more disturbing.

When the Witch locked Hansel into the cage, Małgosia became her favourite. They baked the best cookies together to fatten Hansel up and then the Witch was saying 'It is only for you, my dearest Gretel, to make you beautiful and ruddy forever!' And then she led her to the cage where the plump Hansel was trapped. His flesh was bulging between the merciless grids and Gretel started to bite his skin and eat, eat, eat and drink, drink, drink. . . The more flesh she ate and the more blood she drank, the more ruddy and beautiful she became.

Although Krystyna's versions of these stories were so chilling and bloodthirsty, Romek reassured himself that everyone mourned in a different way, especially after a loss as painful as Grześ. He wondered some nights if Krystyna hadn't tipped over the edge into madness, but after three months of endless crying the peace in the house was such a blessing for him that he dismissed that thought as soon as it crept into his mind.

He had no way of knowing that her behaviour was very far from being a blessing.

'Krysia, have you seen that little Grześ's grave has been dug up again? There's a hole so big you can see the lid of his coffin.'

It was her neighbour Janusowa, an elderly woman with a thin grey bun on the top of her head. 'I saw it this morning when I went to light a candle on Bartek's grave. You need to call the gravediggers to fix it. You can't let it stay like that, can you?'

Krystyna turned and stared at her neighbour. Her eyes were still bloodshot and for a split second Janusowa thought that nobody had ever looked at her with such hostility. But almost as quickly the hostility melted and Krysia smiled and nodded.

'Yes, we're quite aware of that, Janusowa,' she told her, although the tone of her voice made it clear that she didn't really want to talk about it. 'We've reported it to the gravediggers already.'

'Very well, then. It just doesn't look good, that's all. The dead should be separated from the living, for ever. That is why we have funerals, isn't it? That is why we bury them. Of course we want to remember the dead, but we don't actually want to see them again.'

Janusowa hobbled off, without seeing that Krystyna's lips were tightly pursed and that she was staring at her with as much hostility as she had before.

We don't actually want to see them again?

'Krysia, when was the last time you went to see Grześ' grave?' Romek demanded, as soon as he came in through the front door. 'I thought you told the gravediggers to fix it.'

'I did,' said Krystyna, without looking up at him. Her voice sounded blurry, as if she had taken drugs.

'Well, if they did, it's been dug up again, almost all the way down. You need to tell them again.'

'He only wants to be closer to us,' Krystyna whispered, her words barely audible. 'Closer to *me*.'

'What did you say?'

'Never mind. It wasn't important,' she said. She turned around and looked across at Grześ's portrait hanging on the wall. Maybe it was the reflected light from the television, but this evening his face appeared to be more unhealthy, a pale bluish colour, as if he had been dead even longer.

Romek sat down at the kitchen table and took a swig of Żywiec beer as Krystyna set down a plate in front of him with a chicken leg and cabbage and boiled potatoes.

When he cut into the chicken leg, however, he saw that it was almost raw—still slimy and oozing blood. It was as much as he could do to stop himself from retching, and he picked up the leg and brandished it at her.

'Look at the fucking state of this! Did you even show it to the oven?'

Krystyna simply stared at him as if he were speaking a foreign language.

'Have you totally forgotten how to cook?' he asked her. 'That bacon you gave me for breakfast could have come straight off the pig without even saying hallo to a frying-pan. And you never eat dinner with me these days. Are you trying to poison me, or what?'

'No, Romek, no,' said Krystyna, in that haunted whisper. 'It's nothing to do with you.'

After midnight, when Romek was snoring, Krystyna went into Grześ's room and sat down on the bed. 'Little son of mine?' she whispered in a voice that was tired to the edges. She smoothed the quilt with her wrinkled hand. 'Little Grześ?'

The new clothes she had bought for her son were still hanging on the back of the old chair—a Ninja Turtles T-shirt and a pair of bright orange shorts. They were similar to the shorts that Grześ had been wearing on the day he fell down the well, and it was thanks to their bright colour he had been found so quickly in the darkness. But not quickly enough to save him.

'Little Grześ?' she whispered again, and a single tear slid down her cheek. She raised her eyes to the ceiling, with its heavy wooden beams, and stared at it as if she could see right through it to the dark suffocating space above.

As if her beloved little Grzesio was in the attic.

DON'T CRY FOR THE DEAD

The next morning, as soon as Romek entered the chicken coop with a plastic bucket full of feed, he was greeted by the hens cackling all around him, fluttering in panic as if they wanted to run away.

Almost at once he saw why. Three hens were lying dead on the straw, each of them with bite-marks in their necks, their feathered crests soaked in blood.

That fox again. Or maybe that weasel. Romek spat into the straw in annoyance. *I need to seal every gap around this coop before that fucking monster finishes them all off.* He had constructed this makeshift poultry house out of part of the rundown cowshed, and only last week he had caught a weasel trying to dig its way in.

He was about to start scattering the chicken feed when he heard a high-pitched screaming from the house next door.

'Oh my God! Oh my dear God! Mietek is dead! Mietek is dead!'

He looked out through the cowshed doors and saw old Janusowa running towards the village, sobbing in despair.

'They killed him! They killed him! He's dead!'

Romek dropped the bucket amongst the hens and hurried out of the chicken coop, pausing only to latch it behind him. He couldn't believe how fast Janusowa was running for an 85-year-old woman, and he had to gallop to catch up with her. He reached her only as she arrived at the moss-covered fence outside the presbytery. Franek the priest appeared in the doorway, obviously alarmed by her screaming, along with Jurek the organist who was visiting him for morning coffee.

'God bless you, Janusowa. What's happened?' said the priest, raising his arms like the Pope blessing his crowds.

'They killed Mietek! He's dead!' Janusowa sobbed, leaning against the fence for support. 'After breakfast I went to feed the goats, but when I came back—'

'Dead? Are you sure?'

Even though he was wearing only slippers on his feet, the priest came out and took Janusowa in his arms.

'Come on, my dear. Let's go to your house and take a look.'

Together, hurriedly, as silently as mourners, the priest and Janusowa and Jurek and Romek made their way to Janusowa's house on the hill, the last house in the village. It was more of a shack than a house, nearly a hundred years old, with a sagging roof. Janusowa had left the heavy oak doors half open, but the priest pushed them wider. He was struck at once by a strong revolting odour, as if someone had left the house a week ago in the middle of making broth, forgetting about the raw chicken meat that was still lying on the kitchen counter. It was combined with an even more putrid smell, as if a dead tomcat was trapped behind the sofa or stuck inside the old wardrobe.

'Oh my dear God, what *stinks* so much?' said Franek, as if he had forgotten for a moment that he was a priest. He covered his mouth and his nostrils with the sleeve of his cassock and stepped cautiously into the hallway. Jurek and Romek followed him, although Janusowa stayed outside in the front garden.

When the three of them crowded into the tiny living-room, they saw Mietek Janus lying on the faded red Persian rug. His wrinkled face had turned pale yellowish, like crumpled-up sandwich paper, and the odour around him reminded Franek of a corpse that had already started to decompose, even though it was only two or three hours ago that Mietek and his wife Józefa had been drinking morning coffee together.

Thin streams of dried blood had run out of his ears, and his eyes were wide open, as if in fright, but they had both become engorged by dark violet blood, the colour of two shining bruises. Blood had poured out of his mouth and clotted on his chin. Both his fists were clenched in a boxing gesture of defence.

Romek said, 'Jesus,' and cupped his hand over his nose, although it did nothing to block out the stench of death. Franek crouched down beside Mietek's body and made the sign of the cross, reciting a muffled prayer of absolution through his sleeve.

When he had finished praying, all three of them stood looking down at the gruesome sight on the floor, too shocked to speak or even to call the police, as if they knew that even God in person couldn't have spared Mietek from the agony that he must have suffered.

It was two days later, early morning, so that it was still dark, and it was raining again. Jurek came into the kitchen shaking his head as if he couldn't believe how everything in his life could go so disastrously wrong.

'Mania, some kind of creature broke into the chicken house last night and killed five more of our hens. That's the third time in only one week!'

He picked up the towel that Mania had hung to dry on the kitchen stove, mopping his hands and then the back of his neck.

'Jurek! Don't wipe blood on that towel! I've just washed it!'

'Blood? Those poor things had no blood at all! Drained to the last drop, as they say. Only two small holes in their necks where something had bitten them. Maybe it's a weasel. Romek thought his chickens had probably been killed by a weasel.'

Jurek took a tinted glass out of the cupboard, picked up the tiny porcelain pot from the stove and filled the glass with a strong brew of tea. He diluted the brew with hot water and then he sat down at the table and took a noisy sip of it. Mania dragged out a chair and sat beside him.

'Don't you think it's strange, Jurek, that those weasels have been so active lately? We haven't had any problems with them for two years at least, have we?'

'Bad things always come in threes, Mania. First little Grześ, falling down the well. Then Mietek. And now these weasels, killing all our chickens.'

'But do you really believe it was weasels? What about poor Mietek? Are you going to tell me that some monster weasel killed him, as well?'

She wasn't joking. Her voice was shaking and it was clear to Jurek that she was seriously frightened.

'Mania, don't even start with your wild fantasies, please,' he told her. He reached into the breast pocket of his checkered shirt and took out his pipe, which was probably as old as him. He stuffed tobacco into it and then gripped it with a click between his dentures. 'Mietek had a haemorrhage, that's all. Everybody knew how much he liked the hard stuff.'

'You promised not to smoke!' Mania told him. 'You remember what your doctor said! You want to leave me here alone? What if they come back?'

'Oh come on, Mania! It's past! Stop torturing yourself with that again. They've gone and they won't come back.'

All the same, the look on his face seemed to say something

completely different. *Let's pray to almighty God not to let them come again.*

Romek hammered on the front door of the gravediggers' cottage. Adam the gravedigger appeared, his shirt hanging out, his hair messed up, blinking at Romek as if he had just woken up.

'Don't you clowns know how to dig a grave or what?' Romek shouted at him. 'If you can't, go and do something simple for a living, like picking mushrooms or sweeping the streets. Do you want me to lodge an official complaint about you? Jesus!'

Adam's old father Andrzej appeared behind him, smoking a cigarette, and looking even scruffier than Adam.

'What's all this noise about?'

'Do you honestly need to ask?' Romek demanded. 'Haven't you seen that little Grześ' grave has been dug up again? Don't you think it's hard enough, having your own son lying in the cemetery, without his coffin reappearing every few days! You'd better fix it as soon as you can, or else we'll be talking in a different way, believe me!'

With that, he reached out, seized the doorhandle, and slammed the door with a bang in the gravediggers' faces.

'I don't know what the hell is wrong with this grave,' said Adam, leaning against the stone angel that guarded the neighbouring grave and taking a swig of rye vodka straight out of the bottle. 'Is it cursed, or what? We've fixed it over and over, and each time we come here, it's been dug up again! I'm ready to think that every night, this boy digs his way out of it!'

'Don't talk bullshit, Adaśko, and move your arse,' said his father. 'This work won't be done on its own. Otherwise that farmer will be chasing us with his four-pronged fork and we'll be out of a job again.'

Andrzej had already started to shovel soil into the deep hole beside the thick granite slab that covered Grześ's grave. He climbed into the hole to tread the soil flat. A vice-like force gripped his boots and dragged him downwards, right to his knees.

'What the fuck?' he said as he looked up at Adam. He thought at first that the soil had simply collapsed, but before he could start to lift himself out of the hole, he was pulled down even further and faster, as if he were being eaten alive. His body was crushed against the side of the coverstone with a crackling sound of bones that Adam would never forget for the rest of his life.

Adam tossed aside his vodka bottle and jumped down on top of the grave, but he was too late. The last he saw of his father was his face staring up at him like a martyr as his right cheek was scraped against the granite, and then Andrzej was swallowed up before he even had time to scream, with no trace left of him but bloody shreds of skin and a few tangled grey hairs.

'*Dad!*' screamed Adam. '*Dad!*'

He scrabbled in the damp soil with his bare hands, hoping desperately that he would be able to dig out his father alive, but Andrzej was gone. After a while he stopped digging, but stayed where he was, kneeling on Grześ's grave, looking up at the slowly-moving clouds as if he were expecting some explanation from God, too shocked and grief-stricken even to cry.

'Krysia, what the hell are you doing up in the attic for so long?' Romek called out. Then, without waiting for an answer, he started to climb the narrow stairs to the loft, which they used only for storing anything for which they had no more use, like a black-and-white television set or a suitcase that had lost its handle.

When he reached the top of the stairs, he saw Krysia sitting at the far end of the attic, leaning over something that he was unable to see. She was gently swinging from side to side and murmuring a strange melody, as if she were rocking a baby to sleep.

It was dark and dusty in the attic, lit only by a few thin rays of sunshine that broke through the narrow gaps between the roof tiles. Romek was not unduly disturbed, because Krysia had been spending a lot of time by herself lately, singing those peculiar songs, and as long as she had stopped crying all the time and cooked him decent suppers when he came back from working on the farm, he was ready to accept whatever kept her calm.

It was only when he made his way across the attic that he almost felt his heart stop. He could see now that she was holding their son in her arms. The dead son who they had buried in the cemetery.

At first, Romek was too shocked to speak. Their little Grześ's face was puffed-up and mottled yellow and blue, with dark purple bruises. His eyes were closed but he was tightly clutching Krystyna's hand as if he were aware that she was there. Romek could see that his fingers were dirty, with soil behind his nails. His hair and his burial suit were grimy, too, as if he had dug himself out of the wet ground. What struck Romek the most, though, was his unbearable odour, even more pungent than Mietek's body had been.

At last he managed to whisper 'K-Krysia?' covering his mouth and his nose with his work-worn hand. Since his early childhood he had always been tough as a stone, but now he felt like a whimpering runt of a puppy that was about to be drowned. He felt the half-digested sausage that he had eaten for lunch rising in his throat. He simply couldn't accept what he was looking at. Grześ had been dead for nearly three months now, so what he could see contradicted all the laws of biology, physics, and sanity. Even the laws of God.

'K-Krysia?' he repeated, swallowing the bile that had flooded his mouth, but Krysia seemed not to hear him. Still gently rocking the boy who used to be their living son, she kissed his waxy forehead, oblivious to the smell that was oozing out of him.

Romek was about to lay his hand on his wife's shoulder when he saw that his son's hair was thick with a glistening swirl of grubs. One of them had been left on Krysia's upper lip when she kissed him and it was furiously wriggling at having been torn apart from its feeding ground. Romek vomited noisily, so that half-chewed sausage splattered on the attic floor, and that made Krystyna turn around.

'Romek? What are you doing here?' she shrilled, clutching Grześ' floppy body close to her chest as if she were afraid that he would be taken away from her a second time. 'I said, what are you doing here?'

Romek had never heard her speak to him like that before—her voice harsh and hostile as if she would do anything to protect her child.

'Krysia—I—what are you—what's going on here? Krysia? Who is he? He looks like our son!'

'Because he *is* our son, Romek! I told you that he came back but you didn't want to listen! Everyone said that I was crazy or that I was drunk! But no, Romek, merciful God listened to my prayers and returned my beloved little Grześ to me!'

'Krystyna, Grześ has been dead for nearly three months. So that's why I'm asking you who is it? And why is he in such a state? Look at him, he's filthy, and he stinks to high heaven!'

'Romek, he's our son! Our son, who has come back to us from the nether world!'

That evening, just as the sun was going down behind the trees, Janusowa entered her barn to feed her old horse Chestnut with a forkful of hay. He was over thirty now, but she had kept him because she was so fond of him and had never had the heart to give him to the slaughterhouse.

She was struck by the unnatural silence in the barn, and she stood for a moment looking at the specks of dust dancing in the last rays of sunshine and breathing in the aroma of horse and hay. She closed her eyes, still numb from losing Mietek so horribly. She knew that tomorrow she would start to feel the raw agony of grief, but what she needed right now was a deep sense of peace.

It was then, though, that she heard a rustling sound, and when she opened her eyes she thought she saw something moving quickly across the opposite end of the barn, although when she turned around there was nothing and nobody there. All the same, it had frightened her, and her heart was beating fast and hard.

She backed out of the barn and hurried back to her house without looking behind her, ignoring Chestnut who was neighing for his food. Neither she nor Chestnut had seen the blurred outline of a child in the darkness at the end of the barn, a child so pale that he looked as if he had been drained of blood.

It was nearly five-thirty in the morning. Romek and Krystyna hadn't been able to think about sleeping and they hadn't spoken for hours. Romek had brewed them each a mug of coffee but neither of them had touched it and it had gone stone cold. Now they were still sitting in silence at the kitchen table.

At last, as the clock chimed the half-hour, Krystyna looked across at Romek and said, 'You can't tell anyone about Grześ.'

'Krysia, Grześ is dead! Whatever that is, up in the attic, it's not our son. It's impossible! Do you hear what I'm saying to you? Our son is dead!'

'Romek, you don't understand anything, do you? If he's not our son, then who is he?'

'I'm not sure I want to know, for God's sake. Can't you see what he *looks* like? How he *smells* like?'

'Stop it! That's enough!' Krystyna stood up and thumped the table so hard with her fist that her coffee splashed out of her mug. 'You shouldn't say things like that about Grześ. You've no right! Especially when God has gifted you with such a—such a *miracle*. Because it *is* a miracle. I got my son back!'

With that, she started to cry. Romek stood up too and reached out an arm to try and console her, but she pushed him away. Taking her coat down from the peg beside the door, she left the house and disappeared into the pre-dawn darkness.

Romek didn't try to go after her. Instead, he stood in the kitchen, staring up at the ceiling. He was sure he could smell that boy, whoever he was, even down here.

Something's coming this way, he thought, *I don't know what it is yet, but I have such a strong feeling that when it shows up, I'm going to feel like the floor's opened up underneath me.*

Mania was standing in the line that morning for the local bread van when her neighbour Agata came bustling up in her flouncy dress and her floral babushka headscarf. She was carrying her usual two wicker baskets, one of which contained her shopping, and the other her Pomeranian puppy Kosmaty.

'Have you heard, Mania? Janusowa's horse broke its tether last night and ran away into the fields. They found it at dawn, lying by the pond next to officer Cytryna's house. It had drowned, can you believe that, even though only its head was under the water.'

'Oh dear God,' said Mania. She disliked queuing for her morning bread, but her back was too painful these days to bake her own bread in her own cosy kitchen. The only compensation was that she got to hear all the local gossip.

'But what's even stranger than that, Mania,' said Agata, ruffling Kosmaty's ears, 'Andrzej has gone missing! Yes—that old gravedigger. From what I hear he was fixing a hole next to young Grześ' grave with his son Adam when he vanished. Can you imagine that Adam is claiming that his father fell down the hole!

She started to cackle. 'He enjoys a drink or two when he's digging, Adam, so we can only think that he was *narąbany* or else he's gone cuckoo. Or maybe both. That family were always a bit on the mental side.

'The men searched around the pond, because they thought that Andrzej might have stolen Janusowa's horse, but they found nothing. Nothing at all,' she repeated, still cackling. 'It's like something out of a comedy show!'

Mania started to sway. She could hear Agata talking to her, but she sounded as if she were somewhere far in the distance, and she felt as if her knees were going to give way.

'Mania?' said Agata. 'Mania, what's wrong?'

'I'm okay, I'm okay,' Mania told her, leaning one hand against the side of the bread van. 'Something made me feel dizzy for a moment, that's all. I think it's because I haven't been able to sleep recently. There's something strange in the air, although I don't know what it is. Haven't you felt it yourself?'

'I know what you mean. Kosmaty's been very nervous. He won't go out unless I take him. He's never been like that before.'

They had almost reached the end of the queue when a noisy old car pulled up behind the bread van and the driver climbed out. It was Michał Cytryna, the retired police officer. He came up to the serving hatch and was looking grim.

'Michał, what's wrong?' asked Agata.

'I thought you all ought to know that we found Andrzej, the gravedigger. He's dead.'

'You're serious? Andrzej?"

'I'm afraid it's true. He's dead, although I can't go into too much detail right now.'

However, the expression on his face told another story, as if his discovery had appalled him beyond any description, and he was simply too shocked to describe it.

'How did he die? You must tell us!' Agata insisted. 'I have known Andrzej for longer than I can remember!'

'Yes, please tell us,' said Mania, although she was still feeling swimmy. 'We're going to find out sooner or later, after all.'

Michał shrugged his shoulders. 'Well, if you're really sure you want me to.' He took a deep breath, and then he said, 'We did find some evidence on the side of Gregorz's grave. Some blood, and skin, and a few grey hairs. But those were only on the right-hand edge of the coverstone, and the hole was far too narrow for Andrzej to have fallen down there, like Adam tried to suggest, so none of us thought of searching down it. I mean, only a skinny cat could have disappeared down a hole as tight as that.

'It was Krzysztof's dog who found him. He was lying in that field behind the shrine at the end of the village. Or shall I say what remained of him, because he was mostly bones, his skeleton I mean, and they were only held together with strings of skin and flesh.

He took another deep breath. 'We knew at once it was him, because half his face was lying there too, and some bits of his checkered shirt. Jesus. I can still see his moustache in front of my eyes right now, soaked in blood. We have no idea what might have happened to him, but he definitely looked as if some creature had devoured him—a wolf, maybe, I don't know. Anyway, we called the police, because there wouldn't have been much point in calling an ambulance. There wasn't enough left of him, poor fellow.'

The women in the queue stood around Michał Cytryna in silence, and even the skinny young man in the serving hatch was leaning forward, stunned, as if buying bread was now the last thing on anybody's minds.

The days went by so quickly that Romek didn't realise how much time had passed until the morning wind began to feel chilly and the green leaves of the trees around his farm began to turn red and yellow. One early evening, when Krystyna had gone to help Marianna, who had been feeling unwell for some weeks now, he tore a sheet off the small wall calendar in the kitchen and saw that it said, *Hello, October!*

He stood looking at the calendar as if it were a symbol of his life draining away, wasted. What have I achieved, apart from growing vegetables? And where are all those vegetables now? Gone down the drains, like me.

He was still standing there when he heard a scuffling noise from above. *It's that boy*, he thought, *that stinking boy. What's he up to now?*

He climbed the stairs up to the attic, and when he reached the top, he looked around to see what the boy was doing. He saw him standing with his back to him underneath the small skylight. His head was bent forward and he appeared to be holding something in both hands and eating it. Romek stayed where he was, watching him, but he was too frightened to disturb him.

When the boy stopped chewing, he clapped his hands together. Tiny sticks and feathers scattered onto the floor. As soon as he had done that, he reached up into one of the gaps in the plaster ceiling which was stuffed with straw to keep the house warm in winter. He rummaged around in it for a few moments, and eventually he tugged his hand out again, holding a robin.

Romek knew that every year, robins made nests for themselves in the straw, and the boy had clearly discovered that, too. He held this one up for a while in front of his face, as if he were enjoying its futile struggle to get free. Romek heard him whisper, 'How are you feeling, little robin? I have a surprise for you!' Then he bit the bird's head off. A small fountain of blood sprayed up. He crunched the head between his teeth two or three times, and then he clamped his mouth over its severed neck, and sucked.

Romek felt as if his stomach had turned upside down, and he vomited his lunch of green zucchini soup and slimy trails of ham all down the front of his sweater and over his worn-out leather slippers.

The boy heard him gagging and immediately turned around, still holding the decapitated robin in his hand. Slowly, he approached him, his expression blank, staring up at him as if he didn't recognise him as his own father. Then without warning he dropped to his knees and started to lick the vomit from his slippers.

'Jesus *Christ*, what are you doing?' Romek screamed at him, utterly disgusted. 'Stop! Get off!'

He tried to kick the boy away but the boy clung on to his leg, still trying greedily to suck at the vomit on his jeans.

'Get the fuck off me!' Romek shouted, and it was then that he heard the front door open and Krystyna return. She heard the thumping and banging up in the attic and she came climbing up the stairs in a panic, still wearing her raincoat.

'What's going on here?' she shrilled at Romek. 'What the *hell* are you doing?'

She knelt down beside her son and took him in her arms.

'What's going on here?' Romek demanded. 'You tell *me*, for Christ's sake!'

'Stop it! He's simply hungry, can't you see that?'

'Hungry? He's eating my puke!'

'Let the child be fed!'

'Krysia! Have you gone crazy?'

Krystyna sat back and started to sob. The boy stood up and laid his hand for a moment on the shoulder of her coat, as if to comfort her, but then he backed away and stood in the far corner of the attic, staring at them with that same utter lack of expression.

'Why do you do this to me?' Krystyna wept, covering her eyes with her hands. 'Why do you all do this to me? Why? What have I done?'

Romek knelt down next to her. He was totally perplexed. He was still feeling nauseous, too, because the whole attic stank of vomit and the decomposing boy.

'Krysia—'

'Romek, he needs food. I discovered that he can eat some bloody raw meat, but it calms him down only for a very short while. What he really needs. . .'

She bit her lip, unsure of whether she should continue. But he was the only person who could help her, and his bond with Grześ was unbreakable, whether Grześ was living or returned from the dead.

'What?' said Romek. 'I have to get out of this stinking sweater.'

'He needs living food. He needs people's flesh and blood. When he feeds on such things, he reminds me of my son again, the way he was, smiling, laughing, with his ruby-red cheeks.'

'Living food? What are you talking about?' But it was then that Romek thought of Mietek, and of Andrzej the gravedigger. He turned to look at the boy, who was staring back at him, still clutching the headless robin in his fist and sucking at it.

Please, dear God, thought Romek, *don't tell me it was him.*

DON'T CRY FOR THE DEAD

They were eating the supper in silence, although it was hard to call it 'eating' when Romek had no appetite at all. He was digging into his scrambled eggs with his fork, but when Krystyna slid four slices of black blood pudding out of her frying pan onto his plate, his throat tightened and he pushed his plate away.

'I tried to feed him with some of these, uncooked,' Krystyna told him. 'But it wasn't long before he was hungry again.'

She raised her reddened eyes to Romek, and her voice was hoarse and pleading. 'He's our son, Romek. Don't you love him anymore?'

He tried to read her expression. He had the feeling that she had some kind of idea hatching in her mind, but she was afraid to tell him what it was, in case he thought that it was far too gross.

To keep the peace, though, he said, 'Yes, Krysia. Yes, I love him.'

'You can't deny now that something bad is happening, Jurek, can you?' asked Mania as she came out of the kitchen, wiping her hands on her apron.

'I was hoping that I was wrong,' said Jurek. 'But, yes, you're right. It does seem possible that they might have come back. Or one of them, at least.'

'I warned you, didn't I? I warned you that all this endless mourning would bring us bad luck. You have to let the dead go and find their own peace—'

'Mania, we couldn't have predicted it.'

'But *I* did! *I* did! What did I tell you about Krysia's endless crying?'

'Calm down, Mania, please. All we can do now is keep our eyes open and stick together.'

It was nearly midnight when someone rang the doorbell of Janusowa's house. Although it was so late, Janusowa was sitting in her kitchen in her dressing-gown sipping a cup of very strong sweet tea and staring at her picture of the Mother of God. After losing her dearly beloved husband and her favourite horse, too, she badly needed comfort. She was about to pick up her rosary and say a grace when the doorbell jangled a second time.

'Who's there?' she called out, standing up from the table. Nobody answered, so she called out again. 'It's late! What do you want?'

Again, there was no response, so she went to the front door and opened it. And there, standing in the porch in a muddy blue suit and a crooked bow tie, was Mietek.

'*Mietek*?' she whispered.

'I can't sleep,' he said, in a vibrant voice that sounded as if he were talking to her from far away.

'Oh my dear Mietek! How is this possible?' Józefa gasped, and in spite of her age she rushed up to him like a lovesick young girl and threw herself into his arms. She hugged him so tightly that she didn't see how bloated and blue his face had become, or the wriggling grubs that were dripping out of his eyes.

He kept Janusowa locked close to him, but he didn't kiss her. Instead, with an audible scrunching sound, he bit into her nose and her upper lip so deeply that his front teeth clashed against hers, breaking her palate and penetrating her nasal cavity. Before she could draw in enough breath to scream, he started to suck at her face with the thirst of a man who has crawled across a desert.

Early the next morning, Krystyna was standing in front of the meat delivery van, stuffing two chickens and three rings of raw black blood sausages into her shopping bag when Mania came hurrying up to her.

'I thought I might find you here,' she panted. 'Can we talk for a while, you and me?'

'What about?' Krystyna snapped at her. 'I'm already late.'

'Please—just give me a minute.'

'All right,' said Krystyna with a theatrical sigh. 'If you really have to.'

'Come—come to my house,' said Mania. She took hold of Krystyna's sleeve and almost dragged her along the street. When they reached her house, she took Krystyna's shopping bag away from her and helped her out of her coat.

'Please, please sit. I'll make us some coffee.'

'I thought you said a minute,' said Krystyna, testily, even though they had been friends for years and Mania had done so much for her. Mania laid both her hands on Krystyna's shoulders, almost as she were forcing her to sit down. She had the strange impression that someone different was speaking to her through Krystyna, like a ventriloquist.

'I know I did. But listen. This is important.'

Krystyna tried to prise Marianna's hands off her shoulders. 'What are you talking about, Mania?'

'Don't be angry, please. I know that the pain of losing your precious child was almost impossible to bear. But your despair—all those weeks of mourning—that woke up something very, very bad.'

Krysia twitched her head in annoyance, as if she were shaking off a fly. But it gave away her realisation that Mania had discovered her secret, or at least guessed what it was, and that she knew why she was so desperate to talk to her.

'I think it would be better if you kept your mouth shut,' said Krystyna. She had never spoken to Mania with such hostility before.

'Krysia—he's not your son anymore. Don't you understand that he's a *spirit*, an evil spirit. He's primaeval and he has no mercy. He may seem small and weak now, but with time his power will grow, and he will do whatever he can to suck the life out of us, one by one.'

'Don't even dare to meddle! Otherwise you will be the first!'

'The first? That spirit is already a killer and you are a killer, too! It was your endless mourning that brought it back to life, and I'm afraid that means those people who have died are your victims, too! Mietek and Andrzej the gravedigger, you have their blood on your hands as much as that creature from hell!'

Krystyna was furious. She pointed her finger at Mania and screamed at her, 'You! I'm warning you, you saintly witch! Stay away from me and stay away from my son or you will suffer more agony than you can imagine!'

With that, she picked up her shopping bag, tugged down her coat from the hook in the hallway, and stormed out of Mania's house, leaving the front door wide open behind her. She pushed her way past Jurek, who was coming home for breakfast. He said, 'Krysia! How are you?' but she went off without even looking at him.

When he came into the house, he found Mania in tears.

'Mania, what's happened? Did you and Krysia have an argument?'

Mania wiped her eyes. 'I tried to tell her, like we agreed, but it made her so angry. She spoke to me as if I was her enemy.'

Jurek held her close. 'For as long as she's protecting that thing, I'm afraid that you *will* be her enemy. We all are.'

Late that afternoon, storm clouds began to roll over the sky from the west, and Romek went out to guide his cows into the barn. He was crossing the field beside the church, leading a black and white Holstein on a rope, when Jurek called out to him from the porch.

'Romek! Long time no see! How's it going?'

Romek stopped and waited as Jurek came up to him. 'Hi, Jurek,' he said, reluctantly. 'Looks like we're in for a storm.'

'I haven't seen you in church lately,' said Jurek, trying to sound natural and calm. 'Has something happened?'

It didn't escape Jurek's notice that Romek hesitated. Then, 'No. . .' he said, but almost as if he didn't believe it himself, and simply didn't want to talk about it.

'That's good. And I'm glad I caught you. Can I ask you for a favour? There's a really heavy table which I have to move before vespers this evening but Franek is going to be late so he won't be able to help me.'

'Okay. Just let me shut up this cow in my barn.'

Jurek accompanied Romek to the barn. As they came closer, he noticed that the cow was becoming increasingly agitated, and as they reached the barn door, it started to kick and moo as if it was seriously frightened.

Romek pulled at its rope, digging in his heels and struggling to stop it from running away. 'Calm down, you stupid animal! Easy! I said *easy*! You want me to process you into a sausage?'

Jurek gave Romek an uncomfortable smile, and he shivered. *It's here, it's close by, and this poor cow can sense it. That's why she's so terrified. It's here.*

DON'T CRY FOR THE DEAD

'So, where's this table?' asked Romek, looking around the church.

'I'm afraid I was fibbing,' said Jurek. 'There is no table. I simply wanted you to come into the church so that I could talk to you. You'll have to forgive me, but I thought that in a sacred place you wouldn't try to avoid telling me the truth, and the whole truth, too.'

'What do you mean?'

'I mean that you have to stop your wife before that creature you're hiding kills us all.'

Romek almost choked. 'Excuse me?' he spluttered. 'What creature?'

'Don't play the fool with me, Romek!' Jurek shouted at him. This was the first time he had lost his temper in years. 'Don't think I don't know what's going on! But then maybe I'm not sure that you do!'

'I—that is—we—Krysia and me—'

Jurek calmed down. 'Romek, I love you as if you were my son. So listen to me, my dear friend, before it's too late. That creature in your house—it's not your son.'

'How do you know about that?'

'I've seen what's been happening for months now. People have died, and they've died in such a way that there's only one explanation. There's no way that Mietek and Andrzej and Janusowa were attacked by animals, whatever the pathologist had to say. The hole that kept appearing by your son's grave confirmed it, and so did the change in your wife's behaviour after your Grześ was drowned. Every woman in the village has remarked on the way Krystyna keeps talking about him as if he were still alive, and the children's clothes that she's been buying, and how much food like liver and hearts and tripe. She's trying to feed the beast, but one day before too long, you and she will be food for it, too. You mark my words.

Romek couldn't find the words to answer him, but looked around the church again, as if the Angel Gabriel would suddenly appear to give him an explanation.

'I can understand that you're confused, and how hard it is for you to deal with,' Jurek went on. 'But in the name of merciful God, it's not any divine miracle. On the contrary, it's the beast awakening.'

'Beast? Awakening?'

'Yes, I'm afraid so. I'm sorry it happened to your son, Romek. But as you know, evil never sleeps, unlike God, who made us in His own image. He sleeps, just as we do, and while God is asleep. . .'

Romek was silent for a long moment. Then he said, 'Tell me more, Jurek. I need to know everything.'

'You're sure? Then let's go to my house.'

They were sitting upstairs, in a room with a high ceiling and huge windows on two sides. The windows filled the room with sunlight during the day, but when it grew dark it felt as if they were out in the middle of an ocean, with no sight of land. It was dimly illuminated with a single lamp, and three candles in a silver candle-holder.

'Want some coffee?' asked Jurek. 'Mania always tells me not to drink coffee in the evenings, but I just love coffee!'

He poured vodka into two coffee cups, topped them up with espresso, and then lifted one of them and said, *'Na zdrowie!'* Romek could see that he was trying to be cheerful, but his strain and his tiredness was showing on his face. He was not a young man, after all.

'It's like a bad dream,' Romek told Jurek. 'I was working in the field when Krysia came running to me shouting that the doctors were mistaken and that Grześ was still alive. No—what she actually said was, "He came back!"'

'Well, he did come back, but only in a way. It's his body, yes, but it's not him.'

'So who is he? I said more or less the same thing to Krysia when I found them together in our attic.'

'Your attic?'

'Yes, during the day Krysia lets him hide there. But man, when I saw him—he has the face of my son, but he looks terrible. Talk about the living dead! And how he stinks! Like carrion!'

'Everything indicates that this creature is not your son, Romek, but a specific and unusual kind of vampire.'

DON'T CRY FOR THE DEAD

As he said that, thunder growled outside as if they were in a horror story, and that none of this was real.

'A vampire? Are you serious? What, like Dracula?'

'Yes, I'm serious. Not like Dracula, who was only a character in a book, but an actual vampire, and this kind of vampire doesn't care if you believe in it or not. In fact, it would rather that we didn't believe in it, because we won't go hunting for something that we don't believe in. In any case, they regard us as nothing more than a bag of blood and flesh, to feed them.

He sipped his coffee, and then said, 'I think it's time to light the *gromnic*, the protective candle. They'll come for us, for sure, and we need to be ready to stop them before they kill any more of us.'

'Vampires, Jurek. I feel as if I'm going mad! How is this possible?'

'Vampires is the generic word for all kinds of spirits that nourish themselves on living humans. They've lived in our lands since forever, and their graves can be found in many towns and villages. Our village is no exception. Many, many years ago they appeared here and hunted, scores of them, and they killed many of our former generation. Didn't your mother or rather your grandmother or your great-grandmother ever say a word to you about it?'

'I'm sorry, but I'm finding it hard to believe any of this,' said Romek, shaking his head.

'Even though you have one of them hiding in your attic?'

'But vampires? Here?'

'Yes. But like I told you, they're not like the vampires you see in scary movies. We're not talking about biting your neck and sucking a few litres of your blood. These vampires can devour you in the blink of an eye. They don't only suck every single drop of blood out of your body, but the marrow out of your bones, and your liver, and kidneys, and all the fat from your stomach. They'll kill your animals, too, like poor Janusowa's horse.'

'But nobody's seen them doing it.'

'No. They usually attack you when they catch you alone, and they'll take not only your blood and your flesh, but the one thing that would have given you eternal life. They'll take your soul.'

'If they're really real, though, Jurek, where do they come from? How did one of them manage to possess my poor little Grześ?'

'We don't exactly know,' said Jurek, pouring more vodka into their coffee cups. 'But it's said that the dead return if you mourn them for too long. It means that their spirits can't go through to the world of the dead. You're always holding them back.'

'I thought it was good to remember the dead.'

'To an extent, yes. But they can hear endless crying like Krystyna's. And it doesn't help if you keep too many pictures of the dead at home, and if you're always thinking about them, or calling them, or hugging and smelling their clothes. Anything they left behind when they passed away is a way through to the world of spirits. And of course, not all spirits are good and merciful. Some of them are angry that they have died, and others are angry because your mourning won't let them go. Some of them feel that if they can't find peace in the world of spirits, they'll continue to inhabit the land of the living, but for that they need to feed on human life. Those are your vampires. And that includes your Grześ.'

Romek sat in silence. Regardless of how frightening Jurek's words were, and how incredible, he knew deep in his heart that everything he had told him was true. His whole house now reeked of the boy in the attic. But he had no idea of what he and Krystyna should do. Run away?

'I'm afraid that running away is not going to help,' said Jurek, as if he could read Romek's mind. 'At the moment, he's not so dangerous as he will be, when he grows up and gains even more strength.'

'So what do you suggest?' Romek asked him.

'The decision is yours, my friend,' Jurek told him, just as another grumble of thunder rattled the windows and one of the candles was snuffed out.

Three days went by. After what Jurek had told him, Romek was unable to sleep and had no appetite at all. When he came home in the evenings, all he could do was sit and watch Krystyna bustling around the house, cleaning and cooking as if nothing had happened.

As he lay awake at night, he could hear her in Grześ' bedroom, murmuring those strange fairy tales. And day or night, there was always that rancid smell.

DON'T CRY FOR THE DEAD

'Krysia—' He tried to speak to her, but each time she looked at him with her bloodshot eyes, he couldn't think what to say. He knew that if he suggested they leave the house and run away somewhere, she would flatly refuse.

His life had become so unreal that he wiped any thought about Grześ from his mind, and every morning he went trudging off to the fields with his brain blank, like a zombie himself.

'Krysia—' he repeated.

She was coming out of the kitchen with a bowl filled with raw liver.

'I know what you're going to say, Romek. But he needs to live. He needs to eat. He's only a child. Children must eat.'

She recited these words as if she were enchanted. Then without saying anything else, she started to climb the stairs to the attic.

Romek stayed silent, but he was beginning to feel that this house was a tomb, and he was trapped in it, along with the dead. He stood up, lifted down his jacket and left the house. Perhaps Jurek would be able to give him some idea of what to do.

Nobody answered when he knocked at Jurek's front door, but it was slightly ajar, so he pushed it open and called out, 'Jurek?'

He found Jurek sitting in his kitchen, his face hidden in his hands as if he were crying. On the table next to him was a bottle of vodka, nearly empty.

'Jurek?' Romek's voice caught in his throat. Jurek was always so calm and in control, so he could tell that something seriously bad had happened. 'Jurek, what's wrong?'

Jurek lowered his hands and looked at him, and his eyes were almost blinded with tears.

'He took her,' he sobbed.

'Sorry? What did you say?'

'He took her. He took Marianna.'

Romek shivered. He sat down next to the organist, took hold of his hand and squeezed it.

'Oh my God, Jurek. I should have believed you. They *are* vampires, aren't they? Well, sort of vampires, like you told me.'

Jurek poured out the last of the vodka.

'Nobody knew where they came from. War's a great breeding-ground for every evil that infests this world, and maybe it was the disturbance of World War Two that brought them back to life. Some of the shells landed in the cemetery, and maybe the explosions dug up the graves. My mother told me that was when they first appeared in our village, but of course it was difficult to tell who had been killed by a bomb and who had been killed by a vampire. Both bodies were ripped to pieces.

He swallowed the vodka and was silent for a moment. Then he said, 'Mourning those who passed away for too long doesn't allow their souls to rest in peace. They remain suspended in between, in what you might describe as purgatory. It's then that they're vulnerable to being possessed by any one of so many malevolent spirits. These spirits take on their dead bodies as a disguise to enter our world, and once they've entered our world they use their grieving relatives as servants, because their relatives are overjoyed to have them back, no matter what kind of a state they're in.

'During World War Two they slaughtered nearly half our village before we discovered who they were—or should I say *what* they were—and got rid of them. They had to have their throats cut and their stomachs cut out, too, so that they could no longer feed.'

'Jesus,' said Romek. 'So what kind of vampires are they, exactly?'

'They're called *martwce*—the vampires of mourning. They have an insatiable craving for all God's creatures, human or animal. They are always hungry and their hunger only increases the more they feed.'

Romek sat back and stared at his friend with sympathy and horror. 'Holy shit,' he said, shaking his head. 'So that's what happened to my Grześ.'

Romek spent the rest of the day digging up beets and, when it grew dark, reluctantly returned home.

He found Krystyna in the kitchen, stirring a large cooking-pot, although there was no flame underneath it.

'Krysia, do you know that Mani is missing?'

'Ye-e-es,' she said, vibrantly, so that it sounded as if she were singing.

'And? She's your best friend. You're not worried?'

DON'T CRY FOR THE DEAD

When he came closer to the stove, Romek could see that the cooking-pot appeared to be full of dark glutinous blood, with ragged slices of meat floating in it.

'He must eat, Romek. He must be fed properly.'

'Krysia—' he began, but then he saw the chopping-board on the kitchen table. At least thirty small bones were scattered on top of it, like finger-bones, but what made Romek's heart lurch was the gold ring that was lying amongst them.

Krystyna turned away from the stove and saw what he was looking at.

'He *must* eat properly, Romek,' she repeated in that sing-song voice.

Robert was sitting in his living-room watching a football match when Romek knocked frantically at his front door. His wife had a cold and had already gone to bed.

He went to the front door and opened it. Romek was standing on the porch with his hair scruffed up and his shirt collar torn. Robert couldn't help noticing that both of his hands were bloody.

'Romek? What's happened? Don't tell me you've been in a fight.'

Romek was so short of breath and so overcome with emotion that he could barely speak. He pressed his hand against his chest, and then he said, 'Robert—tell me. Is it against the law to kill somebody when they're already dead?'

The moon shines
The mourning vampire flies
The tiny dress up up up
The little lady aren't you afraid?
     The Slavic Bestiary, part one and two

It's amazing, that the mourning turns even the luckiest
memories into the sharp knives that hurt.
       Akira

GRAHAM MASTERTON & KAROLINA MOGIELSKA

[. . .] for the redeemed souls the human blood is for nothing.

Henryk Sienkiewicz, With Fire and Sword

The time will come when all who lie in these graves will awaken.

The cemetery inscription

Karolina Mogielska *is a Polish writer who lives in the south of Poland, in Nysa city. As a clinical psychologist with ten years experience, she undertook to co-operate with the British writer Graham Masterton to write a novel on domestic abuse as a way of helping people trapped in such situations. To develop her fiction-writing experience, they started to create short horror stories together which bore fruit with their very first story* Mr Nobody. *Since then they have published nine more, including the best-selling* Gloria *and* Boneless, *and they will be bringing out a collection of stories based on Slavic mythology. Apart from that, Karolina as a psychologist has published articles on the maladjustment of children and teenagers in Polish scientific magazines. She was inspired to write about a graveyard because her grandfather was a gravedigger who founded a cemetery in the rural village of Wegryzn, in Świętokrzyskie, which is still in use today.*

Graham Masterton *is mainly recognized for his horror novels but he has also been a prolific writer of thrillers, disaster novels and historical epics, as well as sex instruction books. He became a newspaper reporter at the age of 17 and was appointed editor of Penthouse magazine at only 24. His first horror novel* The Manitou *was filmed with Tony Curtis playing the lead. Graham also turned his hand to crime novels with* White Bones, *set in Ireland, and this has been followed by thirteen more novels featuring Detective Superintendent Katie Maguire, the latest of which is* Pay Back The Devil. *In 2019 Graham was given a Lifetime Achievement Award by the Horror Writers Association. Ten years ago he established an annual prize for short stories written by inmates in Polish prisons. Graham's latest horror novel in the series featuring Det Sgt Jamila Patel and Det Jerry Pardoe is* House of Flies.

40

HAMMERED HALLOWEEN

JONATHAN GENSLER

I ALWAYS THOUGHT I'd be the one to save my daughter. That's what fathers do, right?

Protect their children from monsters. I believed this with every chamber of my hungover heart as, gearing up for the evening ahead, we strung up black lights, nylon spiderwebs, and a giant TRICK OR TREAT sign in goofy black and orange letters outside my run-down saltbox.

The first nail was my ex-wife's face. Now *there* was a real monster—one who took, took, and took some more. Since the split, that meant taking the only thing I really wanted—time with Annie.

WHACK! One swing smashed it home, despite the residual headache from my Friday night date with Mister Beam.

I moved the ladder over, stretched out the string of lights Annie'd ordered on her stepdad's dime.

I looked down at my girl opening the boxes of decorations. With her black clothes and ever-present midnight dark eyeliner, she seemed built for the holiday. We were going to scare up my old place like we were up on the Southside Hills, where rich folks like Little Miss Lawyer and Mister New Guy sat around talking down at folks like me.

I grabbed a reused nail from the box. The next would be *his* face—the bastard.

What would you do if you caught your old lady shacking up with a douchebag partner at her law firm? I turned to my old friends James and Jack and all the rest. Sue me.

Turns out he was a divorce lawyer and did just that. I didn't stand a chance against them. Or with the bottle, after they stripped my drunk ass of almost everything.

One weekend a month with Annie.

A father needs more than that.

Releasing the rage building behind my eyes in a single THWACK, I drove the nail home.

Annie called out as I was readying the next nail.

"Daddy! The big package came!"

"Dammit, honey! Can't you see I am up here working? I ain't doing this for me."

I was, though.

The house would be perfect and Annie'd see how much I loved her and her momma would see I wasn't the total fuck-up she claimed. I'd get a second weekend. Maybe some weekdays. If I could do this, hell, everyone would see I could kick the bottle to the curb, too.

This next nail was going to be my need for the drink. Right hand reared the hammer back, expecting to drive it home in a single strike like the others. Left hand held the just-tapped-in nail steady.

"Daddy, you have to see what I got you!"

My head throbbed from the previous night. I half-turned to face her as I swung.

"Jesus, girl, let me work!"

My attention splintered. The right foot slipped off the worn ladder step. The left hand struck out, grabbing the wooden frame to steady my fall, right hand swinging a two-pound claw hammer right at the jagged head of the nail.

The metal scraped into my left palm the instant before the hammer hit the nail dead on. The weighted hammer head simply ignored the hand, bashing into the head of the nail through the pancake thickness of my palm.

The ladder fell as my flailing legs kicked it. I didn't follow it to the ground.

For a second: no pain, no sound, no blood.

The nail head sliced out through the back of the left hand as my flailing fingertips gripped the two-by-four the nail had just been pounded into.

My right hand dropped the tool to the ground and reached for the two-by-four as well, but by then my 210 pounds of out-of-shape muscle and bone were swinging from the nail impaling my other hand.

At least the frame is solid, I thought before a raging inferno exploded in my mind.

Rivulets of blood ran down my forearm, soaking the rolled-up sleeves of my blue flannel shirt. Blood that almost certainly had a bit of my whiskey party left over from the night before.

I hated my little girl for a second. But I hated myself more.

I didn't scream—Annie did.

"Daddy! Oh my god ohmygod ohmygod!"

No answer.

"Hold on! I'll get help!"

The pain scoured everything else from my awareness. Blood flowed from my hand in a steady stream, fingertips slipping off the two-by-four. Right hand reached for left wrist rather than the wooden frame, and left hand slipped off the wooden structure, my weight pulling everything down through the nail.

Which slowly sliced through the flesh holding my fingers together.

A tendon popped. Skin ripped. White flashes filled my vision.

My own scream brought me back to the moment.

Right arm reached for the frame, legs kicking to reach a bit higher, the swinging dragging the nail farther into my flesh, until it ripped all the way up between the second and third fingers.

I hurtled toward the ground, a ten-foot fall onto concrete.

My arm reached out to break the fall, and I landed precisely wrong, smashed onto the gaping wound. I swear you could hear cartilage and bone warp, twist, break.

Next thing I knew Annie was carrying a box over to me. The box rattled, almost jumping around in her small arms.

"I'm sorry, so sorry, Daddy. I wanted to surprise you."

All I could think was *what the hell is in the box?*

Not the first aid kit I expected.

Annie was carrying a wooden crate, which was not only shaking, but also emitting a high-pitched wail.

The remains of my left-hand gushed blood and my thoughts wandered, separated from self. Call it woozy, bleeding to death—I needed to wrap my hand ASAP. I didn't have time for whatever she was trying to do.

I'd fucked up, again.

Facing away from her, I tried to stand.

A CRACK exploded from behind as something small and light hit my back. It was up and over my left shoulder, a black streak of furry lightning launching to my hand, smelling of copper and earth.

My eyesight blurred, while the pain from the bite was nothing less than exquisite.

The creature enveloped my wounded appendage with translucent black wings. Its small head burrowed into the center of my flayed open hand.

"This was for you, Daddy. For us."

A numbness flowed up my forearm and into my shoulder, an iciness creeping in, flowing through my veins. My chest froze as the absolute cold struck my body into a rigid and broken shape, once again prone on the concrete driveway.

I have no idea how long I lay there, suckling Annie's surprise. In that moment, time became meaningless.

Annie eventually came around to me, half smiling. "See, Daddy? I knew you'd be surprised!"

"What is this?" I asked, even as I felt the answer rising in my mind. An addict knows—I felt the new craving, the need, almost immediately.

I suddenly saw Annie with different eyes. She was already there waiting for me amid our newborn infinity, her pretty face darkened by a shadow from the inside.

I always thought I'd be the one to save my daughter. Not the other way around.

That first evening together, we made a trip up to the Southside Hills and ensured the *real* monsters were taken care of.

And she showed me how delicious it could be to be so absolutely wrong.

Jonathan Gensler (he/him) grew up in a haunted house on the outskirts of a cursed town. He's published nearly 20 short stories since 2023 in venues such as Cosmic Horror Monthly, On Spec Magazine, *and* Creepy Pod, *among others. An Army combat veteran, recovering entrepreneur, and Active Member of the HWA, he lives and writes in the Rocky Mountains with his wife and three children. You can connect with him online at* jonathangensler.com.

GENE OF THE OBSCENE

NICK ROBERTS

MY GRANDPA KILLED eleven people in his lifetime and got away with it. Could be more. We don't know if he's still livin' or not. If he is, he's pushin' seventy.

Tim, he's my older brother by two years. He's fourteen, so that rightly makes me twelve. My mom says that Tim was their plan—hers and my dad's—but I was God's plan. Took me years and a talk with Tim to understand what she meant by that. And it wasn't no compliment.

I get it now. I was a surprise baby. Sometimes Mom tells me our house is too small 'cause I wasn't on their minds when they bought it. Meanin', I don't have my own room. She likes to tell me, that right after I was born, they put me in a crib in their room, and I'd wake them up all night. Was like that for eighteen months, so she says.

I can't confirm it with Dad 'cause he left, too. One thing that stands clearest about Dad was his belt. It had a star on the belt buckle. Thought it was mighty cool until he hit my face with it. I didn't even do nothin' neither. We was in the livin' room—me, Dad, and Tim—and Dad had NASCAR on the TV. He made us watch it even though I got so bored watchin' them dang cars drive in circles. Tim thought it was cool when they wrecked. He laughed at that.

I told Tim there wasn't nothin' funny about people gettin' hurt. I said it at the wrong time 'cause this one driver that Dad hated wrecked and couldn't finish the race. Next thing I know, Dad dropped his beer 'cause he stood up so fast. He cussed and yanked that belt off like he was pullin' a lawn mower rip cord. I turned right into that star. Never felt no pain like that before in my life.

Tim didn't laugh at that. When Mom came home from work and saw my face, she made Dad leave. He didn't even put up a fight, and he never came back. Thought he was dead or in jail or just started a brand-new family somewhere else. He disappeared just like grandpa did. Everyone in Hinton knows about the killin' Grandpa did and got away with.

Seems like there's nothin' but secrets here, under all them pleasantries and church talk about lovin' your neighbor. Lots of houses have family graveyards out back. Not all them people are kin, though. You gotta watch who you do wrong in this town, that's for sure. You could end up disappeared and buried beside someone's vegetable garden. We only got a few cops around here, and they don't do much of nothin'.

Only time I ever seen them in action was when everyone found out about Grandpa and them little girls. That's where the town draws the line, I reckon. Little girls. By the time they figured out it was him that done it, he was already gone, and we ain't seen him since.

I asked Tim just the other day if he thought Dad was with Grandpa somewhere. Like maybe Dad knew what Grandpa had been up to all along out there in his barn and never said nothin'. Like maybe they had a plan that if Grandpa ever had to make a run for it, Dad would know where to find him.

'Cause when you're pushin' seventy, life on the run ain't somethin' that seems easy. I asked Tim if that's why Dad hit me with his belt and left the star-shaped scar beside my eye. Like maybe Grandpa got caught, and Dad didn't wanna make it look obvious that he knew where his daddy was hidin', so he gave it time and then gave Mom an excuse to kick him out of the house. That way it wouldn't look like Dad just left town after his Dad went on the run. Tim said I was smart, but he didn't think Dad would do that. When Tim told me nice things, I believed him.

That's what gave Tim the idea that got us into trouble. After the cops found those three dead girls who was half my age hangin' by their feet in Grandpa's garage, they searched his land for more bodies. No one in Hinton was missin' though, so the cops didn't know where Grandpa got them girls from and if there was any more out there.

Even though we wasn't supposed to, Tim and I snuck over the hill and through the woods to look down on Grandpa's farm to watch the cops diggin' around and lettin' their dogs sniff around. Tim said they were lookin' for more bodies. I only knew about the girls because Tim showed me the newspaper that had a picture of Grandpa's farm and lots of words tellin' what he done to them.

'Cause Tim ain't as good a reader as me, he asked me to read it to him. Tim gets real embarrassed that he can't read, but it's his own dang fault for skippin' school all the time. So I read the paper and it talked about the girls bein' from out of town 'cause no girls in Hinton was missin' and how these girls were hanging upside down and hollowed out like Dad used to do to deer when he bagged one and skinned it in our garage.

I had a nightmare once that it was me that Dad was huntin'. I was runnin' through the forest, and he shot me in the back with his rifle and dragged me back home and hung me by feet in the garage. He used his knife to cut off my clothes and put a big metal bucket on the floor to catch my blood and guts when he emptied me out and put my meat in the freezer.

But anyways, after we read that paper, we snuck over there every day just to see if the dang cops had left yet. New newspapers came out each day and talked about more bodies the cops found. Most of them was under his house which made sense 'cause his house smelled like dead pigs sometimes.

It took a few weeks, but one day the cops was just gone. They left the yellow crime scene tape around the property, though. Probably just to keep people like me and Tim away. It didn't work though.

After Dad left, Mom got in the worst shoutin' match with Tim that I ever heard. She even cussed him, and he cussed her right back, and I ain't never seen him do that. She smacked him so hard he fell and tipped over the kitchen table. I laughed at that 'cause he laughed at me when Dad whipped me.

So that day when Tim and me snuck to Grandpa's and saw no cops, we went straight to the barn. Tim was excited to see what was in there. I didn't know why. We'd watched them take those girls out in bags, so we knew there wasn't no bodies still hangin' in there. I guess he just wanted to see if there was still blood stains or somethin'.

We went in, and all of grandpa's stuff was still there. There wasn't no blood or bodies. I asked Tim if he thought there was badness inside Grandpa, and it got passed to Dad. I couldn't get it outta my mind that Dad was into killin' too, but he just didn't get caught. Tim didn't think anyone was born bad like that. He said they had to be taught to be bad. That there wasn't no gene that made you like killin'.

He was wantin' to leave, but I told him we didn't check the hayloft.

And that's where I killed him, my brother.

I waited until he was lookin' over the railin' and I hit his head with Grandpa's hammer. He just fell straight forward over the railin' with that hammer still stuck in the back of his head, somehow. One arm was bent the wrong way.

I never planned on killin' him until Dad left. Once I found out about Grandpa and then my suspicions about Dad, I knew one of us had to have the badness in us. Tim was my older brother by two years. He could easily kick my ass if he wanted, and he did sometimes, but not all the time, only when we got into really bad fights. I knew the badness wasn't in me, so that meant it had to be in Tim. If I didn't kill him first, he woulda eventually killed me and lots of others probably.

I left him there and went home and told Mom what I done and the reason I done it. I hated seein' Mom cry. She told me I was jokin' and kissed my star-shaped scar and then made me tell her it was just a joke me and Tim was playin' on her.

I told her I wouldn't joke about nothin' like that ever. She made me ride with her to Grandpa's to show her Tim's body 'cause she didn't think I done it. She ran over to him and cried and screamed so loud that I thought my eardrums was gonna pop. I tried to tell her that it was all right now, that the badness was gone from our family for good.

But she just kept cryin' and told me that I ruined her life 'cause I wasn't planned and that if I was never born, her and Dad would still be together 'cause he'd never do nasty things like his Daddy if it was just them two and Tim. I went crimson and took Tim's pocketknife and made a mess of her throat. She fell on Tim, and that's where I left her.

I didn't know what was gonna happen with Tim and Mom dead and me havin' the whole house to myself. I just went home and made Mac 'n Cheese and watched TV while I waited on the cops to come, but they never did.

Grandpa came though.

GENE OF THE OBSCENE

It was late at night, and I must've fallen asleep on the couch 'cause he just snuck in and woke me up. He said he went to the barn earlier that night to get some monies he'd hid that he needed and saw Mom and Tim's bodies and asked if I done it. I told him yes 'cause Tim had the same badness in him that he and Dad had in them.

He told me Tim didn't have the badness. Said that *I* did. He said his older brother was a good man his whole life. He told me Dad's older brother, Howie, was a good Christian man who wanted nothin' to do with Dad. I reckon his point was to convince me that the second born son gets the gene.

I told him I didn't feel like no killer. I just done what needed to be done 'cause Tim was the real killer, and that Mom woulda been sad the rest of her life with just me, so I did her a favor. He smiled at me and told me I was comin' with him, and he'd take care of me. Told me the cops would come for me as soon as they went back to the crime scene and opened them barn doors.

So I agreed to go with him. Get outta town for good. I asked where Dad was, and he said Dad was at a cabin they owned right outside Bluefield. He said the two of them would take care of me because I was like them.

I told him again that I didn't have no badness in me. I had good reason to do what I done. He laughed until he saw the star-shaped scar on my face and asked what happened. I told him the truth, and I could tell he wasn't happy about that.

The car ride to the secret cabin felt like it took forever, but as soon as we made it there. Grandpa parked the truck and told me to hand him the pistol out of his glove compartment. I asked why, and he said no one lays a finger on his grandson and left the car. I didn't know if I was supposed to go with him or not, so I waited until I heard the gunshot before I got out of the truck and walked to the house.

Dad was on his side on the couch crying cause there was a big hole in his belly. Grandpa had already taken off Dad's belt. He handed it to me while Dad cried and called Grandpa bad names. I knew what Grandpa wanted me to do though 'cause I wanted to do it too.

I smacked Dad in the face with the star-shaped belt buckle. Dad cussed me, so Grandpa told me to keep going until Dad didn't have no face left, so that's what I did.

I woke up the next mornin' and asked Grandpa if he felt bad for doin' what he done to those little girls and them other people he killed.

He asked me if I felt bad about what I done to Tim and Mom and Dad. I looked at Dad's body on the couch and didn't feel nothin'. Not good or bad. So that's what I told him.

He smiled because he knew I just figured it out.

The not carin'. . .that's the gene.

I asked him when we was gonna go on killin'.

He told me we ain't in no rush, but he'd let me know when the time's right.

Nick Roberts *is the award-winning author of* Mean Spirited, Anathema, The Exorcist's House *trilogy, and other novels and collections. His works have become international bestsellers, translated into multiple languages, and are in various stages of film/TV development.*

A native West Virginian and a doctoral graduate from Marshall University, Nick currently lives in South Carolina with his wife and three children. When he's not reading or writing, he enjoys exercise, going to the theater, and is an advocate for people in recovery from substance use disorders.

Follow him at www.nickrobertsauthor.com

LAST DAY FREE

Viggy Parr Hampton

THE SMELLS OF POPCORN, funnel cake, and corndogs are the same, but everything else is different.

Jason grew up coming to Funland of Georgia. Every few months, his mother would splurge on two tickets, and she would allow them to both escape for a day into the colorful tents, the calliope jingles, and the whoosh of roller coasters, all of it scented with butter, frying oil, and sizzling sausage.

As Jason walks down the main thoroughfare, he has to blink rapidly, wondering if the act of squeezing his eyelids together tightly enough will make the scene in front of him change, shift back to what it was before, to what it should still be.

The colorful tents are now streaked with mildew, worn thin, and flapping limply in the fall breeze. The calliope has been replaced with some teenager's Spotify playlist, sending trashy pop tunes floating through the air, as unpleasant as dirty fog. Even the whoosh of the roller coasters feels stale, accompanied every time by the creak and groan of the aging wooden struts.

I shouldn't have come here, he thinks. He shuffles to the right, trying to dodge a woman muscling a stroller through the trash-strewn street, but she clips him in the shoulder anyway.

"Ow," he says reflexively.

The woman stops, staring him down. "Ow? Really? You want to trade places with me?" In the stroller, which Jason now realizes has a wonky wheel, a toddler with a face covered in what he hopes is chocolate ice cream starts to wail.

The woman is still staring at him, clearly expecting an answer.

For a second, he considers saying, 'Why yes, ma'am, I would gladly trade places with you.' There's a wedding ring on her finger, small but nothing to sneeze at, and despite the toddler's wailing, the child is clearly well-dressed and much-loved. Despite her frustration, this woman must have people who love her, a home to return to at the end of the day that is no doubt full of the warmth of other people. Maybe there's even a family dog, a mutt with an overeager tail, who likes to lick the toddler's face clean whenever his mother isn't looking—

"Hello?" The woman is waving her hand in front of his face, her annoyance shifting to a mixture of suspicion and concern. "You in there?"

"Have a good day," he finally manages to mumble, as his hand moves to the shoulder she bashed with her elbow, rubbing the old injury.

The woman gives him one last skeptical glare and continues on, pushing the stroller laboriously through the street toward the exit.

Jason glances at his watch—3:52pm. The park will be closing for the last time in one hour and eight minutes. He wishes he could have gotten here sooner, but his boss demanded Jason cover a shift at the restaurant this morning, the dreaded brunch crowd, and after making barely $25 in tips for four hours of work, not to mention the extra time cleaning and prepping for dinner, Jason was lucky to make it to Funland at all.

He keeps walking, past a haunted house ride that looks like someone raided the clearance section at a Halloween store, past a Ferris wheel moving so slowly, it appears nearly stationary, past an ice cream stand with a disturbing amount of fluid leaking from the cooler to form an iridescent puddle on the pavement.

In the midway, instead of smiling barkers cajoling the crowd into trying their luck at a game or two, there are only a handful of bored teenagers, hunched over their phones, ignoring even the customers who look like they want to play.

It hurts Jason to see Funland like this. People used to come from hundreds of miles away to visit the park, the biggest of its kind in Georgia. The best thing about his childhood, apart from baseball, were the Saturdays spent with his mother at Funland— back when his life brimmed with possibility, crackled with joy, vibrated with enthusiasm for living.

LAST DAY FREE

Jason's hand finds its way back to his shoulder, massaging the joint, which the woman with the stroller set to aching again. Not for the first time, or the second, or even the hundred thousandth, Jason wonders what his life would have been like if he hadn't taken Tony Castro up on his dare, if he hadn't grabbed that fraying rope and swung high above the water, hadn't lost his grip and gone sailing to the dark depths, if he hadn't felt his shoulder crunch against the rock hiding just beneath the surface.

"It probably would have been a lot better," Jason says, quickly moving to cover his mouth. He's been doing that a lot lately, accidentally speaking his thoughts out loud. In the restaurant, it's easy enough to hide it under the din of diners, but here, where the crowd is beginning to thin in the late afternoon of Funland's last day, it's much more conspicuous. A teenager with a nose ring turns to look at him, opens her mouth to say something, then thinks better of it and walks off quickly in the other direction.

When he gets to the Twirling Twisters ride, he stops, gazing up at the spinning compartments, transfixed. The ride seems to spin much slower than it did thirty years ago. I certainly spin much slower than I used to, he thinks and chuckles aloud. Luckily, nobody is close enough to hear him this time.

He continues on, letting his feet take him wherever they want to go. He expected more of a crowd, with the 'Last Day Free' promotion and all, but then again, it is late in the day. Children are tired, teenagers are bored, parents are ready to get home, cook dinner. The magic has run out, the spell broken.

"Jason? Jason Ryder?" a voice from behind him catches him off guard, and he has to steady himself against a railing to keep from tripping. Whipping around, he half expects to see the street behind him empty, the voice all in his head.

But no—there's a woman standing there, about his age, glossy, shoulder-length brown hair. Bright blue eyes.

He knows those eyes.

"Jason?" she says again, taking a few steps toward him. "Is that you?"

When she smiles, he's transported back to high school, back to math class, where Jane Ransom is asking if she can borrow a pencil, smiling and looking at him sincerely with those piercing blue eyes.

"Jane?" he says.

She laughs. "I knew it was you!" She closes the distance between them and, to his great surprise and delight, pulls him into a hug. The feeling is strange but welcome—he can't remember the last time someone hugged him. Not since his mother died, at least.

She pulls away, holding him at arms' length, and gives him a once-over. "Jason, you look great!" she says, and even though she's lying, his body warms at the compliment.

"Thanks," he says, grinning. "So do you!" This, at least, is not a lie. Jane does look great. The years have been kind to her, and before he can help himself, his eyes flick to her left hand. A simple gold band encircles her ring finger, and Jason feels some of the warmth in his core start to dissipate.

"What have you been up to?" Jane asks, and Jason can't help but think that her last name must not be Ransom anymore. Would it be weird to ask her who she is now?

"Oh, you know," he says. "I'm still nearby. Been working in the service industry."

"Great," she says, her head cocking at a questioning angle. "Are you still playing baseball?"

Jason's face crumples in on itself like a dying star. How does she not know? He thought everyone knew. . .

"Oh," he says, swallowing past a knot in his throat. "No."

Her smile falters, and she looks at him curiously. "No? Had enough of it after college?"

He bites his lip, tries to keep the tears at bay. That's all twenty years in the past—why are the tears still so close to the surface? "I. . . I, um." He clears his throat. "I didn't go to college."

Jane's eyebrows shoot up, making her blue eyes look as big and shiny as the slippery balls of ice Jason clinks into diners' Negronis at work. "But. . .didn't you get a scholarship to UCLA? Right?" Jane shakes her head. "That was you, I know it was! Jason Ryder, baseball star!"

He knows she's not trying to be insensitive, but rage and resentment twist in his gut. Even here, he can't escape his failures. "I thought you knew," he finally chokes out. "I thought everyone knew."

"Knew what?" Surely she's not being deliberately ignorant?

"I, uh, I had an accident. A month before I was supposed to leave for California. I was on a rope swing and I fell into the water, landed on a rock, fucked up my shoulder. Doctors said it was a rotator cuff tear, a really bad one. I thought I would get better. . .but it just didn't happen. Lost my scholarship."

He's staring down at the ground now, ashamed, and he can feel Jane's secondhand embarrassment, her pity. He hates her for it. "Oh, Jason," she says. "I'm so sorry. I didn't know. I think I'd left for Vanderbilt by then. I had no idea."

"It's okay," he says, because that's what people say in situations like these, even though nothing is okay and he wishes he were anywhere but here.

"Well," Jane says awkwardly. "I'm glad you're doing well now."

Is he doing well? Is a nearly forty-year-old man with no wife, no girlfriend, no family, and no real friends, stuck working a server job for meager tips, with a shoulder injury that still makes it difficult for him to raise his right arm, 'doing well?'

"Thanks," he says.

"I better get going," she says, pulling her phone from her pocket and glancing at the screen. "I promised my husband I'd meet him at the ice cream stand in ten minutes."

"Yeah," is all Jason can manage. He considers telling her about the leaky ice cream freezer, maybe making a joke that she should avoid the ice cream here at all costs, but he doesn't.

Let her eat it. Let her feel some small shred of the pain he feels, the pain she has made him relive.

The sign in front of him is faded and decaying, like everything else in Funland, but it's still legible.

"The Terror of the Seas," it reads, the letters a deep blue, the rest of the sign festooned with cartoon sharks.

"This one's got one ride left, if you wanna get on."

Jason looks up into the pimpled face of yet another teenager. Is Funland completely run by children?

"Oh," Jason says. "Okay."

The teenager is wearing a name tag that says, "Jeremy." His uniform shirt is covered in some sort of dark stain. Jason isn't close enough to catch a whiff, but he imagines the smell coming off that fabric is nothing short of rank.

When Jason doesn't move, Jeremy prods him again. "Sir? You gonna ride, or what?"

Is he going to ride? As a child, "The Terror of the Seas" was his absolute favorite ride. After his accident, even though his mother tried to take him to Funland to cheer him up, he refused to get on the little boat, refused to let her drag him aboard. The dark water, the hidden monsters looming just beneath the foaming surface, the stench of chlorine and metal. . .it was too much. He couldn't bear it.

"Man, come on. Last ride of the day. Well—last ride forever, I guess. I gotta get home, man."

Jason looks up at Jeremy, at the whiteheads spangling his face. What waits at home for Jeremy? A mother, a father, perhaps a younger sister? The kind of sibling Jeremy pretends to scorn, but who secretly delights him with her quick wit and unabashed kindness? Is there a meatloaf on the table at Jeremy's house, home-cooked by his mother? Is there homework waiting on his desk, begging to be completed? Is there a shining future waiting just outside the Funland gates for Jeremy?

"Yeah, I'm going," Jason says, and his tongue feels fat and foreign in his mouth. The popcorn-funnel-cake-corndog smell has shifted into a stench, something rotten and greasy, and his stomach lurches even as he climbs aboard the little boat, which rocks gently with his weight.

There are no other passengers, and Jeremy doesn't wait for any.

"Have fun, man," Jeremy says, and before Jason can change his mind, before he can leap off the boat back to the safety of dry land, Jeremy is pressing the GO button, and the boat jerks forward into the green water.

The boat is wobbly but sure of itself as it seesaws into a tunnel. Jason tugs at his collar, heat rising up his neck. The air is stale, fetid. Despite the darkness, he can see the cracks in the black paint where the plaster is showing through.

Tinny sound effects pipe through ancient speakers. As a child, this ride was the kind of scary that made you feel braver for tackling it. The kind of scary that made you feel empowered instead of small, invincible instead of achingly vulnerable.

Now, all Jason feels is a crushing sense of despair.

LAST DAY FREE

The boat emerges from the tunnel into a large room painted to look like the ocean during a massive storm. Alongside the narrow canal Jason's boat staggers through, fiberglass sculptures of roaring polar bears, fierce penguins, and an inexplicable seven-foot Yeti, the fur balding and dirty, sit rotting in the dim light. The sound of waves crashing erupts from the speakers in a spray of static.

Jason shifts in his seat, and the boat rocks with him. He doesn't think it should be able to do that, but what does he know? He hasn't ridden this ride in nearly twenty years, and back then, he had his mother with him to clutch his hand, even when he was old enough for that to be embarrassing.

Now, there's only the polar bears, the penguins, and the Yeti to keep him company.

The boat wends its way laboriously around each curve, getting closer to the ride's exit.

Not far to go now.

Jason knows what awaits him here at the end, the final jump scare, the true "Terror of the Seas." He knows, and yet it still startles him.

The boat is five feet from the exit when the animatronic Great White Shark erupts out of the water, so close Jason could reach out and touch it. Decades of being water-bound have turned the shark a diseased greenish hue, and one entire side of its head has rotted away, exposing the metal ribbing beneath. One black eye has caved in, and the open jaw is full of holes where jagged teeth have fallen away.

But the black void of its throat is still there, still gaping.

Still beckoning.

He's not sure if it's the physics of the shoddy boat and the uneven weight distribution with only one passenger, or if it's his own startled reaction, the way his body involuntarily jumps back, or, more gruesomely, if it's a death drive hidden deep in his own psyche. Whatever it is, the result is the same.

The boat rocks alarmingly, and, with a quiet splash, Jason falls into the dirty water.

The water is lukewarm, full of leaves and debris that collide against Jason's skin, and he feels as though he has slipped into a bathtub recently vacated by someone much filthier than him. He's slipping down, down, down—*Shouldn't there be a bottom here? How deep does this go?*—and the water grows cooler as he descends, and he really should start pumping his arms, start swimming, start cresting above this tepid pond, but a lightning rod of fear strikes him limp.

The disgust evaporates, replaced entirely by an animalistic terror. He's stuck in this dark water, effectively blind and deaf, and he knows there are things down here with him, there are rotting things, decaying things, the kinds of things that will swim inside you and taint your insides.

Dear God, he thinks. *Dear God, get me out, get me out of here—*

His hand touches something solid, and there's a beat of relief, but it's mercilessly brief. His fingers grasp at the object, trying to find purchase, but instead they push through the rubbery material, colliding with sharp metal wires.

His legs start to kick furiously, windmilling against what he now knows is the shark, the fucking Great White Shark, he's put his motherfucking hand through it, and he knows he must be face to face with that destroyed eye, with that mouthful of broken teeth, with that dark abyss that promises nothing but death. He knows it's there, but he can't see it, and somehow that makes it worse, far worse, and panic is constricting his lungs, and he tries desperately to pull his hand back, but his injured shoulder is too weak, and he's stuck, stuck so solidly underwater, with this shark-thing, and Jeremy has probably already left for the day, and no one is coming for him, and no one will ever come for him.

Jason doesn't expect to ever open his eyes again, but he does.

Painfully bright light sears his retinas as fingers pull apart his eyelids.

"Normal pupillary response," a gruff male voice calls.

There's a crushing pain against his ribs, once, twice, three times, then a pair of sweaty lips encase his own, sending hot salami-flavored breath down his windpipe. Then he is heaving, water rushing out of his stomach, surging through his mouth and onto the ground next to him. At the taste of chlorine and salami, he retches again, this time bringing up a thin soup of bile.

When he's finished, he sucks in a lungful of air before wheezing it back out.

There's a hand on the back of his head and another on his elbow, pulling him up to sitting.

"You're going to be fine, pal," the salami-breathed man says, giving him a rough pat on the back. "You had us pretty scared there for a minute."

"What," Jason tries, but is beset by a coughing fit. When he catches his breath again, he manages to ask, "What happened?"

"You fell in, buddy," the man says, and Jason's vision has returned to normal enough so he can see the paramedic uniform. "Fell right in, yep. You were down there for quite awhile, too. Had to stop the ride and get you out."

"Oh," Jason manages, and it's only then that he looks past the paramedic to take in his surroundings. The sky overhead is blue and clear, and there's a brightly striped building directly in front of him. Have they taken him to the hospital? Or somewhere else? "Where am I?" he asks.

"Funland of Georgia, of course! We had to triage you right here. You were pretty bad, but—"

A female voice cuts through the atmosphere. "Jason!" A woman appears at his side, with pretty shoulder-length brown hair. Her blue eyes, full of worry, sparkle with tears as she looks down at him. "Jason, I thought we'd lost you!"

"Jane?" he says, now more confused than ever. Clear, jaunty calliope music drifts toward him, and now he can smell something fresh and delicious and fatty wafting through the air, too. There's a raucous peal of laughter in the distance.

"Of course it's me!" she says, starting to cover his face with light kisses. "Jason, we were so terrified!"

"We?" he says, and surely this must be a dream. Surely, he has died down there, and this is the afterlife. Was he really good enough to get into Heaven?

"Me and Tessie, of course!"

Before he can ask who Tessie is, a small girl of about six leaps into his arms. He hadn't noticed her before—she must have been standing behind Jane. "Daddy!" she yelps, snuggling close to him, completely unbothered by his chlorine stench or his soaked clothes. She starts to sob, repeating "Daddy, Daddy" until Jane finally pulls her off of him.

He sits up straighter, looks around more intently. "The Terror of the Seas" is at his back, and this can't be possible, but the paint is fresh, the queue is full of people staring at him with concerned expressions, and he now realizes the thoroughfare of Funland is teeming with happy families, teenagers holding hands, and children sucking on colorful ice cream cones. Not one piece of tarp is stained with mildew, not one sign is missing a letter, not one employee is hunched over a phone.

This is not possible.

"Does he need to go to the hospital?" Jane is asking the paramedic. She clutches Tessie close to her.

"No, Mrs. Ryder, he'll be fine."

Mrs. Ryder? Jason's eyes flick to his hand, and sure enough, there's a gold wedding band wedged on his finger. Incredulous, he lifts up both hands, and he's even more shocked at the smoothness with which his shoulder joint responds, at the complete and total lack of pain. On the ring finger of his right hand, an MLB championship ring glitters like a rare jewel.

"This can't be real," he breathes, but nobody hears him.

He died down there. Didn't he?

He looks around again, taking in the smiles of parkgoers, the obvious health of the park itself, the shining auburn hair of Tessie, who has her mother's blue eyes.

He gulps, his mouth still tasting of bile and salami.

If he didn't die down there. . .who did?

Viggy Parr Hampton, MPH is an epidemiologist, host of the podcast "Horror Humor Hunger," and the author of A Cold Night for Alligators, Much Too Vulgar, The Rotting Room, *and* A Veritable Household Pet. *She is a graduate of Georgetown University and Emory University's Rollins School of Public Health. Connect with her at her website,* http://www.viggyhampton.com, *or on Instagram or TikTok @ viggyparrhampton.*

THERE IS NO HEAVEN, ONLY HELL

S. C. FISHER

"CAN I LET you in on a secret?"

Dr. Nichols leans forward and the leather couch squeaks obscenely with the seismic shift of his ass. He is not embarrassed. In fact, he barely notices. He tents his fingers in front of his nose, which—much like the rest of him—is long and slender.

I elect to humour him.

"Please," I say. It is an effort to sound engaged.

I await the standard, psycho-babble preamble. This time, there is none: he strikes for the heart.

"There is no Heaven, Abigail. Only Hell."

On the coffee table that separates my couch from his, a metronome sways. This is how I identify the exact moment when the adrenaline kicks in and my heart rate spikes.

"What?"

I blink, dumb with confusion. Whatever this tactic is, I don't recognise it. On our quest to address my laundry list of issues, we have explored many avenues—mindfulness, hypnosis, a cocktail of meds—but not this twisted form of reverse psychology. Dr. Nichols is the epitome of professionalism. He has never cursed, never grown frustrated, never so much as passed gas in front of me. He has certainly never been cruel. Until now.

"I think you heard me." His smirk suggests that I'm not imagining the sarcasm that drips from his words like warm honey.

Taken aback, I pick at the skin near my thumbnail. The bloom of pain focuses me, allowing me to formulate a response that is not rooted in panic.

"Why would you say that!?"

"Because it's true."

I should get up. I know I should leave—cuss him out first, maybe, then storm out the room—however, I am frozen stiff. An ice sculpture on an ugly couch that has seen better days and countless patients.

"But, my anxiety. . . I. . .you can't. . .you shouldn't. . ." I trail off, gawking at Dr. Nichols' grin. It brightens by the second.

"I see what this is," I announce with faux confidence. "You want me to convince myself that death is nothing to be scared of. Self-healing crap, right? Shouldn't be afraid of something we can't change."

He laughs. It's the cruel kind of laughter that reminds me of my childhood bullies, in all their forms, so I conceal a shudder by rounding my shoulders. I notice that the metronome has stopped marking time, then the office darkens as if the sun has ducked behind a cloud. I glance toward the window, though I can't see much through the misted glass except a crimson streaked sky. It seems unlikely that the weather has changed drastically enough to account for the long shadows that ooze out of the woodwork.

"Oh, Abigail," he croons, and nausea balloons in my gut so fast that I worry I'm about to puke on my lap. "This is no such thing."

Irritated, I roll my eyes and fold into the cushions at my back. It's an immature reaction that sets Dr. Nichols off chuckling again. He reaches out to pat my knee, thoroughly patronising, and I'm too slow to evade the contact.

"What is it, then?"

He meets the challenge in my gaze with an arched brow and the kind of devilish smile that shows off how handsome he is— sculpted jawline, full lips, cleft chin poorly disguised by a peppering of auburn stubble. Clearly I have noticed him before, in the way a woman notices a man. It's obvious from how the tip of his finger circles the peak of my knee, tickling playfully, that he's not oblivious to this. For a moment, I wonder where this encounter might go, if I wasn't so crazy and he wasn't so strange.

"This is me being honest." His tone has softened. "You deserve that. Every human being does. I've never lied to you, Abigail, but I've withheld certain things I wasn't sure you could handle."

"Things?" I parrot. I try to swallow and must force the reflex with very little saliva to aid me. "What kind of things?"

THERE IS NO HEAVEN ONLY HELL

There is no more noise from outside. The ever-present hum of afternoon traffic and the buzz of pneumatic drills from the construction site on the corner have faded away, as though the world has been muted by the touch of a button. There is only us, now.

Dr. Nichols sighs as he hikes up the hem of his pants so that he can cross his legs. I observe him carefully, as the fly watches the spider.

Despite the gloom that ensconces us, when the doctor inclines his head towards the window, I catch a glimpse of something I have never noticed before in the six months I have been his patient: a tattoo, running along the arch of his neck, right where the muscles cord. It is a serpent twisted around an apple. As I stare at it in wonder, the snake writhes and a forked tongue flicks out of its mouth. I grip the arm of the couch so tight that my nails add to its collection of scars.

Dr. Nichols turns back to regard me and I cannot dismiss the flames burning within his pupils. I hear them crackle, fracturing the silence, and I worry that I may be incinerated where I sit.

"There is no Heaven, only Hell," he repeats and, deep down, I believe him.

I think of my greatest fear—the black dog that nips at the heels of my joy, daily—and I'm filled with the terror that comes whenever I contemplate the possibility that all that awaits me in death is endless nothing. It started when I was ten, after I held my mother's hand whilst her body grew cold and her chest still. The idea that everything I was or am, every last feeling, desire, and dream, will be snuffed from existence, is more than I have been able to stand since.

I long to be more to the universe than a smudge that will be wiped clean by time.

"Why?" Through a haze of tears, I watch as Dr. Nichols sets down his notepad on the table with fingers that end in tapered talons. They are black, and they take my breath away as he drums them on his thigh.

"It's the order of things." He shrugs, a brief lift of the shoulders. "Evil endures. Can't say the same for righteousness."

My heart drops into my toes. Sensing my devastation, Dr. Nichols offers a smile that peels his lips away from his gums to exhibit a row of serrated incisors. He scrubs a hand over his stubble, contemplative, whilst I melt into the couch.

"There is one way." The words have scarcely cleared his lips before I pounce on them.

"Anything!" I feel the darkness reaching for me, swiping at my ankles, so I tuck my legs beneath me on the couch. The shadows howl with mirth at my expense, but my attention is locked and loaded on the doctor, whose credentials I am beginning to question.

"Sin." A simple word. A complicated concept.

I pause, uncertain.

"There's no rest for the wicked," he states slowly and, though this should be all the clarification I need, I want him to spell it out for me. A moment lapses, then he obliges. "Sin, and you will endure. This world burns through decent folks like kindling at a cookout, then it blows them off as smoke. That's not the way you want to live, if that's not the way you want to die. Sin, Abigail, and you'll be reborn. That's the best I can offer you, and that's no word of a lie."

I look at the static metronome. I cannot help but picture fire and brimstone, rivers of blood, bodies tormented and tortured by whip and chain and claw. It is alarming—horrifying, even—but it is something, and that is the part I cannot dismiss easily. My eyes swerve back to Dr. Nichols. In the light bleeding through the window, his horns are resplendent. I gasp at the sight of them, towering above his head in columns of bone that stretch for the ceiling. There is beauty in all things.

"You know what you have to do," he says, quietly. The metronome returns from the grave. "That's our session for this week."

I leave his office on autopilot, feet carrying me to the street outside the building before my brain has a chance to catch up. The sky is perfectly blue and the clouds skate by, fluffy and white. A car horn blares, drawing my attention, and I remember that I have to drive myself home. Nearby, a baby squawks from its stroller, an old lady hobbles along leaning heavily on her stick, and a teenager pauses at a hydrant so her dog can relieve itself. I watch them all far longer than is decent, mind working overtime.

So many souls, so many possibilities, and me—the devil in the details.

I have never felt so alive.

THERE IS NO HEAVEN ONLY HELL

Welsh horror author **S.C.Fisher** *is the creator of the YA series* Base Fear, *which delves into the haunting histories of three real-life military bases and the experiences of the families living at them.* Fisher *also has work featured in anthologies from Voices From The Mausoleum, January Ember Press, House of the Macabre, and Infested Publishing. Most recently, her short story* Mother Never Liked Dead Things *appeared on season one of the Haunted UK Fiction podcast. Fisher is working on her first adult pink horror novel, featuring zombies, toxic friendship, and the perils of skincare during the apocalypse.*

CLOSER THAN THEY APPEAR

TOM DEADY

"**T**HANKS, MAN.**"** I slip the receipt into my pocket without a look. All that matters is that my baby is fixed. The cashier replies with nothing more than a smirk—a smirk I don't much care for. And why does he look so familiar?

The Arizona heat envelops me as I start across the lot toward my baby: a vintage metallic-blue Pontiac Firebird. The sun highlights the paint job, turning the car into a giant gemstone. I go to the passenger side first, running a hand along the smooth paint on the sideview mirror. The heat of the metal matches the torrid rage I'd felt the other night when I'd come out of the bar to find the mirror smashed and dangling from the car. Some asshole must have sideswiped it on the way out of the parking lot.

I toss the heavy duffel bag into the trunk, slide into the driver's seat, and fire up the engine. The jungle-cat purr is music to my ears. I roll down the windows and crank the AC to high and the stereo even higher. Bon Jovi blares out from the speakers, drawing looks from the few people within range. I slip my mirrored shades on and start out of the lot. On my way by the office, I flip the cashier a wave. The only response is that creepy, *knowing* smirk. "Fuck off," I mutter, rolling up the windows and leaving the lot in a cloud of smoke and burnt rubber.

I have a long drive to Gallup ahead of me. The Bird will get me there in plenty of time for the meeting. It better. Then I'll be flush with cash, enough to travel, chill for a while, whatever I want.

Route 40 East is a lonesome desert highway with nothing but Winslow—as in "standing on a corner in Winslow, Arizona"—and the Petrified Forest National Park to break up the hot, dry monotony. Its claim to fame is being part of "historic Route 66" but that just means a bunch of hokey tourist traps and honky-tonk souvenir shops. I chuckle as I pass the "Entering Winona" sign; I might have enjoyed that back in her prime.

I step on the gas. The speedometer reads just under eighty as I rocket toward the blazing fireball in the east. Fast enough to make good time but not so fast as to attract unwanted attention. That's the last thing I need considering what's in the trunk. The meeting is set for 2 p.m. and the ride is only about three hours. I want to get there early and case the drop site to make sure Mendez doesn't have any tricks up his sleeve. I glance at my watch, it's just after 9 a.m. Plenty of time to grab lunch and still be early for the drop.

I'm just past Winslow, humming *Take It Easy*, of course, and heading for Joseph City when I notice the pick-up truck in the sideview mirror. There isn't much to notice, really. It's an old, beat-up-looking thing, a shitty tan color with darkly tinted windows. It is in the right lane and far enough back that I can't make out the driver, especially with the sun glaring off the windshield. Still, a seed of apprehension tingles in my gut.

I goose the gas pedal, sending the needle to eighty-five. I want that damn pick-up out of my sight. My gut is never wrong about these things.

The radio goes staticky. I must be out of range of the classic rock station, so I fiddle with the dial until I find something tolerable. When my eyes shift to the sideview, the pick-up is right where it had been—about seventy-five yards back. I wipe sweat from my forehead and edge the car a little faster, pushing ninety. The pick-up keeps pace. What the fuck?

The most likely explanation is that Mendez has a tail on me. It even makes sense. I'd mentioned my desire to get out of the business, so maybe he thinks I'm going to steal his drugs and freelance sales to make more cash to finance my exit. I'm not *that* stupid. But it doesn't help settle my nerves. There is something about the truck. When my eyes slide again to the sideview, the memory hits me.

It was the night I'd met a few friends at The Chalet, a dive bar just outside Flagstaff. The place was packed and the gravel parking lot was full, mostly of shitboxes and jacked-up pick-ups. I'd squeezed the Bird into a spot between an ancient Monte Carlo and an old pick-up. When I'd exited the bar a few hours later, completely wasted, with one of the waitresses on my arm, she'd pointed out the smashed-up sideview dangling from the passenger door.

My gaze once again finds the sideview mirror—I can't see the truck in the rearview because of the "FIREBIRD" decal I have covering most of the back window. "It's the same fucking truck," I hiss. I realize I can't possibly know that. . .yet I am still sure of it. "Son of a bitch."

Gotta be one of Mendez's guys. But that does nothing to allay the slippery dread that has taken root in my gut. My eyes shift back and forth between the road ahead and the sideview mirror. The truck keeps an even distance behind me no matter how fast or slow I go, so I ease down to five miles above the limit. I realize just how isolated this stretch of Route 40 is. Nothing but desert scrub and rocks as far as the eye can see. I desperately search for a gas station or rest stop to pull into. The only sign I spot is for the Painted Desert Indian Center. Better than nothing. At the last possible minute, I jerk the wheel to the right, cutting across the slow lane and onto the access road. I make the turn into the parking lot, grab my Glock out of the glove box, and jump out of the car. The pick-up truck is nowhere in sight.

I walk slowly to the rear of the car, trying to spot the pick-up on Route 40 or pulled over on the access road. It is gone. Just. . .gone. I scan Route 40 to the west, thinking maybe the truck had stopped when the driver saw me swerve onto the access road, but there is nothing there. The truck must have sped by, I realize with a laugh. "Fucking paranoid bastard," I say, and get back into the Bird. I keep the gun on the passenger seat in easy reach.

I am just over an hour from Gallup. There isn't a car in sight in either direction when I pull back onto Route 40, immediately getting in the left lane and leaning on the gas hard. All I want is to get out of the fucking desert and get the drop done. The little scare has me thinking it might really be time to get out of the business. There are only a couple ways it ends for people who stay with it too long. One is prison, the other is in a shallow grave right out here in the godforsaken land I'm driving through. The payoff for this drop is enough to get me out. I can move out of state, out of Mendez's reach. He's a lunatic, even for a drug dealer, always talking about hoodoo and shit. Yes, time to get out, maybe as far as the east coast, find a straight job—

CLOSER THAN THEY APPEAR

The truck is back, now only about forty yards behind me. Where the fuck did it come from? I still can't see who is driving, but I can sure as hell imagine. A scary-looking Mexican with a scar on his face and death in his eyes. Probably more than one of them. All packing AR15s or whatever the preferred weapon of the cartel is these days. Shit. They'll wait until there is nothing around, not even some shitty Painted Desert Indian Center, because of course they know exactly where to do it. They'll run me off the road and pepper the Bird with automatic weapon fire until there is nothing left. . .of me or the car. They'll take the duffel bag and pay nothing. They probably already have my grave dug and waiting. Suddenly the prison option doesn't sound so bad.

Without warning, my terror turns to rage. No fucking chance am I going out this way. Not in the middle of this stinking desert inferno, not by a bunch of shit-for-brains drug dealers driving a shitbox pick-up. I know I can outrun them in the Bird, but that isn't how this ends either. Time to send Mendez a message.

I slow the Bird down to fifty-five and keep one eye on the sideview mirror. The truck holds its distance at about forty yards, matching my speed. I ease off the gas pedal a little more, watching the truck as I do. Somehow, it seems to stay exactly the same measure behind. I scan the road ahead and spot a small dirt shoulder. At the last second I pull in, slamming on the brakes and raising a cloud of dust in my wake. I grab the pistol off the passenger seat and step out of the car, weapon raised. My plan is to fire a shot in the air to get their attention. Then, depending on their reaction, well. . .I'm not sure what comes next. Whatever it takes.

As impossible as it is, the truck is gone. It didn't pass me, didn't pull in behind, and is nowhere to be seen on the road. It is just. . .gone. I blink, unable to stop jerking my head back and forth in search of the truck. Waves of heat shimmer off the asphalt but a body-wracking shiver runs through me. Every instinct is telling me to run. Back the way I came. Whatever waits ahead is. . .I don't know. But I can't. That would be suicide. I slide back into the Bird, crazy ideas spinning and jumping in my head, but I can't hold onto any of them long enough to make sense of them. I set the gun on the seat between my legs, pull the door shut, and speed back onto the road, raising another cloud of dust behind me.

I know I shouldn't be driving in my current state of confusion, but sitting idle on the side of the road seems like a worse idea. All I want is to be in motion, getting out of the desert and away from. . .*what?* Some haunted truck? My thoughts begin to clear and I try to come up with something, *anything* that could reasonably explain what is happening. Nothing comes. I realize why: because what's happening is simply not possible. I decide I just won't look at the sideview. Let the truck be there. As long as it isn't real, as long as I don't *acknowledge* it, it can't hurt me.

My resolve crumbles within three minutes. My eyes are drawn to the sideview, then go wide. "Yes!" The truck is gone. Wait. . .not gone, but a distant speck. Maybe I just didn't see it when I got out of the car. The thought makes me giddy. I bang my fists on the steering wheel in relief, cheering. I look again, just to be sure. Something cold coils inside my chest. The truck is almost out of view it is so far behind, yes, but that isn't what chills me. There is a man walking along the shoulder of the road. But I hadn't *passed* a man on the road. Logic—if you can apply logic to a situation like this—tells me it has to be the driver of the pick-up. "No, no, no. . ." I slam my foot to the floor, pinning the accelerator. The car leaps forward. The needle passes a hundred and hovers at one-oh-five.

I keep my eyes glued to the road, refusing to look at the sideview. "Fucking Mendez! What are you doing to me?" My eyes shift, almost involuntarily, to the mirror. The man is closer. It is impossible. His gait is slow, ambling, as though he has nowhere to go and nothing but time to get there. Yet he is somehow catching up to the Bird doing over a hundred. *What is he holding?* "Fuck this." I take my foot off the gas and let the car slow, then brake, pulling over to the side of the road. Knowing it is futile, I grab the gun and get out. It feels like the temperature has gone up twenty degrees: sweat pops out on my forehead, soaks my shirt. It's not the heat, though, this is the stinking sweat of fear. Of course, there is no man walking on the highway. And no pick-up in the distance, either.

I stand on the road, panting, and wipe my arm across my forehead to clear the sheen of sweat when an idea strikes me. I lean inside the car and look across at the sideview mirror. The man is there, strolling along. His steps are steady, not hurried, but somehow purposeful. He is close enough that I can see what he's holding: a huge knife, maybe a machete. I'm also close enough to make out his features. He looks Mexican, with a black goatee.

"Holy shit," I say when I recognize the man. It is the guy from the body shop, I am sure of it. Another memory slams into me like an anvil. That same night at the bar. I'd caught some asshole staring at me a few times. *This guy.* Had he been there, parked next to me, and smashed the mirror when he left? Knowing his body shop was the closest one to take it for repair? With that thought, that *knowledge*, comes the next. "It's the fucking mirror," I say, a hint of triumph in my voice.

I shut the car off and move around to the rear, glancing back down the highway to make sure there is no sign of the man. I pop the trunk and grab the tire iron. In three quick strides I reach the passenger side. I raise the tire iron, and with just a small pang of regret, bring it down on the sideview mirror. Two more hits are all it takes to dislodge it completely. It lands in the dry dirt on the shoulder with an unceremonious thump and the tinkling of glass. Careful not to look at the mirror itself, I pick it up and, with a cry, throw it as far into the desert as I can. It raises a small cloud of dust when it hits. "Problem fucking solved."

I toss the tire iron back into the trunk, get in the driver's seat, fire the engine, and peel back onto the road, laughing as I do. With a "just in case" glance to where the sideview mirror used to be, I pump a fist. "Fuck you, Mendez." I crank up the radio and settle in to finish the rest of the drive. I am out, I decide. This is the last drop, then I am gone. I'll have enough money to move, settle somewhere far away, find a job that won't get me killed. Fuck Mendez and whatever shitty cartel he works for.

Feeling better than I have all day, I head straight for Gallup. No more fucking around. I'll park at the diner and do the drop right out front where nothing can happen. Then I'll be taillights, heading east and not looking back.

I am just a few miles past Chambers, about a half hour before Gallup, when I need to piss. There is nothing around, just the desert foothills before the New Mexico border. I pull onto the shoulder and walk to the passenger side of the Bird in case any cars pass while I'm doing my business. I realize as I relieve myself, I haven't seen a single car all day. Other than that pick-up. With a cautious glance at the spot where the sideview should be, I move back around to the driver's side and jump in. I utter a squeal and hot bile rises in my throat when I see the sideview mirror on the passenger seat.

I look around frantically, knowing there is nobody but me. For miles, probably. Dread weighs on me like a bad decision. With something that feels like surrender, I reach for the battered sideview. Slowly turning it so I can see in the mirror, a hot, fetid breeze caresses my neck. I realize the doors and windows are closed. *It's his breath.* I see the man's grinning face in the mirror as he raises the machete.

Tom Deady's *first novel,* Haven, *won the 2016 Bram Stoker Award for Superior Achievement in a First Novel. He has since published several novels, novellas, a short story collection, and the first book in his middle grade horror series. Most recently, he compiled* The Rack, *an anthology celebrating the bygone days of mass market horror paperbacks. He has a master's degree in English and Creative Writing and is a member of both the Horror Writers Association and the New England Horror Writers Association. You can find out more about Tom and his work at www.tomdeady.com*

RACING THE MILK

ROBERT FORD

Robert Ford *has written the novels* The Dead Pennies, Burner, Blood Roses, The Compound, *and* No Lipstick in Avalon, Inner Demons, *and* The God Beneath my Garden. *Under the pen name Gideon Stone, he has written the westerns* They Rode Pale Horses, *and the* Clover Hollis: Bounty Hunter *series. He has co-authored the novella* Rattlesnake Kisses, *and* Cattywampus, *and* Black Salve *with John Boden. He can confirm the grass actually is greener on the other side, but it's only because of the bodies buried there.*

You can find out more about what he's up to by visiting robertfordauthor.com

LATE NIGHT CIGARETTES

GAGE GREENWOOD

I don't believe in the devil, but I see him every day.

"While the lamp holds out to burn,
The vilest sinner may return."
—Hymn 88, Issac Watts

AT TWO IN the morning, I slip out for a cigarette. My last of the day after brushing my teeth. Afterward, I go inside and check the locks on the front door and the sliding glass one in the back. I check the range dials to ensure they're all in the off position, and I check the freezer door because its suction is loose, and sometimes it pops open when someone uses the fridge door above it. It doesn't happen often, but on a few mornings, I've discovered water dripping from the freezer drawers, and the cardboard packaging on our frozen dinners slightly warped and soggy.

After I do my security rounds, I head to bed, where I toss and turn for an hour or so, thinking of all the day's mistakes, and I wake up to an alarm at 6:45, which hardly gives me the time I need to wake the kids and rush them out the door for school. I yearn for a life where they can eat their breakfast slowly. In peace. But I am not the man to deliver it. I cannot fall asleep early, no matter how exhausted I am, and they don't offer schooling for the children of night owls, something that starts at 11:00 A.M. Although they should.

The 2:00 A.M. cigarette is something of an important ritual, even more so than the freezer door check. If the food goes bad, more can be purchased, but if I don't have my cigarette, I go bad. Rotten and decaying.

We used to live in Cranston in a second story apartment. I smoked on the upstairs porch, watched the neighbors, many of whom were still up at the late hours. Cars drove by out front. There was movement, a dance, a thrum, and the last cigarette of the day pulsed tendrils of smoke into the party of life.

Seven years ago I moved to Richmond, Rhode Island. We had a two-acre yard and deep woods surrounding it. There was a house about a quarter mile down the road on the other side, but otherwise we were alone. I loved it for all the reasons one might love such a thing. The thrumming in Cranston wore thin, and the crime rates were rising. Richmond offered peace and quiet, calmness. Well, not inside our house where we still had to rush out every morning to get the kids to school on time, or while we danced around the small kitchen, bumping into each other, me making the kids pasta for dinner, and my girlfriend making her coffee, which for some reason has six hundred ingredients.

There never seemed to be a time without chaos, but it was our chaos, and we welcomed it.

But then we had to move again.

During a rowdy windstorm, a tree collapsed onto our house, crashing through the ceiling and destroying the wall that went from the den to the kitchen. We weren't home at the time, thank God. We were in Newport, playing video games at Ryan's Family Amusements. When we got home, washed over and spent, we saw the branches driving out the den door, crawling off the kitchen counter, and then we saw the shattered glass and ceiling pieces. Then we saw the bees.

We hurried the kids out, back into the car, and called the landlord. We stayed in a hotel for a few days while the landlord hired someone to clear and clean it all out, then we had to pack up our stuff because he had to repair everything, and it was gonna take months and months.

Needing a place in a hurry, we found a seasonal rental in Charlestown just to buy some time. A lot of wealthy folks bought houses by the beach just to stay in them during the summer, then for the off seasons, they rented the houses to college students, or in our case, a chaos family.

It's a small house, too small, and too expensive, but we don't have the luxury of choice in the current market, so we are where we are.

At 2 A.M. the yard feels bigger than it does during the day. The front yard is lined with decorative pine trees whose needles are a pain in the ass to clean. Rich people love inconvenient accessories because they can pay someone else to do the work. They have thousand-dollar lounge chairs on the back deck, and you wouldn't even want to sit on them. As a note, the more expensive the furniture, the less comfortable it is.

The pine trees end at the small dirt driveway. An old boat sits on a metal rack, wrapped in a tarp at the other side of the driveway, and behind it are more pine trees, this time stretching from the road to the garage, blocking the house entirely from the view of any neighbors.

I have to go to the very end of the driveway for my smoke. The owners will be back in a few months, and they had a strict no smoking policy, even on the property.

The road is dirt and pockmarked from April's heavy rains. Four houses line the opposite side of the road, and three on my side before the road spills out onto the main artery of Charlestown. No one lives in those houses off season, though. We are completely alone.

I sit on a green plastic lawn chair, smoking and flicking the ash into a half-filled Pepsi bottle. Rabbits hop through the shrubbery all day and night. Raccoons and possums creep into the backyard where my girlfriend leaves wet cat food for the strays.

I've seen weird shapes in the sky at night. Sometimes drones, I think, other times, I'm not so sure. Triangles, glowing and pulsing.

Occasionally, a boat horn blares. It's a beautiful sound, loud and hypnotic.

I sit with my thoughts. Afraid of them. What did I do wrong today? What did I do right? It's hard to answer my own questions.

I remember yelling at the kiddo because he dropped frozen fruits on the ground when he went digging for an ice cream cup in the freezer. It was probably me who left the bag open enough for the fruits to spill out, but still, I said, "YOU HAVE TO BE MORE CAREFUL," in a voice louder than the situation warranted.

Eyes peek through the dense shrubbery under the pines. I see them all the time. Looking at me. Judging me. There is something stalking me. It knows my routine and it waits each night to examine me while I smoke. But why doesn't it do anything? Why hasn't it come out yet? What is it waiting for?

I sometimes worry I'll be homeless soon, that things won't ever "pick up." That I spent a life chasing a dream that could only be defined by the walls around it.

As a child, when my anxiety reached unbearable heights, I'd recite lists to calm my nerves. I liked the Muppet Babies. *FozzieScooterRowlfPiggyGonzoKermitAnimalSkeeter. . .*

I suppose I still do that, but now it's more abstract. I'll list my failures one two three.

My son cries to me in the evenings, He doesn't know why. I just hug him and let him. I can feel his limbs trembling under the weight of his heavy emotions. He doesn't know how to carry what he's inherited, and I don't know how to teach him to.

Sometimes we cry together.

On the neighborhood Facebook pages, there's been a lot of videos posted of teenagers from Connecticut rolling up and robbing the cars in the driveways. Usually, they break in and take whatever they can from the vehicle, but sometimes it's the vehicle itself that gets taken.

I wonder what would happen if they rolled up while I was outside having my smoke. Would they drive away in a hurry, or would they beat me up or kill me? I bring stuff out with me for protection. Mace. A stun gun. My car keys.

I'm afraid all the time. Not just of the car thieves. I fear disease, and not always the big ones, although cancer is on my mind quite often. But the ones you can get from mouse poop, from bats, from rusty nails, things I don't usually see and that's what makes them all the more terrifying.

I watch car wreck videos on my Reels and TikTok. That and freak accidents.

I watch them to torture myself. To be afraid.

To add layers of fear onto my soft and fragile tower of anxiety.

The eyes are there again tonight, coming from the road. Could be a coyote or a small mountain lion. We have those here. Could be a fox or even a deer.

Could be. But it's not. It's the devil. It's everything I carry with me. It wants to take.

I'm afraid of people. I'm afraid I can't breathe.

Tonight, the moon is near full, and it helps me see my surroundings. The ocean waves provide a constant melody. A metronomic swooshing.

The devil creeps closer, his eyes blinking behind the sheath of summer green.

We'll be moving out soon, I think. *I won't see you anymore.*

But I will. The devil doesn't belong to the house. He belongs to me.

My son watches YouTube videos about the American Presidents. He sings a song to help him remember them in the order in which they served. His favorite is Grover Cleveland because he finds the name funny. I respond with, "Millard Filmore."

We laugh.

I think about my son while I inhale on my cigarette. I want to hug him, let him know everything will be alright, even though he's asleep and went to bed feeling fine.

Maybe I'm projecting.

More eyes appear under the devil's, too. I thought they were eyes, but the more I look, the more I realize they're teeth. He's smiling now. I'm not.

"We can't live like this," I say to him. "Constantly scared. You have to leave now."

He doesn't hear me. Never does, despite always listening.

Then it gets really scary. I hear it breathe. A shallow, raspy inhale and exhale. I don't run, and not because I'm frozen in fear, although that might be there too, but because if I do, then I must believe it. I can't go inside and pretend it was just a deer, or a bobcat. It was the past catching up to me. It was the devil, but not the biblical guy, fallen angel, horns and a pitchfork. It was my devil, all of mistakes and mental flaws born into a beast that wants to eat me alive. Maybe it comes in the form of a hideous monster or maybe it looks like a guy robbing cars. Either way, I'm in its path, and I see its teeth.

I'm too far from the house. It'll catch me before I can make it inside and slam the door shut, click those locks.

I used to sleep so soundly. I felt like I owned my body and life, but now that I'm older it feels like I've handed over the keys and I'm just hoping the ride doesn't end soon.

The driver of my car is behind the pines, hunched in the

shrubs. He's rattling the branches, and his smirk shows off his glow in the dark teeth.

A puff of smoke pours from my nostrils. I see the garbage barrels at the end of the drive and worry I haven't taken the trash out in a few days. We'll get fruit flies and probably ants because of it.

I used to buy pills from a guy in fluorescent pants, who took my money and put it in a fanny pack, but he kept the pills in little baggies up his sleeve at the elbow. I used to carry around a two liter of Pepsi that I'd partially emptied and mixed with cheap vodka. I used to overdo it on purpose until I couldn't walk, and I'd lie on the living room floor, feel the dust and dirt on the back of my head, staring at the ceiling and wishing I could float through it.

The bushes rustle and the eyes move a little closer. The breathing comes again, wet and harsh.

The head falls off my cigarette, plops in the driveway dirt. The breathing comes again, this time clearer, no liquid in the lungs. It's a long, relieved sigh. It's got me.

Do you feel that, too? The pain in your knees and weird thing in your throat when you swallow? Do you feel the way your heart sometimes stutters from doing too much? Do you feel your teeth giving up on you? Do you remember when it wasn't like this? When you sat in the back of your friend's car, all seats taken, and the lot of you sang "Africa" by Toto in unison? Do you remember when the weekend was forever, and the drinks were stronger, and the cigarettes did something to you? Made you dizzy? Do you remember when dizziness was sought after and not something that made you concerned? Do you remember when you laughed until you choked? Do you remember crying alone because you knew every moment wouldn't be realized until it was over? Have you ever been *in* the moment? What's that like? How does it feel to stay put with your surroundings and not in an infinite universe of future possibilities, each populated with their own versions of dread.

Do you feel it now? Its hand is on you.

Its breath moves the hair on your neck. It's here.

I run. I run inside as it laughs, and I lock the door, check it twice, lean against the wall and catch my breath.

I remember the sliding glass door, and I charge at it, making sure it's locked tight. It is, thank God. Then I run to the freezer and the oven because who knows where the devil might come from.

GAGE GREENWOOD

I see a light on in the bathroom, the door cracked open. The soft glow slices across the living room. I follow it because I hear a voice whispering inside, a sniffle.

As I get closer, my heart plummets. It's my son's voice. He's crying. I peek inside. He's sitting on the toilet, seat down, his knees brought up to his chest, arms wrapped around his calves. He's rocking. Crying and rocking.

Then I hear what he's whispering.

WashingtonAdamsJeffersonMadisonMonroeQuincyAdamsJacksonVanBurenHarrisonTylerPolkTaylorFilmorePierceBuchananLincolnJohnsonGrantGarfieldArthurCleveland. . .

My God, no. I fall back a step. Then, I leap forward, push the door all the way open. My son looks up at me, eyes wet and bloodshot. I open my arms, and he opens his. We cry to each other for a while, hugging and bawling.

I had locked those doors so tightly. I don't know how he got in, but the devil's inside.

He's here.

Gage Greenwood is the best-selling author of the Winter's Myths Saga, *and* Bunker Dogs.

He's been an actor, comedian, podcaster, and even the Vice President of an escape room company. Since childhood, he's been a big fan of comic books, horror movies, and depressing music that fills him with existential dread.

He lives in New England with his girlfriend and son, and he spends his time writing, hiking, and decorating for various holidays.

Find out more, or contact me: www.gagegreenwood.com

MR. WHITE

LARRY HINKLE

"**Y**OU'RE LATE. That's going to cost you a finger."

"Come on, it's only a couple days," Billy whined. "You know I'm good for it."

"'Only a couple of days' is why you're only losing one finger." Charles nodded, and two burly men threw Billy into a chair. "You knew the rules when you borrowed money from Mr. White. Every two days that you're late, you lose a finger."

Charles nodded again, and the goons wrapped a belt around Billy's chest to strap him in place.

"Which one is it going to be, Billy? I'll let you choose, since it's your first time. But you have to choose fast." He waited a beat. "Too late. Left pinky." One of the men slammed Billy's hand onto the table. He folded Billy's fingers under his palm, except for the pinky, which he wrenched to the side. Charles smiled at the sound of Billy's finger snapping. He picked up a meat cleaver, raised it above his head, and swung down. *THWACK!* The slight rocking of the boat threw his aim off, and he had to push down on the back of the blade to cut through the last strip of flesh.

Billy screamed, then passed out.

"Missed it by *that* much." Charles chuckled as he wiped the blade.

He tossed the pinky into a bucket, then used a sponge to sop up the blood from the table. This he squeezed into the bucket as well, drizzling it over the dozen or so fingers and toes laying in a pool of congealed blood.

"Wrap that and get rid of him," Charles said. "I need to give these to Mr. White."

Billy woke up in an alley near the wharf. His finger was bandaged, but blood was already seeping through the wrap. How was he going to explain this to Mary? He'd only borrowed the money from Mr. White to cover the poker losses he'd racked up since swearing to her he'd quit. He should've kept his promise, as the other players ate him like chum in the water. Turns out he was more of a minnow than a shark.

Charles finished washing his hands, then dried them off with a clean white towel. Being the front man for a loan shark certainly had its perks. He loved seeing the fear in his victim's eyes as he told them what was about to happen. He'd actually developed a taste for it.

He picked up the bucket and walked into Mr. White's office. "That was the last one for the day, Mr. White," he said. He showed Mr. White the contents of the bucket.

"Excellent work, Charles." The computer interface gave Mr. White's voice an artificial tone. Some called it creepy, but Charles didn't mind. He was amazed Mr. White could talk at all, let alone run such a smooth operation. Charles hadn't worked for him long. A mutual boss, someone higher up the food chain than either of them, had assigned him here after Mr. White's last front man had met an unfortunate demise. At first, he thought it a little odd that Mr. White operated from a ship, but he soon saw the logic behind the decision. He'd never been on the water before this assignment, not even a canoe, but it didn't take long for him to get used to it. Half the time, he even forgot they were tied to a pier.

Billy had decided to come clean with Mary after Charles had taken a second finger earlier that afternoon. Sure, it would cause problems between them in the short term, but what choice did he have?

If he could only talk to Mr. White! He had to figure out a way to get past Charles, though. He knew if he and Mary could speak to Mr. White alone, just the three of them, they could come to some sort of "agreement." She'd do that for him, wouldn't she? If it meant he got to keep the rest of his fingers. . .?

The next evening, after he'd given Mr. White the day's collections, Charles was tidying up his desk when an alarm dinged. He looked over at the monitors. Two people were climbing onto the ship. It was that idiot Billy Barnes. And was he actually bringing his wife with him? Oh, Mr. White was sure to find this a delicious turn of events.

He reached down to the console and buzzed the lock on the port-side door. Charles worried Billy might be suspicious that it was unlocked and suspect a trap, but his worry was unfounded. Billy and his wife slipped into the passageway.

Billy ran his hand along the wall and found a switch. A single light in the middle of the ceiling came on, illuminating the ten-foot passage.

"Billy, are you sure about this?" Mary asked as the door clicked shut behind them.

"Course I'm sure," he said. She'd seemed okay with the idea at home, but now that they were here, Billy worried she might back out. "Like I told you, Charles should be gone, and Mr. White's a reasonable man. I just need you to talk with him and see if we can work something out." He held up his mutilated hands. "You don't want me to lose any more fingers, do you?"

"Of course not. It's just. . ."

"It'll be okay, I promise. Now let's take a look at you." He fluffed her hair, then tugged at her top. He'd picked one that was a tad too small to better show off her tits. Something wasn't right, though. He unbuttoned another button. Now the red lace edges of the bra he'd chosen were clearly visible. "That's better," he said. "How can Mr. White say no to those?"

Charles chuckled as he watched Billy pimp up his wife on the monitor. He walked over and opened the door. "Come on in, Billy. You too, Mary." He licked his lips as she slunk by. "Why, you look good enough to eat."

Billy blanched. Mary was trying to make herself smaller as she struggled to button her blouse. Charles pulled her hands away. "Oh no, Mary, we mustn't do that." He unbuttoned another button and cupped her breasts. "Mr. White is definitely a breast man."

Mary crossed her arms. "What does that mean?" Her voice squeaked, like a mouse cornered by the cat.

"Didn't Billy tell you? He's offering you to Mr. White."

"*Offering* me?" She stared at Billy, comprehension slowly crossing her face. "Billy, you said I just had to talk with him. Bat my eyes, maybe bend over a few times, and Mr. White would call it even." She looked back at Charles. "He said Mr. White can't even walk. How can he. . .?" Her voice broke.

"Is that true, Billy? Do you think Mr. White would forgive your debts because you let him see the top of your wife's bra?"

Billy stared at his feet.

"Listen to me, Billy." He grabbed Billy's chin and lifted his face. "I'm only going to ask once: are you sure you want to go through with this? Are you really offering your wife to Mr. White?" He squeezed Billy's jaw. "Think carefully."

Billy's eyes welled up. "I can't lose any more fingers!" he cried. He grabbed Mary's hands. "Please, honey, just this once?"

Mary yanked her hands away, then turned to Charles. "Do I really have a choice?" she asked.

"Not anymore, I'm afraid," Charles said. "The offer has been made."

She sighed. "Fine, I'll have sex with Mr. White," she said through gritted teeth. "Maybe *he'll* actually know what to do."

Charles laughed, then buzzed the intercom. "Mr. White, Billy Barnes is here. He has a gift for you. She looks quite tasty."

"Bring her to me," Mr. White's metallic voice answered. "Her husband, too. I want him to watch."

From his position beneath the boat, Mr. White looked up through the water into his "office." The ship's moon pool was large enough for a team of divers to drop in, which made it more than big enough for his needs.

Prior to this job, he'd been used to "disappear" enemies of the organization. But after his boss's lab rats used a CRISPR program to boost his intelligence and implanted a chip that enabled him to speak through a computer interface, he'd immediately asked to be put in charge of loans for the wharf area. He might be the smartest great white in the world, but like most sharks, he was also quite literal.

So far, he'd limited himself to the handful of severed body parts and blood drippings Charles collected for late payments. After all, it wasn't smart business to eat the customers. But a customer's wife? He couldn't pass that up. Besides, Charles was right: he *was* a breast man.

***Larry Hinkle** is a copywriter living with his wife and two doggos in Rockville, Maryland. When he's not writing stories that scare people into peeing their pants, he writes ads that scare people into buying adult diapers so they're not caught peeing their pants.*

His work has appeared in Dark Recesses Press, Deep Magic, and The NoSleep Podcast, among others. He's an active member of the HWA (his short stories have made the preliminary Stoker ballot twice in the past three years); a graduate of Fright Club and Crystal Lake's Author's Journey program; an HWA mentee; and a survivor of the Borderlands Writers Bootcamp.

Look for his debut collection, The Space Between, *in February, 2024 from Trepidatio Publishing.*

You can stop by and say hi at writtenbylarry.com.

ASK ME ABOUT MY CRYPT, NOW ON SALE FOR HALF PRICE!

GWENDOLYN KISTE

ARE YOU ONE of life's lonely hearts? The kind that just can't catch a break in love?

Always the bridesmaid, never the bride? Or maybe once upon a time, you were the bride, and now you're just another lost divorcee, sitting up all by yourself after midnight?

Then come on down to Greywood Cemetery and try on our vast inventory! We've got crypts like you've never seen before. Big crypts, little crypts, in-between crypts—you can take your pick on our lavish grounds. So long as you don't mind a little company.

Because here in our gorgeous graveyard, we promise you'll never be lonely again.

It's three in the morning, the television flickering before me, my eyes bleary, my mind blank, when I see the first commercial.

It's grainy and half out of focus, but it's still undeniable: there's a man with a toothy grin on the screen, doing his best to sell me a used crypt.

"A joke," I murmur to myself. It's got to be a joke.

I blink hard, trying to take it all in, but just when I'm sure there's about to be a punchline, the commercial fades to black, and I'm alone again.

ASK ME ABOUT MY CRYPT...

I'm still in my pajamas at noon the next day when Jackie wanders in through the back door.

"Hey, you," she says, as if I've been expecting her. These days, she rarely speaks my name. It's like she doesn't quite remember it anymore.

"Hey, yourself," I say, because I can play along, too. I can pretend I don't know her either.

I only wish that were true. Jackie waltzes through the house like she owns the place. I watch the way she moves, elegant as a ballerina, determined as a razorblade, and I feel it all over again, my heart twisting in my chest. I should have asked for that key back. When it comes to Jackie, I should have done a lot of things.

"Have you seen my yellow sweater?" she calls to me from the bedroom.

I exhale a quiet sigh. "You took it with you when you left."

She already knows that. We both remember how she took everything that was rightfully hers—and a few things that were rightfully mine—when she moved out three months ago.

Jackie drifts down the hallway and into the dining room where I'm sitting by myself at the table. She gives me a small smile. "How are you, Laura?" she asks, and for a moment, I'm almost convinced she means it.

She takes the seat across from mine. I pick at my cold oatmeal with a spoon, the bits congealed like old glue.

"You won't believe what I saw last night on television," I say.

"What's that?" she asks absently, and I can already tell she isn't listening. Jackie never listened. It's one of the reasons she and I are in the past tense.

"It was a commercial," I say, mostly for my benefit than hers, mostly because I want to hear these words aloud, to make them real. "For a crypt. This place was literally selling graveyard crypts."

She's looking right at me now. "You mean like a funeral home?"

"No," I say. "Not exactly. They were selling used crypts in a cemetery."

Jackie snaps her tongue. "That can't possibly be legal," she says, her lips pulled to one side of her face. "What cemetery? Maybe we should call the police."

Dread clenches in my throat. "It's not that big of a deal," I say. "Probably some kind of satire that went over my head."

This was just supposed to be funny, a bit of small talk. A way to make her stay another minute, even though I know she shouldn't be here at all. Sometimes, I like to pretend nothing's changed between us. We were good for each other until we weren't. A year and a half ago, she breezed into my life like a hurricane, a mixed media artist with wild hair and wild eyes. I'd never witnessed anything like her in my life. Two weeks after we met, I quit my cushy job and my cushier marriage to run away with her.

"We'll be like those influencers who travel all the time," she told me, and for a while, that's exactly what we did, vacations by the sea, mixed drinks at sunset. Instagram photos with her kissing my cheek one day and me kissing hers the next. We burned through her savings in six months and mine six months later, and then suddenly, for the first time, we had to really look at each other and figure out who we were together. I didn't mind what I saw.

"We can make this work," I said, but she apparently didn't agree. I barely had time to use my alimony checks to put the down payment on this house before Jackie decided she had no interest in settling down after all.

"I'm sorry," she said on her way out the doorway.

If only she'd stayed gone. Jackie's in the kitchen now, rifling through the refrigerator.

"I still think you should call somebody about that commercial." She takes a drink of the kombucha I've been saving. "If not the police, then maybe the cable company."

"It wasn't on cable," I say. "We don't have cable, remember?"

"Well, the streaming station then. You should call them."

I do my best not to roll my eyes. This isn't turning out how I planned. Just like everything with Jackie.

"It's fine," I say. "Everything's fine."

She heads out the way she came in, the house key still tucked in her pocket. I never asked for it back. She already knew I wouldn't.

Be honest with us, Miss Lonely Heart: we know you're thinking about calling. We know you can't get us out of your mind. That's why we advise you to be quick before our sale ends.

You wouldn't want to miss out on the deal of a decade, would you, Laura?

I jolt awake at the sound of my own name. I've been half dozing on the couch for the past hour, but I'm awake in an instant when I see his face. It's the same man from before, that ugly grin curled on his lips. He's standing in front of a stone archway, surrounded on all sides by dusty coffins, the shadows practically closing in around him.

I keep staring at him, and I swear he's staring at me, too. I move back and forth on the couch, sliding this way and that, his eyes always following me.

"Are you really there?" I ask, and then I shake my head, because what kind of response am I honestly expecting? Just to be sure, I creep forward and flick the flatscreen. It doesn't respond. Instead, the commercial simply ends, the same as last night.

With my breath tight in my chest, I flick off the TV and climb into my empty bed. "It's just a joke," I keep repeating to the ceiling. "It's got to be a joke."

The next morning, I decide to talk to somebody else about it. Somebody who used to understand me.

Paul answers the door on the first knock. "You know, you could call first," he says.

I shrug. "Where's the fun in that?"

I knew he'd be here. Paul works from home, the same as me, which means he's a captive audience. Jackie stops by my house unannounced, and I stop by his. The circle of life.

He puts on a pot of coffee, and we hunch together at the table that used to be mine, drinking from mugs that I bought us. When I left, he told me I could have them—"Take anything you want" were his exact words—but I was already taking myself away from him. It seemed almost cruel to take anything else.

"I saw this commercial," I tell him. "A couple commercials actually. About a sale on used cemetery crypts." I hesitate. "But here's the weird thing."

He frowns at me. "*This* is the weird thing?"

"Listen," I say, leaning forward. "I was half asleep, so I can't be sure, but I think the guy on the commercial said my name."

Paul considers this for a long time, his hands tightening around his mug. "Maybe it was a personalized ad. It seems like companies know everything about us these days. Algorithms and all."

Relief trickles through me. It's the first explanation that actually makes sense.

"That could be it," I say. Although it doesn't make me feel much better that my TV thinks I want to hear about places to visit once you're dead.

Paul breathes deep, his cheeks flushing a little. "Is there something else you want to talk about?" he asks, and I realize he's hoping this is a cover story, the excuse I made to show up at his door. As if I'm returning to the scene of the crime.

"There's not much else to talk about," I say, and it's true. These days, I'm mostly in stasis. I used to work at the same accounting firm as Paul. After I crumpled my life and tossed it in the trash to be with Jackie—and after she left me like I always feared she would—the firm hired me back, but only as a part-time consultant. Now I'm doing the same work for half the pay. I'm like a magician's assistant, and the world just keeps sawing me in two.

But I won't bring up any of that. Instead, I stare past Paul, at the Vegas green accent wall behind him. I chose that color. I painted that wall. He and I bought this place together. It was supposed to be our forever home. I guess it could still end up being his forever home.

Things weren't supposed to turn out like this. Paul and I were college sweethearts, a meet-cute in the campus Rathskeller, drinking two dollar drafts our junior year and bonding over Terrence Malick films.

"*Badlands* all the way," I remember telling him. "My favorite."

Paul only waved me off. "*Days of Heaven* for sure," he said. "That's Malick's best."

We huddled together beneath the beer lights, the neon glowing like a kaleidoscope on our skin, and I swear it couldn't have felt more romantic if it had been the Aurora Borealis. Paul could smile like he really meant it, like you were the only person in the room, maybe even the world. Back then, we had the kind of dreams that weren't meant to come true. Those big hopes that you're going to conquer the conquerors, topple the system, make some flea speck of difference in this life. Maybe we still have those dreams, and that's why we're lingering here together in a house that used to be ours.

Paul reaches across the table, his hand on mine. "You sure you're doing all right?"

I let out a ragged laugh. "Was I ever doing all right?"

He pulls away from me, and I see it there, the flash in his dark eyes, the small curl in the corner of his lips. Every look he gives me is like a condolence. Paul didn't want the divorce. If I'm being honest, neither did I. It just seemed like the right thing to do. He can't help but blame Jackie, but it wasn't all her fault. He and I barely knew each other anymore. Though once he was gone, I realized I barely knew myself, too.

The truth is I can't hold on to people. Or maybe they can't hold on to me. Either way, it always turns out the same.

"Maybe you should try to get some sleep, Laura." Paul looks hard at me. "Then you won't have to worry about commercials on late-night TV."

"Maybe," I say and finish what's left of my coffee.

I'm driving across town, Paul's words still ringing in my ears, when the sign appears like a mirage up ahead.

Greywood Cemetery.

I've never noticed it here before, nestled on the edge of town in the old business district. Part of me wonders if that's because it wasn't here before. If it simply materialized out of the ether, just to torment me.

"That's ridiculous," I murmur as I pull into the parking lot. I'll prove it to myself. I'll walk right in and see that there's nothing inside.

The office is at the end of the parking lot, and a purse-lipped woman about my age reclines behind a front desk. "How can I help you?" she asks.

I seize up in the doorway. "I'm not sure," I say.

She tilts her head at me. "Then why are you here?"

I edge a step closer, my head whirling. "Because I saw your commercials."

"Is that so?" She squints at me. "What if I told you we've never run a commercial for this place in our lives?"

I force a smile at her. "Then I'd tell you that you're missing out on valuable advertising."

I take a few steps down a nearby hallway, searching for that man with the toothy grin, searching for proof that what I saw on late-night TV was real. Then I nearly laugh aloud at myself. My life has become so absurd that this doesn't even seem like the strangest thing that's happened to me this year.

The woman behind the desk is still watching me. "So," she asks, her arms folded, "what did this alleged commercial of ours say?"

"That you had crypts on sale."

"You mean, like burial plots?"

"Sort of. Only the commercial said they were used."

Her mouth contorts. "As in, there was already a corpse inside?"

I put up both hands. "I'm just repeating what I saw."

"Nice try," she says and nods at the exit.

I walk through it without another word. No one else is here anyhow.

At least no one I can see.

I stay up all night. I try all the channels. There's no commercial this time. No sign of that dubious man anywhere.

"I know you're here," I whisper to the television. "I know you can hear me."

But even if I'm right, it doesn't matter. He's not whispering back.

It's almost two in the afternoon when I open my eyes and find Jackie standing in the bedroom doorway, her hair as tousled and wild as the day I met her.

"You look terrible," she tells me.

"Thanks," I say and roll out of bed.

"Good thing I stopped by," she says, "or else you never would have gotten up."

She's back again, still claiming she can't find that yellow sweater.

I loiter next to the window, the afternoon sun blazing on my skin. "I went to that cemetery yesterday. The one from the commercial."

Jackie shudders. "I wish you'd stop talking about it."

I instantly bristle. "And I wish you'd stop making excuses to come by," I say before I can stop myself.

Hurt flashes across her face. "Is that your way of saying you want your key back?"

"That's up to you, Jackie." I hesitate, before adding, "Everything's always been up to you."

She searches through another dresser drawer before turning back to me. "I never wanted things to end up like this between us."

I gape at her. "And you think I did?"

"You never try, Laura," she says. "You're just on cruise control all the time, going wherever the inertia of life takes you. For a while, it led you to Paul. Then a little later, it led you to me. But you never go anywhere because it's what you want."

I grit my teeth. "That's not true," I say, even though it is.

Jackie doesn't say another word. She just gives me one last look, sadness fermenting in her eyes before she disappears out the back door. It takes almost five minutes before I realize she still didn't leave her key.

Tonight, I don't turn on the television. Not after dinner and certainly not after midnight. I head straight to bed instead.

But that doesn't mean I'm safe. The moment I close my eyes, the world falls away, and I know exactly where I am. I'm inside the commercial.

I'm inside the crypt.

There are stone walls everywhere, crumbling to dust, and silent coffins lined up one after another.

A hand reaches out for me, plucking me out of the darkness. My head spins, and I'm suddenly standing in front of the camera. Of course I am. After all, they need to recruit new faces if we want to stay in business.

"Why me?" I ask no one in particular.

"Because," a distant voice says, "this is what you wanted, isn't it?"

I squint into the darkness, suddenly spotting him there in the corner. The man with the toothy grin, waiting among the shadows.

"And if I take you up on your offer?" I keep watching him, my gaze never faltering. "What happens to me then?"

"You'll live with us, of course," he says.

You'll live among the dead, he means. He's telling me this is a place I could belong. A place where people won't slip away from me so easily. A place where I won't slip away from them either.

"Think it over," he says as the crypt fades away from me, and I fall into a deep, dreamless sleep.

I stay at home the next day, shuffling in my pajamas from one room to another, not even bothering to check the mail.

I pick up the phone three different times, desperate to call Paul, to hear his voice, to hear his explanations.

"It'll be all right, Laura," he told me a few months ago, back when Jackie and I had wasted our savings and had to retreat home. Paul was the one who gave me the money for this house, an advance on my alimony checks. He wasn't even mad about it. In fact, he wrote the check in person, inviting me out for dinner at the Italian restaurant where he proposed.

"Why don't you bring Jackie?" he asked. "Maybe we can all be friends."

"I'd like that," I said, and it seemed like the most cosmopolitan thing to do, taking your new girlfriend to meet your ex-husband. Paul bought us a round of drinks, and we sat together like old pals until closing time.

"*The Tree of Life*," Jackie said when Paul asked her about her favorite Terrence Malick film, a rite of passage in our world.

"You two have the worst taste," he said with a laugh.

I remember smiling at Paul and really meaning it. I missed him then, and I miss him now. But I miss Jackie, too. That's the problem. Paul and I lasted almost fifteen years. Jackie and I lasted almost fifteen months. My heart's broken the same way over both of them.

It's suddenly three in the morning again, and I'm back on the couch. On the television, an ad appears in front of me, the stone archways achingly familiar. I assume the next thing I'll see is that same man and his ugly smile. Only that's not what's waiting for me. Instead, I'm staring at my own face on late-night TV.

"Why me?" I ask, the same way I did in my dream.

I swallow hard, leaning closer. Leaning toward myself. But this isn't a regular commercial. It's not really a commercial at all. It's an audition maybe. An unlikely casting call, whether I like it or not.

And it doesn't last. A moment later, the screen fizzles out, and I'm gone.

✦

As soon as it's light out, I'm in my car, driving across town. Back to Greywood Cemetery.

It's Sunday morning, and I expect the office will be closed. I'm also wrong. That same girl is still sitting behind the desk. She's already scowling at me before I even walk in the door.

"You again," she says.

"Yes, me again." I edge closer to her. "I need to talk to someone."

She scoffs. "That's for sure."

"I mean your management."

She rolls her eyes. "Frederick!"

There's a rustling down the hallway. I glance in its direction, toward a door I didn't notice before. Maybe because it was too dark. Or maybe because it wasn't there. Either way, a man emerges from it now.

The same man from the commercials.

I shrink away from him, my heart clutched tight in my chest. "We've met before."

"I know," he says, inspecting my face. "You were a big hit with our fans."

I clasp my hands in front of me, trying not to shake. "Is that so?" I ask, pretending to play along.

"Absolutely." He gives me that wide grin, the one that's so familiar. "We hear you only have a part-time job right now. We want to invite you to join us full-time."

This can't be real. This can't be right.

"No thank you," I say, and bolt outside.

I need help. I need someone to bring me back to earth.

I'm pulling into Paul's driveway, desperate to tell him everything, desperate for his advice, when my breath catches in my throat.

Jackie's car is parked out front. I tell myself it doesn't mean anything. I already know it does.

I trudge up the front steps and knock once. It's still early. They're not expecting anyone. They're certainly not expecting me. That's why Paul turns pale as fresh paper when he answers the door.

"Laura," he says, regret oozing through him.

I nod at Jackie's car. "How long?" I ask.

He won't look at me now. "About three months."

About the time Jackie and I broke up. No doubt the reason we broke up. My ex-girlfriend and my ex-husband, hooking up behind my back. My life is no better than a punchline.

Footsteps, lighter than spring rain, coming down the stairs. "Who is it, Paul?" Jackie asks, and there she is in front of me, her hair a tangle of briars. She's wearing her yellow sweater. I wonder if she forgot it here and blamed me for it, or if it was always just an excuse.

Jackie hides behind Paul, as if somehow, she can still conceal this. "We didn't want you to find out this way," she whispers.

"And what way did you want me to find out?" I seethe at her. "Is there a more convenient way to tell your ex that you're fucking her other ex?"

I don't wait for them to answer. I'm already back down the front steps, traipsing over the gladiolus I planted myself, crushing what's left of my past behind me.

At home, I turn off all the lights and sit among the shadows. The only flicker of life is the television screen. I keep waiting for that commercial. I keep waiting to see my own face again.

It's long past sunset when Jackie sneaks through the back door.

"Laura?" She murmurs my name like it's an apology. "Where are you?"

"In here," I say, and she comes rushing toward me.

"I'm so sorry. Paul's so sorry." She's kneeling in front of me now, her eyes rimmed with red. "We kept wanting to tell you about it. We just didn't know how."

I stare straight ahead. I stare right through her. "There's nothing to tell," I say without inflection.

I wish she would go away. I wish she would leave me alone with my TV.

But she won't let it go. "Laura, come on," she says. "You're scaring me, all right?"

"Well, maybe that's not a bad thing." My voice even as the tides. "Maybe you should be scared."

"Please," Jackie says, taking my hands in hers. "You've got to listen to me."

"Not anymore," I whisper, wrenching away from her.

I don't bother to ask for her key back. Instead, I leave her mine, the silver glinting up from the end table.

"What are you doing?" she asks, her throat clogged with tears, but I only turn away. There's nothing left to say now anyhow.

I've tried everything. A husband, a house, a white picket fence. A lover, a lark, a hopeless second chance. Nothing's worked out. That's because I've always been a lost person, the piece that just doesn't fit. I don't belong anywhere. I don't belong with anyone.

Except maybe that's not true. Before I can stop myself, I'm out the door, driving across town one last time. Back to the edge of the old business district.

Back to Greywood Cemetery.

The man with the toothy grin is waiting in the office. "Glad to see you again, Laura," he says, his eyes glinting gold as he leads me toward that strange door in the hallway.

I hold my breath as he opens it, revealing a narrow staircase that spirals into shadows.

"After you," he says, and I don't hesitate. All the way down the stone steps, Jackie's words echo in my head.

But you never go anywhere because it's what you want.

That's not true, not anymore. I'm here because I want to be. I'm right where I belong.

The crypt is roomier than it looks on the commercial. The elegant archways seem to stretch on forever, and the scent of death and decay is sweeter than I ever realized. Like spun sugar at a carnival.

And I'm not alone down here. There are coffins all around me, far more than I can count in the dark. "Hello there," I say to them, as one by one, I hear the voices whispering inside. When I look again, the man with the toothy grin is gone, but that's no matter. He was just a glorified real estate agent. I've got what I needed from him.

"I'm ready," I say to no one in particular, and upstairs, the door slams shut behind me.

There's a blinking red light in front of me, no more than ten feet away. It tells me we're recording. It tells me it's time.

I don't know where the camera operator is. I don't even know if there is one. This place exists outside of time and space, the lights so bright they're nearly blinding, the walls closing in from every angle.

But I don't mind. I just turn toward the lens and flash my biggest, brightest smile.

Is your new relationship proving to be the same as your old one? Did you think you settled down but it turns out you simply settled?

Then I've got just the thing for you! Come down to Greywood Cemetery first thing tomorrow, and I'll show you the latest and greatest in homeownership: your very own crypt! Sure, it might be a little packed, but let's face it: two's company and three's exactly the kind of crowd you're looking for. Isn't it, Paul?

But act fast if you want to catch this once-in-a-lifetime opportunity. I promise you'll like what you see, Jackie.

Somewhere, out across the city skyline, there's a couple curled up on a couch that used to be mine. He's got a smirk on his face like he means it, and her hair is always as wild as the wind.

By now, they've noticed I'm gone. They might have knocked on my door or called my phone ten times or even filed a missing person report. Tonight, they're sitting up late, maybe wondering where I am, maybe not thinking about me at all. At least not until I've materialized right in front of them.

Not until I've called out their names.

"Do you see this?" Jackie will ask, as she leans forward, her nose already turning pink, those salt tears threatening to fall all over again.

"I see it," Paul will whisper, but he won't know what to do

about it. He might even reach out for the screen, but by then, I'll have faded out, no more than a fever dream.

And tomorrow, when they try to explain it, try to confess where I've gone, their ex who vanished into thin air, everyone will just shake their heads, and nobody will believe them.

"A joke," someone will tell them, but Paul and Jackie won't accept that, not for a minute.

"But it's true," they'll say, and they won't be able to help themselves. They'll come looking for Greywood Cemetery, the same way I did, and they'll find it, just not how they're expecting it. They'll show up in the office, arguing with that bored girl behind the desk, a Charon all her own, and what they won't realize is that beyond a door they can barely see, I'll be waiting for them.

And somewhere in the dark, I'll be smiling.

Gwendolyn Kiste is the four-time Bram Stoker Award-winning author of The Rust Maidens, Reluctant Immortals, Boneset & Feathers, Pretty Marys All in a Row, *and* The Haunting of Velkwood. *Her short fiction and nonfiction have appeared in outlets including* Lit Hub, Nightmare, Best American Science Fiction and Fantasy, CrimeReads, Titan Books, The Lineup, *and* The Dark. *She's a Lambda Literary Award winner, and her fiction has also received the This Is Horror Award for Novel of the Year as well as nominations for the Shirley Jackson, Premios Kelvin, Ignotus, and Dragon Awards. Originally from Ohio, she now resides on an abandoned horse farm outside of Pittsburgh with her husband, their excitable calico cat, and not nearly enough ghosts. Find her online at gwendolynkiste.com*

SAY WHAT'S INSIDE

Ramsey Campbell

"**C**OULD I ASK you what the contents are?"

"Nothing worth mentioning." The woman peered at Henry through his window on the counter. "Nothing of value," she said.

"Could you tell me anyway? I'm afraid I have to ask."

"Just old snapshots for the children."

He felt more awkward with the question. As he planted a stamp on the package the customer behind her turned away from glancing at the headlines on Madge's section of the counter to point out to his friend "They're not just robbing money now, they're dealing drugs as well."

"And some of us aren't doing either," Madge objected.

"Not saying about you, love," the second man said.

"Kindly don't imply it about my husband."

When the pair reached his window the first man said "You want to watch out what you're touching, all the same."

"I've never taken anything." Henry thought it best to add "Not money, not drugs."

"You don't know what you may have touched. You can't be sure what people are sending, whatever they tell you it is."

"Some of the stuff they're using these days," the second man said, "just the smell would send you off."

Henry hoped to end all this by saying "What can I do for you gentlemen?"

"He'll have a grouse," the first of them said.

Henry refrained from commenting they already had. The bottle of whisky proved to be all they'd come in for, unless that included troubling him. His next customer dropped an obese parcel bound with tape on the slab that weighed mail. "First class in our country, if you please."

"Could you tell me what's inside?"

Her eyes grew as blank as the glass of his window. "Just what do you mean by that?"

"Nothing personal, I promise you. We have to ask everyone."

"You didn't ask your friends you spent so much time talking to."

"They weren't my friends, and besides—"

"I was using the term loosely. I can see why they wouldn't be."

Henry felt lured into a dialogue that would lead to no good. "I do need to know what the contents are."

"An outfit for a grandchild. Does that satisfy your requirements?"

"I'm sure it will theirs as well."

Her brusque nod accepted the postage he read off the screen. Once she'd gone, leaving them alone, Madge protested "What was all that supposed to be about?"

"As the other lady said, nothing worth mentioning."

"We know you'd never do anything wrong." More fiercely still Madge said "And that's all that matters."

He wished he could feel it was. The inverted headlines drew his gaze away from her resolutely optimistic small round face, whose cheeks she pinched before the mirror every morning to erase traces of age. MORE POST OFFICE THEFTS and SIX MORE POSTMASTERS JAILED hemmed in POSTAL WORKERS NETWORK OPERATES DRUG RING. "Shall I make some tea?" Madge said. "Things always look better after a cup."

He hoped they would once he managed to achieve a night's relatively uninterrupted sleep. For weeks even telling himself he'd no cause to worry had kept him awake, ever since the post office half a mile away had been investigated, and the nearest in the opposite direction too. Surely the lack of an inspection meant he and Madge weren't suspected of wrongdoing, but it felt as if a pincer movement had yet to close on them. He did his utmost to sound heartened as he said "If you're having one I will."

At least no more customers made an issue of his question, but the prospect of accounting for his daily take trapped him with a threat of panic. Once the shop was locked he stayed at the computer until his eyes began to ache. A second scrutiny convinced him the takings tallied, unless it was the third, at which point he gave way to Madge's urging to come upstairs for dinner. "Good?" she said anxiously more than once, and he echoed her less like a question, though her casserole's French accent seemed a little amateur. After dinner they watched some of the quiz shows she liked. When she began to nod rather than racing to call out the answers, he suggested bed. Every penny, he kept repeating in his brittle skull, a formula that brought him intermittent slumber.

In the morning the daily bundle of newspapers was squatting on the doorstep. When he cut their bonds he found no headlines about post offices. Were the raids finished? Perhaps they were waiting for someone to make a mistake, but it wouldn't be him. As a parade of early risers bought groceries and newspapers and infrequent packs of cigarettes, he tried not to feel nostalgic for the years before he and Madge had decided the Mad Hen should be a post office as well.

The first postal customer was a youth whose chin together with the turfy outline of his mouth appeared to be compensating for his shaven cranium. He dumped a bulging puffy envelope on the scales with such force the reading leapt beyond its weight. All too soon Henry had to say "What's in the parcel, please?"

The answering stare resembled a bid not to blink. "You're the feller thinks everyone's posting drugs."

"I don't know where you could have got that idea." Closer to what he hoped was the truth Henry said "I'm sure I've no reason to think so."

"You made my nan feel like you thought she was dealing."

Henry saw why the stare had looked familiar. "I wasn't thinking that, you have my word."

"She says she's not coming to yours any more."

"Then I can only apologise." Having hesitated in the hope of appearing polite, Henry said "So what was in the parcel?"

"Dope."

"You really shouldn't say that. I know the lady wouldn't go anywhere near that kind of thing, but I was asking what's in yours."

"Dope."

"You mustn't keep saying that or I won't be able to accept the item."

"If you said that going through security they'd arrest you," Madge told the customer.

"Sounds like you've got none here."

Henry tried to fend off the remark by saying "I'll ask you just once more. What's in there?"

The stare grew defiant if not challenging. "Baby stuff."

"That's what your grandmother said."

"Right, cos my sis is having one."

Henry had to accept this, however eager to leave the youth appeared to be—so keen he left without waiting for his receipt. "He thought he was clever, didn't he," Madge said. "So long as he wasn't really."

"How would he be?"

"Saying there were drugs as if it was a joke when there really are."

Henry felt driven to sniff at the parcel, but smelled only paper and the same reduced to pulp. He'd asked what he was required to ask, which surely absolved him of any complicity. He dropped the parcel in the sack for the postman to collect. "Don't stop me trusting people," he said, only to wonder if Madge should indeed disabuse him.

A jangle of bracelets announced a young woman who placed a wrapped box on the scales so carefully she might have been anxious not to disturb the contents. "Can I just ask what you're sending?" Henry said.

The corners of her wide smile might have been striving to indicate how guileless her eyes were. "A necklace."

"And what's the value?"

"I couldn't say."

"How is that? How can't you know?"

"My cousin lent it me for an occasion. She didn't say how much it's worth."

"An occasion of sin." To suppress the phrase she'd dislodged from somewhere in his memory Henry said "What occasion would that have been?"

"My friend getting wed. Is that all you want to know?"

"I'm obliged to ask these things. If you don't like it, complain to head office."

"Maybe I will."

He hadn't intended to suggest she should. Why was Madge watching him? She had no cause to spy on him when he was simply doing his job. When he seized the parcel it emitted a surreptitious rattle. "What did you say the contents were again?"

"You heard me, didn't you?" the woman said, but not to him. "My cousin's necklace."

"That's what you said."

He needn't assume Madge was saying she believed it. Perhaps she was being craftier than his customer. As he turned the package over to reveal the return address he gave it a sly shake that roused a shrill rattle. "It doesn't sound like one."

The eyes on him were still denying any culpability—the customer's were. "What does it sound like, then?"

"I'd go for pills in a bottle."

"Well, it's not." The eyes were growing moist, however deliberately. "It's been passed down our family. It's an heirloom."

As Henry opened his mouth Madge said "I'm sure everything's all right."

Did she mean with him? She had no business telling a stranger so. He wasn't about to be deterred from saying to the customer "Then I expect you'll want to insure it."

"I was going to."

"In that case you'll need to set a value on it."

The eyes had taken back their moisture and grown fixed. "Two hundred pounds."

"Quite a sum." He wished he hadn't said this, having been reminded of the calculations the day's end would bring. "Is that the sentimental value?" he heard himself enquiring.

"That's more than I can tell you."

He glanced at Madge, but she seemed to have heard no admission. "We'll say two hundred, then," he said and felt as if he wasn't aiming to placate just the customer.

Once she'd gone he dropped the item in the collection sack. He wasn't going to let Madge see him sniff the parcel, since the pills would have no odour. Instead he demanded "What did you mean, everything's all right?"

"Isn't it?" Her gaze looked like a plea or was designed to resemble one. "I hope you'd tell me if it wasn't," she said not far from a rebuke.

Why should he have to do so? She ought to be able to see what was going on, but now she'd made him feel he had to hide it from her so that she wouldn't grow concerned. Whenever he sniffed a parcel he took care to ensure she didn't catch him in the act. He was glad when the postman came to empty the sack, but accounting for the day was already gnawing at his mind. He stayed at the screen until the numbers began to writhe and Madge tramped downstairs to discover why he wasn't responding to her calls to dinner. "Like you say, it's all right," he hoped he'd reassured her.

He had to devote himself to tasting his steak as vividly as he could. No doubt lingering over it mimicked enjoyment, though he was mostly striving to postpone the quiz games on television. All too soon the questions began to gather, lodging in his mind even after Madge or somebody trapped in the screen had answered them, piling up in Henry's skull as if the quizmasters had only pretended the answers were correct. When he retreated to bed they merged into or were ousted by a solitary question that relentlessly prodded him awake, and he felt it was demanding what was inside him.

The newspapers he released to sprawl across the counter displayed headlines that had nothing to do with him—various summations of a crazed or otherwise galvanised driver who had rammed a car into a crowd. Henry assisted Madge with their early clientele until a man planted a parcel on the scales with a muted metallic clank. "Inland by one o'clock tomorrow, thanks."

This sounded efficient enough for officialdom, and Henry thought the blandly watchful face might signify that too. He strove to seem professional by asking "What's in the package, please?"

"Chocolates."

Henry accepted this and the value he was told and attached the stamp to the rectangular package. He was preparing to consign it to the sack when the customer looked back from the door and then strode towards the counter. "What do you think you're doing there?"

Henry snatched the parcel away from his face. The contents seemed to have no odour, which was suspicious in itself. His guilty gesture provoked him to retort "What did you tell me was in here again?"

"I told you chocolates."

Henry shook the parcel. "How is it they aren't loose in the tin?"

"Because they're in the box they came in."

"It sounded like a tin to me." Henry rapped it with a knuckle, only to produce a cardboard noise. As he realised the metallic clank must have been emitted by the scales the man said "I asked what you thought you were doing."

"Checking the contents as we're meant to."

"I hope now you know they're exactly what I said. A birthday present for my mother."

The observation this roused came out before Henry could suppress it. "You do seem fond of your families, some of you."

A frown squeezed the man's eyes more watchful. "Some of whom?"

"Whoever you may be."

"Police."

For a moment Henry thought the man was calling them. The assertion seemed no more trustworthy than the description of the parcel. "So why aren't you in uniform?"

"We're still the law on our days off." The man reached inside his jacket for a card to flash. "That's what we show anyone who needs to see it."

How much of a threat was this meant to be? Henry thought it wisest not to respond, and contented himself with dropping the parcel in the sack to encourage the man to leave. As the door shut behind him a woman who had paused loading a wire basket sent Madge an incredulous grin. "Was your man really sniffing at that parcel?"

Madge pressed her lips together as if she would rather not have spoken. "Were you, Henry?"

"I said what I was doing."

The woman added a packet of tea to her basket, which she carried to Madge. "No wonder your shop's called what it's called."

"The name was my idea," Madge objected.

The woman peered awry at Henry. "If you ask me she wants to tell you something."

"We weren't asking," Henry said.

She evidently took his wife to endorse the retort, which he hoped Madge did. As soon as the woman left the shop Madge turned to him. "If you keep on doing that we'll be losing custom."

"Doing what exactly?"

He could have thought age had seized her face. "Being peculiar with people," she said. "We can't afford to have you driving them away."

So that was what the woman had known Madge wanted to tell him. Surely they couldn't have discussed it in advance somehow. Realising how Madge felt about his wariness was bad enough. Did she want them to be arrested, or would she hope to be exonerated? He mustn't start thinking such things when he had too much to suspect as it was. At least he'd thought how to distract Madge from the investigations he had to perform. Whenever he accepted a parcel he contrived to include her in chatting to the customer, then let them carry on their dialogue while he turned his back on them so as to bring the item to his face unobserved. If by the end of the afternoon his conversational gambits had begun to feel forced, even grotesquely unnatural, he needn't care so long as nobody else thought they did.

When at last he managed to abandon scrutinising the restless digits on the screen before Madge could follow her calls downstairs to him, it was only to resume the pretence that nothing was amiss. He mimed relishing his dinner and let her answer all the questions in the quiz shows that she could, even when she frowned at him for not responding. There was just a solitary question in his brain, and he took it to bed with him, where its secrecy felt like a wall between him and Madge, despite her arm clinging to his waist for reassurance—hers or his, he didn't know. What's inside? What's inside? The voice she mustn't be able to hear interrogated him throughout the night, but he had a sense that it was telling him a solution if he could only understand.

Somebody had blown up a truck and himself in the midst of a crowd. At least he'd banished any mention of post offices from the front pages of the newspapers Henry unbundled. While serving early customers he strove to devise conversational gambits he could use to distract Madge later. He oughtn't to repeat any of his bids to start a chat in case they made her suspicious, but the new ones turned progressively feebler and more unnatural as parcels piled up in the sack. Though he was increasingly uncertain whether any of them betrayed an odour when they were pressed against his face, he thought a faint secretive smell was gathering around the mass of them. He would have asked Madge about it if he could have been sure of her response. Why was today's collection so late? The topmost parcel was protruding from the sack as though to mock him—to challenge him to hide his suspicions from her. At last the door lurched inwards to admit not still another customer to thwart his hopes but the postman. Henry was about to demand why he was late when he saw the man in uniform had donned a different face. "Who are you supposed to be?" he blurted.

The man's pudgy bag of a head arranged its lips in a fat straight line. "He's sick."

Was he saying this to Henry or to Madge about him? The man's eyes were dodging the question. "Who is?" Henry said low enough to swivel them to him.

"Ken till next week. I'll be picking up his round."

"Nobody told you to be late."

"I know that. I'm still learning his route."

"I'm asking if anyone told you to be."

He felt Madge's gaze cling to him. "Why would anyone do that, Henry?"

The furtive smell seemed to surge in response, provoking him to speak before he could exercise caution. "They might have their reasons."

As Madge's gaze grew heavier the man who wasn't Ken despite his outfit protested "I said I'm just finding my way."

"So long as you haven't found the wrong one." This sounded emptier of meaning than Henry had intended. "There's your bag," he urged. "Don't leave it so long next time."

"Sorry if it's been bothering you."

Henry stared at this so fiercely his eyes felt as hard as the window. "Why are you thinking it would do that?"

"Not thinking anything."

Henry barely managed not to accuse him of having been told to take his time—Henry's time. He might have said as much if Madge hadn't been listening, a good deal too closely for his taste. He unbolted the gate in the counter and made room for the man to heft the sack. Nobody spoke until the man returned with the empty item and left the shop, and then Madge muttered as if she hardly even wanted Henry to hear "What was wrong now?"

"Nothing worth mentioning," he had the impression he was remembering aloud.

He felt she hadn't stopped watching him even once she looked as if she had. He refrained from sniffing the parcels until her attention was held by a customer. He forced himself to turn his back on the swarm of numbers on the screen once he heard her anxious footsteps on the stairs. Miming enjoyment of his dinner proved to be a prolonged task, if less of one than directing some of his mind at the questions the television posed rather than the interrogation that resounded in his cranium. What's inside? By echoing some of Madge's answers he hoped to appear engaged by her quizzes—the broadcast sort, not the kind he sensed lurking in her head.

The question he was carrying everywhere with him grew more insistent in the dark of the bedroom. What's inside? He moved as far out of Madge's reach as he was able to retreat in case this helped his brain work if not find some species of calm. He had no idea how many times he'd jerked awake out of a mockery of sleep when he was met by the answer. The question wasn't only for him, it was about him. It explained everything, not least his sleeplessness. A customer had told him the truth days ago—that some drugs could infect you just by their smell.

For as long as it took to release a slow breath he welcomed the explanation, and then the implications overtook him. Since he'd been left with no excuse to doubt he was handling drugs, didn't this make him an accomplice? He'd exhausted so much of himself in refuting any bids to convict him of theft, but could he face conviction for the crimes he hadn't realised were implicating him? Perhaps at that very moment workers in the sorting office were investigating the items he'd accepted yesterday. The possibility amplified every sound in the street: footsteps that might belong to police assembling to raid the shop, the hushed approach of vehicles carrying equipment the police would use to break the door down. When one halted outside he lost all ability to breathe, especially as someone tramped to the shop and dealt it a thump that must be the preamble to forced entry. Not until the van drove off did he manage to grasp that he'd heard a bundle of newspapers fall on the pavement, if indeed the incident hadn't been designed to trick him into feeling safe. He had to sneak down to confirm it had been a delivery, and now he was out of bed there was no point in going back. At least for a little while Madge wouldn't be watching him, unless she was pretending not to spy on him when he crept into the bedroom to get dressed.

He tried to appear eager for the day, but even serving early customers was no comfort any more, since they were merely delaying the first of the parcels he would have to handle. His attention drifted to the headlines inverted on the counter, where topsy-turvy words kept addressing him at random. STOP STRESS—how could he achieve that? Hardly by realising they were POST and ARRESTS, but why was FATE spelled so oddly? Because it was THIEF. RUEFUL was FURTHER, which was more than he wanted to understand. When the rest of the headlines lapsed into incomprehensibility he felt they'd revealed they were written in an unknown language. It was one more effect of the drugs, of course.

The carriers began to bring their merchandise in before he could think how to identify which they were, let alone prevent them. How innocent were they determined to look? Might the dealers be employing relatives or friends, who had no idea what they were posting? Could he invent some regulation that directed customers with parcels to the main post office? He might have tried if he'd been certain Madge wouldn't overhear. At any rate she wouldn't catch him smelling parcels now that he knew how it had been affecting him; even handling them made his eyes flare like embers. Surely the authorities couldn't prove anything against him, even if they sent the man who wasn't Ken to trick him into betraying himself as he nearly had. He just had to bide his time until tomorrow—Sunday, when the shop was shut. He nearly groaned aloud at realising only the post office would be. When was he going to be left alone to plan? How would he need to achieve it? He fought to quell his desperate thoughts in case they were apparent, no doubt especially to anyone who was using him for crime. He could only take refuge in his question, however false he knew the answer would be. "What's in here, please?"

"A china doll."

The woman might have been describing herself, her thin pale brittle face, her eyes like stones faded by polishing. So much tape crisscrossed the bloated parcel there was barely space for an address, let alone her tiny counterpart on the back. It was evident to Henry that the contents were protected from investigation, a thought that prompted him to squeeze the packaging. The contents yielded as he thought leaves might have, certainly not like china. He squeezed harder, producing several sounds: a tiny crack, a muffled splintering, a cry beyond his window. "You're breaking it, you stupid man. You've broken the doll."

"No need to repeat yourself." With an effort Henry succeeded in relaxing his grip. "I have to check the contents."

"You've damaged them." The woman rapped on the window with a signet ring. "Give it here. Give it back at once."

The shrill sounds—the tapping and her voice—seemed to impale his brain. "You're repeating yourself again," he said and saw she'd given him an excuse to rid himself of the suspicious item. "All yours," he told her and flung the parcel on the weighing slab.

As the woman stalked out of the shop Madge turned on him. "Henry, what have you done?"

"Didn't you hear what she wanted us to think I had? Go and ask."

"I'll go and try and make amends. We don't know who she'll tell about you," Madge complained and ran out of the shop.

He'd meant it as a retort, not a suggestion, and didn't immediately grasp he was alone in the shop. As he heard Madge's voice dwindling into the distance—"Excuse me. Excuse me"—he dashed to lock the door. The instant he swung around he saw exactly how to proceed. The shelves were full of boxes to dismantle, and there were dozens of rolls of tape. It took just a few minutes to block out the eyes that gathered to watch him through the door— Madge's eyes and their crowding companions—as her pleas threatened to drive out of his head the words he'd remembered to say. "Nothing of value in here," he declared, "nothing worth mentioning," but they weren't enough to fend off an intrusion. He should have hidden himself more thoroughly, and he could only shout his assertions louder as whoever was investigating broke into the package that contained him.

The Oxford Companion to English Literature *calls* **Ramsey Campbell** *"Britain's most respected living horror writer", and the* Washington Post *sums up his work as "one of the monumental accomplishments of modern popular fiction". In 2015 he was made an Honorary Fellow of Liverpool John Moores University for outstanding services to literature. His latest novels are* Fellstones, The Lonely Lands, The Incubations *and* An Echo of Children. *His Brichester Mythos trilogy consists of* The Searching Dead, Born to the Dark *and* The Way of the Worm. *His most recent collections are* Fearful Implications, *a two-volume retrospective roundup* (Phantasmagorical Stories) *and* The Village Killings and Other Novellas. *His non-fiction is collected as* Ramsey Campbell, Probably *and* Ramsey Campbell, Certainly. Ramsey's Rambles *collects his video reviews, and* Six Stooges and Counting *is an appreciation of the Three Stooges.* Limericks of the Alarming and Phantasmal *is a history of horror fiction in fifty limericks.*

DEATH'S DOOR

Ben Eads

TALKING TO LITTLE dead boys and girls had to stop, and Rachel hoped this would be the last. *Dead or a few months away from dead. There's no difference at that point. And somehow, the parents look even worse...*

Prior visits on behalf of the Smiling Children charity brought acid up Rachel's throat. Not long after she'd read the first chapter of the new book, all of them had nodded off from the chemo. Either that or the painkillers. Their breath a dull whistle their mom and dad tried to fix by tucking them in a little tighter, propping up pillows.

That's what hope brings: pain.

Rachel scratched her bandaged wrist. The wound she'd made with the razor was still healing. Itching. *Next time, I'll cut up the arm, not across....*

Her GPS pinged, startling her out of her own thoughts, compulsions. It said her destination was on the left. She rubbed her belly, where three months ago a faint heartbeat slowed, then died. So had her husband, Gary, after he ate the barrel of his Glock.

Spotting the aged Victorian's house number, she brought her hands together and blew hot air into them. New Hampshire's version of winter had already burrowed into the marrow. The cold outside crept between her ribs, caressing her heart, her lungs. Snow began to fall, etching spider web patterns over her windshield. Rachel took a deep breath and hunched over her steering wheel, looking for the house.

The neighborhood was all Victorians of various sizes. Behind them, barren maples and withered red oak rose like broken teeth. The sky, a band of white haze, like the gauze around her wrist.

The last child's father she had visited asked her for money, arguing that since her *Edwin the Choo Choo* book went to theatres, she had enough to spare. *"You know, for medical expenses."* Rachel knew the cost all too well. As she pulled into the front yard, she saw another face with cost written all over it.

Waving from the modest porch with one hand, a beer in the other, the father motioned for her to pull into the driveway. A breeze flapped his Seahawks jersey around his wiry body.

Rachel placed the car in park and pressed the button to shut off. A gale picked up, whining, like a baby. *This is my last one. . .*

Grabbing her purse, and her present, Rachel got out of the car. Wind shut the door for her.

She took a deep breath and coughed. *Smile. . . even if you don't feel it. Pretend.*

"Mr. Stewart?"

November swirled about, soaking through her jacket, her layers. Pulling them tighter, Rachel walked up the weathered steps of the front porch. She carefully avoided stepping on the plank of wood with rusty nail heads sticking up.

"Yep," he said. The boards squeaked as he walked toward her, hand stretched out, eyes looking into oblivion. She could tell they were once blue. Now they just blended in with the scenery, dull and cold as the dirty snow falling from the gutter.

"It's nice to meet you," she said, shaking his gloved hand, which also had the Seahawks logo on it.

"Please. Call me Tom," he said, and finished the rest of his beer. "Well, come on in.

She's been asleep, but I got her up."

Her publicist said the father was twenty-seven, but he looked twenty years older. Even his stubble was salt and pepper.

Tom opened the front door for her and followed her inside. He grabbed another beer from his cooler, cracked it open, and drank it, as well.

Rachel closed the door behind her, and the heating system began to warm her up. A cobwebbed light bulb lit a clean and sparce mud room. Seahawks hoodies hung on a coat tree. She looked beyond the mud room. A large fire in the fireplace. Pale yellow squares marked the walls, cleaner than the rest. Rachel wondered if pictures of the family were once there.

"May I take your coat?" Tom said.

"Please, thank you." Rachel took off her coat and handed it to him.

"Thank you so much for coming, Mrs. Swift. This means the world to us."

Tom placed her coat atop an empty coat tree and motioned for Rachel to follow him up the scarred, wooden stairs.

"You've got a nice house, Tom." *Where is her mom?*

"Thanks. She's right up here." Taking the steps two at a time, he motioned for her to follow him. A belch echoed off the faded yellow walls as they ascended.

Her hand began to massage her belly again. *You can do this. You can do this.*

Stopping by her door, Tom turned and pointed his finger at Rachel. "Be careful with her.

She's very delicate."

"I understand, Tom. The last thing—"

"One more thing." Rachel heard his teeth grinding. "This isn't easy for me. . . or her. My wife—her mother—she went the same way." Tom's eye began to twitch, hands clenching and unclenching, his breathing more rapid.

"I'm so—"

His red eyes looked distant, as if caught in a memory. "You'll think I'm terrible, but I can't look at her anymore." Shaking his head as if he had just awoken from a bad dream, tears flowed freely. "The first time she flat-lined, and it looked like they couldn't resuscitate her, I was happy because she was finally at peace."

I know the feeling. . .

She knew better than to share her pain. The miscarriage. How every morning Gary used to sing songs to her that he would come up with on the spot. How thoughtful and beautiful they were. They always started with, *"I love my Rachel. . ."* Now? Gary's vocal cords wouldn't let him sing, and the hole he left in her grew every goddamn morning she had woken up after he bit the bullet.

"I—I'm so very sorry, Tom. I had no idea—"

"And I wish I could just curl up with her in that little coffin when she *does pass.* How quiet it would be. No more pain. God, I'm so sorry for dumping this on you."

Rachel embraced him, patted his back. There was a part of her that wanted to share her story, how she didn't even know if the baby she lost was a boy or girl, but she couldn't. Now she was crying, what her therapist called *"Healthy crying."*

Letting go, Rachel composed herself as best she could. *Get it together. Be strong. Be strong for both of them.*

Rachel pulled the manuscript of the latest *Edwin the Choo-Choo* out of her satchel. "I brought a little magic with me."

Tom grunted and gently placed his hand on the doorknob. "We must be quiet."

"Of course."

Tom took a deep breath, as if mentally preparing himself. He opened the door slowly, licking his lips. "Honey?" he whispered. "You sleepin'?"

"Daddy?"

"Honey, Rachel Swift is here. You remember, right?"

"Edwin The Choo-Choo!"

Okay, it's magic time.

Tom motioned for her, and she walked in. The smell of chemotherapy's rot filled her nose, and Rachel doubted she would ever forget it. It always made her wonder if it was contagious. Not the disease, but the way it stripped away at you, carved your heart hollow, until it *became* you. Rachel rubbed at the faint scars across her wrists, arm and belly. She made sure to stop before she stepped into the light. Before anyone could see.

"It's so nice to meet you, Sarah." Rachel walked over to the ten-year-old's bed and saw what was left of her: a husk of a child, with a porcelain doll's face, framed by what Rachel was sure was a black wig. She rubbed her stomach again. "How are we feeling?"

"Fine," Sarah said, blinking slowly. "But a little sleepy."

Tom clapped his hands. "Well, I guess I'll leave you both to it." He stared at the floor, unable to face her. "You gonna be okay?"

"Of course," Rachel said, touching Sarah's withered arm. "We're going to talk a lot about Edwin, aren't we?" She squeezed just a little, like she'd been taught by the nurses.

Tom slowly closed the door.

"Ouch. Not so rough," Sarah said, pulling her arm back.

"I didn't mean to hurt you. Are you okay?"

"Yeah, it happens. The medicine dulls it. . . a little."

Be strong!

"I'm sure Edwin will make you feel better. I brought the latest book for you because *you're* special. Would you like me to read from it?"

"The doctors said Mommy was special. She died." Sarah grimaced. "Guess she wasn't so special. Guess I'm not either."

"No, honey, don't say that. Here. . ." Rachel snuggled up to her and opened the manuscript to read it. "Don't you want to find out what happens to Edwin? After going into that tunnel, who knows what world he'll end up in?"

Grunting at the effort to sit up, Sarah placed a few pillows behind her and got comfortable, even smiled a little. "Edwin's always going to different worlds. It's why I like him so much. He can go anywhere he wants to."

"Yeah! And Edwin finds a way back, with his *friends*," Rachel said, teasing it out.

For a moment, there was color in Sarah eyes, and her cheeks flushed. She drew in a breath. "His friends?"

"Yes!" Rachel laughed, and so did Sarah.

It's working for once!

Fumbling through the manuscript, Rachel searched for the most important scenes to read. And, of course, the end. Always the end. *Edwin the Choo Choo's Big Break-Through!* A fitting finale to a series of books and movies that only brought back the past.

Sarah snuggled her face closer. "No fibbing! They come back?"

"Yeah!" Rachel kept searching for the scene where Edwin saved Andy, his best friend, and one of the most beloved characters of the series. Some even liked him more than Edwin, including Rachel. *Because he came back. . .*

"Can I read it?"

"Of course. Here." Rachel gently handed the manuscript to Sarah.

Sarah coughed. "We're gonna be a family again soon. With my mommy—"

"That's right! Edwin's mommy comes back with his friends. You're very intuitive, Sarah."

The sound of a key locking the door from the outside scraped Rachel's eardrums. *What the hell?* She frowned as Sarah's words replayed in her head:

"My mommy?" Somewhere, flies hummed. Sarah smiled. "I mean I'll have a *real* family again."

Rachel felt as if she was at the top of a skyscraper, and the elevator's cable had just broken, plummeting her downward so fast she had to grab the bedpost for balance. Rachel had her fair share of night terrors, and she hoped this was one of them.

"How—how. . . What did you just say?" Spots danced in front of Rachel's eyes, and the pain from that fateful morning, when the heartbeat in her belly stopped and the little child quit moving inside her, doubled her over. "Shit! Oh, God. . ." *They—they drugged me. . . When?*

How?. . .

"We're going on a trip, Mrs. Swift," Sarah's eyes grew large.

Thumbing through the manuscript, Sarah pulled a black crayon from behind her ear and laid it by her side. A train's horn blared in the distance. Sarah placed her hand under her chin, eyes searching the ceiling in sincere contemplation. "I got so sick that my heart stopped beating." Sarah shrugged.

"Your heart. . . stopped. . ." Rachel faltered, and she wanted to touch her belly again.

Sarah shivered, as if reliving her death rattle. "Yeah." Her tone grew distant. "Did you know that when you die you wake up in a little dark room colder than what's left of you? Only lucky people have something waiting there. Something that's part of them." She stroked the book before her hand moved to the black crayon. Her eyes glazed as a strange smile played upon her lips. She set the crayon to the last page of Rachel's manuscript and began to draw a tunnel.

"Lucky."

"Sarah, are you feeling all right?" *Her father gave her too many pain pills. The parents always give them an extra one right before I show up.*

"In that little dark room, I found this crayon and a coloring book of Edwin the ChooChoo. I thought really hard about Mommy, and how much I missed her. *Still* miss her. It's like the crayon knew what to do. It drew a tunnel in the coloring book. A way back to Mommy after I woke up. But I need to *finish* the tunnel so I can see her again." Sarah finished her tunnel and placed the book and crayon at her side.

Wake up!

Knocking on the door, Tom asked, "Is it safe, honey?"

"Yes, Daddy."

Tom entered the room and sat next to his daughter. He was out of breath, panting. "We know a lot about *pain*, Mrs. Swift. A lot. But that's going to end. My daughter just showed you a way."

"You've lost your mind!" Rachel screamed, making the pain worse, as if she had just swallowed Drano. "You can't—"

The house began to shake, and the siren continued to wail. *Get up! Get the book!* Rachel tried to get off the floor, but the cramping of her insides held her down. Hot liquid ran down her legs.

Taking her in his arms, Tom lifted Rachel off the floor and laid her down on Sarah's bed. "There, there now. Everything's gonna be fine. What you're feeling is part of the price of admission. But soon, we'll both have our families back," Tom said, running his fingers through her hair. "Look." Tom pointed at what used to be Sarah's window. A dark spiral with ink-blot swirls took its place. Growing in size, Rachel could hear the wood stressing until it broke. Plaster and other debris shot across the room.

Fucking hell!

Sarah placed the book aside for a moment. "You never gave her a name."

Tom rubbed Rachel's shoulders. "Now would be a good time. She's waited so long—too long."

Tilting her head, Rachel watched the wall warp, accommodating what was coming through. The smell from the train's smokestack made her eyes water. *Please wake up!*

Placing an arm around Rachel, Tom stood her up. "Hurry, or we're in trouble. Gotta get out of here before it comes through."

Tom picked Sarah up and started toward the door. "Don't want to miss the train!"

Rachel leaned on the dresser for support, the pain ebbing and flowing. Hardwood floorboards split from the stress. *Go! Go!*

She ran downstairs, following Tom and Sarah. Tom opened the door and Rachel followed. A fat, full moon glowed through clouds that looked like they were made of molten pewter, dropping like cigar ashes, as the train ate through the bruised and crimson sky. Yellow lights blinded Rachel from dead sockets of what was left of its desiccated face. Like a permanent marker, its smoke stained what was left of reality. Oil rolled over and blocked the moonlight.

Below it, a bridge kept creating a path toward them. The smell of burned oil and death flooded Rachel's nostrils. She gagged. *Drugs can't do this. . .*

A little hand took hers, stifling a jump. "This isn't real. This is not fucking real!"

Sarah squeezed her hand. "Have you thought of a name yet?"

Curling downward like a snake, the train devoured the house as it came to a grinding stop, smoke billowing and staining the winter sky. It ate away what was left, like a hungry termite. The sounds reminded Rachel of the tornado that ripped apart their house when she was five years old. The floor began to shake, and Rachel had ducked, hoping the house wouldn't come down on them.

The train stopped before them. Its face, pocked and scarred as the moon which kissed it, smiled at them. Jaundiced eyes bulged above teeth that glistened like wet ivory. Rachel watched the grass wither and turn blacker than the night around it. Little faces were pressed up against the windows, looking out. *Not what you created, but close.*

A door on its side opened with a pneumatic *Psssssshhhhh.* Pale lights flickered inside, buzzing like an old movie with cigarette burns and squiggly hairs. Her very own movie. Gary stood in the doorway of the first railcar with a bundle of blankets in his arms under pale light that strobed. "I love my Rachel, she's so fine! Soon we'll be dancing in the sunshine!"

That. . .that can't be him. . . But his voice. . .

Tom grabbed Rachel's arms and pulled her close. "Thank you so much for helping make this happen. Without your inspiration"— Tom took a deep breath and exhaled noisily— "Sarah wouldn't have found a way for all of this to work. For me to see Heather again. . . for Sarah to see her mother again." Tom gently poked her in the shoulder. Tears streamed down his cheeks, and his smile reminded Rachel of circus clowns. "And when we get to Heather's stop, she is going to hug you so hard!"

Gary pulled a rope, and the train blew a discordant whine. "Come on, love. Time for the pain to end. We can be a family here!" He smiled, but his face warped, like a Dali painting. "Our daughter scribbled over my eyes about a year ago. But now I can *see.*" Gary cocked his head in that teasing way that made her swoon back in high school. "Don't you want to *see?*"

Rachel rubbed her belly again, zipped her coat up and crossed her arms. *One little peek won't hurt. I always wondered: Blonde or brunette? Blue eyes or brown. That first smile. . .*

"No," Rachel said, turning from Gary. "I'll wake up soon."

And then she saw them—all of the children she'd visited before shuffled through the doors of the railcar and slowly made their way toward her, feral eyes glowing white. She remembered Amy, of course. Despite the chemo, she still had her hair. *You were in remission by the time I got there, and we celebrated.*

Tom, still wearing his dirty hospital gown, limped forward, and Rachel could hear the contents of the IV bag atop its pole slosh around. She took a step back. The air froze her throat.

"You told me to keep fighting. To never give up. Now I'm here."

Amanda moved toward her, using her walker slowly, favoring her right hip, the one cancer didn't touch. Rachel remembered the last thing she asked her, "Wouldn't it be cool if I got to make one of the Edwin the Choo-Choo books into a movie?" And how her face fell after she realized what she had asked of the universe. *That's where her childhood ended.*

Amanda took a step forward. "You said I was going to Heaven, where all children go." She shook her head and gave her a switchblade smile. "I want to show you a little dark room colder than what's left of you."

All of them, Amy, Tom, Amanda, and four others she couldn't make out, moved toward her.

Rachel heard the bundle in Gary's arms begin to cry. "Love, without you? It's not worth it. Hurry!"

Under the moonlight, she could see Gary's hipster bun, his red beard. He was whole. The *Gary from before.* Memories of the good times raced through her mind, erasing the bad ones.

And her baby was crying for her to finally hold her, kiss her, and be whole again. *He's right. . .*

Rachel ran to her husband and daughter. *What will I name her? Will she grow up?*

Wherever here—

A red-hot poker rammed through Rachel's hamstring. "Fuck!" She turned just in time to see Sarah bring the crochet needle down again. Rachel caught her little wrist, but Rachel's leg gave out and she fell to the ground.

Straddling Rachel, Sarah raised the big needle again. "You lied to all of them! You told them they would live! You're not coming with us!" Sarah moved the tip of the needle to the corner of

Rachel's eye. She began making circles with the point, closer and closer to her eyeball.

Rachel turned just in time for the needle to miss. "No! Stop!" Sarah snarled, her eyes changed, as if they were pulling the moonlight into them, bathing the black in a creamy white.

Sarah kept coming, slashing.

As Sarah brought the needle up, Rachel caught her elbow and leveraged her to the ground. When Sarah went to drive the needle into her neck, Rachel grabbed her arm, twisted it around, and drove it through her head.

I just killed. . . Oh, God. What if it is drugs? And. . . I just killed a little girl. . .

Rachel stood up, and found herself nose to nose with Tom. "You. Fucking. Bitch!" Rachel felt his spit on her face, then she felt his hands around her neck. Fireworks went off behind her eyes as she grabbed Tom's arms. Rachel kicked him right up the middle. He doubled over, grabbed his crotch, and threw up. Rachel pulled the crochet needle from Sarah's head and pushed it through Tom's left eye, then deeper, until he fell over and twitched.

"Rachel! Hurry," Gary said.

As she approached Gary, she could smell his cologne, his sweat. More memories played like a broken reel.

Gary placed an arm around her, and it felt like old times again. "Come on, we'll be late."

Tiny needles began stitching her heart back together. Pain was replaced with a sense of *feeling*.

Being.

Rachel embraced him, ran her fingers through his hair. "I've missed you so much."

"I've missed you too, love." Gary motioned for her to get on board. "This won't take long."

Rachel stepped inside the railcar, grabbing a post for support. She could feel the rust in her hand and almost let go of it. Booths with wooden tables spread before her. Moss grew atop the booths, and termites left the wood looking like puzzles not quite finished. Gary motioned for her to join them.

Rachel sat down, and the smell of black mold filled her nostrils. Springs poked through the decaying leather of the booth. Gary bent down and picked up their daughter.

What her therapist would call *"Healing Tears"* became sobs, wracking her body. "My baby. My beautiful—Let me hold her." She reached out and Gary handed her their baby.

Gary pulled the baby's covers back. Rachel took in the sight before her. Wasted.

Emaciated. It was like a hairless rat, with claws and teeth to match. She almost dropped it.

It began to cry. Sounds of bees in empty soda cans filled her ears. Rachel tried to speak, but only a soft moan came out.

Gary cleared his throat. "Give me a kiss, love. It's been so long."

It felt like Styrofoam was in her throat, expanding.

Gary shrugged again, and she saw he wasn't whole. He wasn't the *Gary from before*. The top right half of his head began to slide open and gray matter oozed down his face. His shirt and tweed pants were covered in blood. "There's no pain where we're going. But here? You'll kill yourself. We both know that. So what's it gonna be? You gonna leave me all alone, too?"

The children shambled inside the railcar carefully. As each one took a seat, staring at her, accusing her, she remembered each and every one of them, and what she told them. What she had hoped would help them beat the cancer.

I said those stupid fucking things to them. "Be strong! You can beat this!" Hope is pain.

And look what I've done. I deserve this. . .

Rachel jumped when the train's whistle blew. Ethereal smoke obscured the night. The door of the railcar slammed shut. Oil lamps, just like in her books, flickered again, as the train began to move.

Gary snapped his fingers. "Rachel? You still with us?"

Rachel pointed at one of the children, the one that was only in stage 1 and began to sob. "I told her. . .that little girl there"— tears spilled down her cheeks— "that she could beat anything. She was just a little girl. . . and she believed me."

When Rachel opened her eyes again, Gary was *Gary from before*. He took her hand in his and squeezed. "And when I told you I was depressed, that I had bad thoughts. . . What did you say?"

Rachel felt her face flush. "That you needed help. You needed to see someone so you—" Gary leaned forward, wiped her tears off her cheeks. "But I didn't do that. I should have. But I didn't. That's not your fault. And here we are. Right here. Together. A family."

The baby began to cry again, and it was the softest music

Rachel had ever heard. She felt whole. Warm. A smile crept up her face. "What's her name?"

"Ruth," Gary said. "We've waited a long time for this."

Rachel looked down at the most beautiful thing she'd ever seen before. She was mesmerized by myriad colors of irises floating around each other, with tiny little black spiders swimming in their currents. Little Ruth smiled and giggled. Rachel gently pulled little Ruth to her chest and hugged her, sniffed her hair. Honeysuckle flooded her senses.

The train shuddered, then moved, jolting Rachel back to the present. She shook her head, as though to wake herself up. "Where are we going?"

Gary laughed as a shooting star raced past one of the railcars windows. He pointed at it.

"Make a wish, and we can go anywhere you want to, love."

As the train began to chug along the tracks, Rachel did just that.

Ben Eads *lives within the semi-tropical suburbs of Central Florida. A true horror writer by heart, he wrote his first story at the tender age of ten. The look on the teacher's face when she read it was priceless. Ben's short fiction has appeared in magazines or anthologies by: Crystal Lake Publishing, Shroud Magazine, Corpus Press, and Seventh Star Press. Ben's horror novellas,* Cracked Sky, *and,* Hollow Heart, *are available now from Crystal Lake Publishing. You can find Ben Eads on the web here:* www.beneadsfiction.com

OUR TOWN

MATTHEW MERCIER

THE LOCAL PEDOPHILE, Brian Hoover, lives in a haunted house but doesn't know this.

We have a theory: he's an evil man who communes with evil spirits and is thereby able to keep the demons at bay. This nugget of scuttlebutt—if true—pisses off the entire population of Norwich, Connecticut.

Norwich is not known for its crime, but we're part of America, so we have the usual hodgepodge of murder, drugs, and racist skinheads screaming about freedom while soliciting the Puerto Rican sex workers at the trailer park.

So, naturally, we also have perverts.

Brian Hoover served a mere fifteen years for buggering children, and after he moved in we thought, "Oh that's sooo perfect. The creep will be driven mad in a few months." But so far it's been crickets. What good is Poetic Justice without the justice?

The house is a rotting heap of aluminum siding and poor framing, cantilevered over the railroad tracks and mere feet from a river that floods at least twice a year. The railroad companies fear the house will collapse onto the tracks, causing a wreck. The neighbors want it demolished since it decreases their property values. But now Brian Hoover rents it, undisturbed.

Tonight, on All Hallows Eve, Brian Hoover will be visited and disturbed by three corporeal bodies

Vinny, our leader, is hunched behind the steering wheel, dressed as Willie Nelson in a jean jacket vest and red bandana. He's our wise elder, a pick-up-driving-high-school-dropout with a penchant for bar brawls. Vinny's sister was murdered by another serial killing douchebag in the 80s, so he's got a lightning bolt stenciled across his heart in invisible ink and whenever he tries to leave town, the lightning bolt pierces his heart, so he's pretty much stuck here.

His half-sister Vivian rides shotgun. She's half everything—half Puerto Rican, half gringo, half-way through high school and, according to her Born Again uncle, halfway to hell since she's a lesbian. Her costume is a white tank top and army issue cargo pants—Vasquez from *Aliens*. She's got the biceps to match.

And me, I'm jostling in the bed of the truck, back propped against the wheel well, a Star Wars stormtrooper helmet cutting off my peripheral vision. It sucks. Vinny said that's what I get for being a fascist tool of the galactic empire.

We park the truck around the corner, in the shade of an oak tree whose roots are pushing up the sidewalk. Below us, a cracked asphalt driveway drops down to the river. It rained last night, so the potholes are filled to the brim.

Vinny unwraps a gun loaded with rock salt. Vivian has a pair of tube socks filled with weights. I've got a water pistol filled with my own urine. The plan is to ring the doorbell, hit the guy low and hard where it counts, then scram.

Except now, when we turn the corner, we see the porch light is on.

A single, naked red bulb is lighting up a series of Paper Mache skeletons that jiggle and dance in the breeze. Hoover is at the door, greeting a lazy ghost (bedsheet, eyeholes) and a Pippie Longstocking, horizontal braids jutting out from her skull.

Children. Grade schoolers. On Hoover's porch. Alone. No adult in sight, unless you count Vinny, who cocks his gun and states the obvious. "What the ever-living fuck?"

Hoover drops treats in the children's bags before they step off the porch and turn right toward us.

My heart is galloping. We part to let them pass, and the freckled Pippi Longstocking glances at me with owl eyes. One of her braids brushes my shoulder. I'm frozen. Only Vivian's touch revives me. She's rubbing my shoulder, a sticky goo webbed between her thumb and forefinger.

"Hey," Vinny whisper-shouts. "Kids? Did he hurt you?"

They ignore us and keep on walking. Fine. We step onto the

porch, hit the doorbell. Hoover's voice bellows, "Again? Right away? Come on, give me a break!"

The door swings open.

Hoover's face is a pink button of fat and five o'clock shadow. He's wearing an oversized purple bathrobe with the sleeves rolled up, and stares down at us through foggy glasses, taped and cracked. He's a balding Ringwraith with tattoos and track marks eating up every patch of visible flesh on his arms. He settles on me.

"Aren't you a little short for a Stormtrooper?" he giggles. "Oh God. Jesus H Chr-"

Vinny whips out the gun and shoots him in the nuts.

Hoover stumbles backward, crashes on his ass. The house trembles. Vinney pushes open the door, wedges it open with a twig. Hoover is holding his junk, but not howling in extreme pain the way he should be.

"You can't be in here," he wheezes.

From inside my helmet, I see a black and white television. A sagging couch. Dishes in the sink. The house reeks of mold and poverty.

"Please," he moans. "Please go."

Vivian steps to him with her loaded sock when the doorbell shrills. Hoover struggles to his feet. We all turn.

The child at the door is a hulking Leatherface, one of those monster kids who's having an early growth spurt. Hoover stumbles to his feet, gives us another pleading look, and then sighs. He picks up a switchblade from the sideboard, then opens his robe to expose a bare shoulder which is a wet hole, white and pulpy. He digs with the tip of the blade, whimpering and wincing as he carves out a piece, flipping a triangle of flesh onto the floor. He picks it up, lovingly tucks it into a discarded Snickers wrapper, and drops it in Leatherface's burlap sack, who turns and leaves.

Vivian gags. Vinny lowers his gun, mouth agape. My bowels loosen.

Hoover puts the knife back on the sideboard, arches an eyebrow. "Okay? Seen enough? Time to go."

No argument. But we're paralyzed.

"Jesus, I'm not going to touch you." Hoover groans, pointing to an ankle bracelet and stomping his foot. "I'm being watched twenty-four seven. Now scram!"

He steps aside so we have a clear path to the door, the belts of his bathrobe hanging loose at his side. As we walk by, I grab one of the belts and yank it hard. Hoover does nothing to stop this. The robe swings open.

Pale hairless thighs dotted with gooseflesh. Where his junk should be is. . .nothing. No stitches, no gash, just a wall of smooth flesh.

He sighs, looks down, scratches his non-existent pubes, then licks goo off his fingers.

We bolt to the porch. Leatherface has already turned the corner and is passing the truck. At our footsteps, he turns and cocks his head to the side, childlike, the way Jason Vorhees always does in the movies when they want the actor to show the boy underneath the monster.

With a palm, Leatherface beckons us, pointing down the driveway.

"No," Vivian gurgles.

But there's a giant magnet in the air, pulling us down. We descend the driveway. The river gurgles in the shallows. It smells of metal and rotting wood. Cat-o-nine tails tower over us. Ahead is the square light of an old fishing shack.

Leatherface holds open the door for us. Inside, Pippi and the ghost are sitting at a table, sorting and labeling their haul with twine and index cards, as if preparing for a tag sale. An earlobe from Jim Malony (our school principal). A ring finger, Carol Dansworth (crossing guard). And three flaccid purple dicks from Father Ross, Father Bob, and Pastor McCarthy.

The children look up, consider us, then shuffle forward and thrust their bags under our chins. They smell oddly sweet, baby powder and lilac. Leatherface points to us, then the bags. Vivian screams.

"But we didn't do anything!" Vinny shouts.

"It doesn't matter."

I take off my helmet as a gesture of peace and grab scissors off the table. I clip a piece of my hair and hand it to Pippie, who grins, a gap between her teeth, and shakes her head.

She takes my hand, rubs a hangnail dangling from my thumb, and rips it off.

I scream as a train rushes, rumbling the whole earth. We get the picture now. Vinny finds a scab on his knuckle the size of a quarter and scrapes it off. Vivian allows the ghost to pop a zit on her cheek and suck out the puss.

Offerings made, Leatherface opens the door and we run into the night, back to the truck, back to the safety of our homes, but we see the children walking the streets all night, visiting the houses of people we know and people we don't, homes that are now marked forever, and we only pray they will never, ever need to visit us or anyone we love.

Matthew Mercier *is the author of* Poe & I *(Crystal Lake Publishing, 2024) a novel loosely based on his time spent as caretaker for Poe Cottage, the last home of Edgar Allan Poe. He's performed true stories about his time with Poe live on stage with The Moth, and he's spun other tales on NPR's The Moth Radio Hour, The Story Collider, RISK, and The Truth. For his fiction, he's been awarded the Leon B. Burstein scholarship from the New York chapter of the Mystery Writers of America and a residency from the Saltonstall Foundation in Ithaca, NY. His work has appeared in various magazines such as Creative Nonfiction, The Fairy Tale Review, Shotgun Honey, and Mystery Tribune. Most recently, he wrote, directed, edited and sound designed a radio drama entitled Poe's Basement for Radio Free Rhinecliff in Rhinecliff, NY. Learn more at matthewmercier.com*

COULROPHOBIA KILLS

LEIGH KENNY

"YOU LOOK TENSE."

Laurel reached a hand across the void and squeezed Ron's knee through the worn denim of his jeans. He stole a glance at her before focusing on the road ahead once more. She was beaming a smile at him, so full of warmth it was as though it, and not the final rays of a waning sun, warmed the interior of the car as they cruised along the dusty country road.

Ron turned his head back towards her, a ghost of a smile on his lips. "I am tense," he said, his eyes leaving the road briefly once more to meet her gaze. "I hate the circus. Correction: I hate the damn clowns." His mouth twisted in a pained grimace as he spat the last word out.

Laurel continued to gaze at him, concern in her eyes. It was taking a lot for him to do this, so it was best not to push. With a final squeeze and a gentle pat, she pulled her hand from his leg and began to fiddle with the radio dial. Out here in the sticks, their choices were Christian rock, fire and brimstone preacher, or static.

The evening sky was ablaze with colour, fiery reds that bled into deepest purple. The sun cast a golden halo as it continued to sink behind the distant mountains. With a steady thrum of tyres on gravel, the car continued along the lane, kicking up a cloud of dust in its wake.

With his mind running a mile a minute, Ron tried his best to focus on the road before him. He knew Laurel would appreciate a little conversation to pass the journey, but the hissing static that leaked from the stereo was soothing. He wanted the quasi-silence to keep his mind from wandering. Needed it to keep himself from slamming on the brakes, turning the damn car around and hightailing it back to their cosy apartment in town, far away from the countryside, the dust and the circus.

As if conjured by his mind, a red and white striped monstrosity rose in the distance, coloured flags perched on its canvas apexes, each one flapping gently in the evening breeze that blew down through the valley from the surrounding hills. A shudder ran through him.

Aware that Laurel was studying him again, Ron swallowed the lump that had formed in his throat and silently urged his pounding heart to normality.

Before them, the valley flattened, and the entire circus compound became visible. Scores of cars lined up uniformly in the grassy patches on either side of the looming archway, a colourful ticket booth standing guard by the entrance. Behind the hastily erected fence, tents and wagons dotted the area. Booths painted in garish colours, that probably hosted games, oddities and a world of fried foods, sat in between them. The huge canvas tent dwarfed it all and drew the eye away from the outer edges of the compound where tired old trailers and trucks looped around towards the back. Probably where the performers lived, spending their days in mouldy old tin cans, and their nights in mouldy old makeup.

Manoeuvring the car into the first available space, Ron switched off the engine. The only sounds in the vehicle were the quiet ticking of the engine and the staccato beat of his racing heart. A breath shuddered from him, and Laurel glanced across sharply.

"You don't have to do this," she said quietly. "I know Doctor Young said immersion was the best therapy, but maybe she's wrong. We can always try a different therapist."

"We've come all this way. May as well keep going," he replied, unable to hide the edge in his tone. A memory flashed in his mind, sharp and hot, and oh so familiar.

Bright red plastic nose.

The meaty thwack of axe against flesh.

His father's grease-painted face contorted in a crazed anger.

His mother's screams.

Oh, how those screams had haunted him as a child. Still haunted him.

Without another word, they both climbed from the car, each

lost in a myriad of thoughts. The warm evening air was punctuated by sound; cheers of delight, tinny loudspeaker announcements, a cacophony of voices mingling as the patrons immersed themselves in all the excitement that the circus had to offer.

At the entrance booth, Ron offered up a silent prayer of thanks that the bored teenager who took their money wore no theatrical makeup. Her eyes never left her phone, and she snapped her gum as she passed the tickets across the worn countertop.

"Looks like we're just in time for the main show," Laurel said, and without looking, Ron knew she was studying him again.

Gritting his teeth, he nodded and took her hand. Together, they strode purposefully towards the yawning mouth of the massive tent. Broken calliope music seeped from the opening, and he wondered why such unsettling music was always used for such a supposedly cheerful place. Maybe it was only Ron whose teeth were set on edge by the grinding notes.

Moving through the darkened tent, he stumbled across the jumble of legs as he aimed for a seat in the darkest corner possible. The darkness seemed to offer the promise of protection. From what, he wasn't sure.

His butt had barely touched the hard bench when the lights came up and a booming voice announced the commencement of the main show. Children cheered, parents smiled, and babies cried. Ron felt an affinity with those tiny, fussing humans.

The show began, and Ron cringed as a trio of clowns tumbled their way around the ring, introducing each act with exaggerated arm flailing. His body relaxed a little as they exited the stage again, and he watched the acrobats sail through the air, their grace bestowing a strange sense of tranquillity upon him. The acrobats were swiftly followed by a troupe of small dogs in various outfits, performing tricks that elicited peals of laughter from the surrounding audience. Next came a woman in an outfit that left little to the imagination, a huge python the only thing covering her modesty. The space erupted in horrified gasps as she completed her act with the massive creature, before leaving the ring to make way for a fresh round of aerial acrobatics.

Between each act, the clowns appeared, their pasty faces and exaggerated mouths filling him with a dread so heavy that it sat in his stomach like a rock. At one point, they began to move into the crowd, whipping up balloon animals for delighted children who greedily snatched at the proffered goods.

As a child, his classmates were always envious that Ron had a real-life clown at home. He was invited to every birthday party, probably at the behest of the parents hoping their kid's chosen form of entertainment would offer a hefty discount with the inclusion of his only child. Ron declined most of the invites.

As one of the clowns, a mass of neon green hair upon his head, closed in on Ron's seat, he shut his eyes. The drumming of his heart, so loud that it almost drowned out the symphony of the circus, only settled when Laurel squeezed his knee. A sign that the coast was clear once more.

The strobing lights were almost blinding as he opened his eyes. The main stage was now home to a gang of men in leotards. One was exhibiting his strength by balancing one of his brethren above his head with an outstretched arm. Another was strapped to a spinning wheel as his blindfolded castmate threw shiny daggers. This elicited more gasps, even the occasional shriek, from the stunned audience.

Ron jolted suddenly, as a shiny red balloon shape floated to his lap. A gentle tap on his shoulder was followed by a small voice, "'Scuse me, mister. Can I have my balloon sword back, please?" Plucking the sword from his knees, Ron turned with a smile to the child behind him. Then froze.

A small face leered at him from behind cracked, white makeup. Large black diamond shapes covered eyes that seemed to bore into his soul, the oversized red mouth frozen in a rictus grin.

Thwack! "Come here, Ronnie! Daddy just wants to talk to you!"

Ron blinked and suddenly the form before him was just that of a small boy, no more than six or seven years old. Blinking again to ensure he hadn't lost his mind, Ron handed the balloon across to the boy, who smiled up at him gratefully. There was a gap where one of his front teeth should be, lending an air of vulnerability to the child. "Thanks, mister!" he grinned, turning quickly away to show off his returned prize to a beaming woman Ron assumed to be his mother.

Sweat beaded on his forehead, and Ron could feel Laurel's gaze upon him once more.

"Everything okay, babe?" she asked gently.

Ron smiled at her in what he hoped was a reassuring way. "Sure thing. Just getting a little peckish is all. This isn't half as bad as I expected it would be!"

Laurel returned his smile with a thousand-watt grin. "I'm so proud of you, Ron. I'll run to concessions and grab a bucket of popcorn and a soda to share. Coke okay for you?"

He nodded, the forced smile still stretched across his face, only allowing it to slide away as Laurel edged her way along the row of seats and towards the brightly lit food stand near the tent's entrance.

Silently scolding himself, Ron had forcibly put himself together when Laurel returned. She sat heavily and dumped an overflowing popcorn bucket on his lap. Leaning across, she kissed him gently, her lips still cold and sweet from the soda she had sipped on the return journey. "I know I already said it, but I'm gonna say it again anyway. I'm proud of you, Ron. You're doing so good."

"I'm proud of myself," he replied, almost believing the false bravado that flowed from him. "Clowns aren't that scary in the flesh." *Thwack.*

"I'm glad you think so, because I have a little surprise for you," she whispered, tilting her blonde head closer to his. The spotlights reflected off the barrette nestled in her hair, the daisy shape twinkling in the coloured lights. "One of the clowns runs the concessions stand. He's a really nice guy, and I told him about your immersion therapy tonight. He's invited you to go back to their trailer after the show to meet the gang. Nothing will cure that fear of clowns faster than seeing them as real people in their everyday environment, right?"

Ron was sure his heart had stopped for just a moment as Laurel's words filtered through his ears and sank into his stomach like concrete. "Sounds great, babe," he said, hating the tremor in his voice.

But Laurel had turned her attention back to the ring, where the dreaded clowns were in full swing.

Tiny bicycles, oversized cannons, tumbles and stumbles; it was a jam-packed schedule that drew cheers of delight and roars of laughter from the audience. Ron watched through widened eyes, feeling his sanity slowly peel away from him like sunburnt skin with every honk of a comically large red nose, every thwack of a juggling club against white-gloved hands.

As they finished out the grand finale and took a well-practised bow, the noise from the crowd was deafening. More than half the tent was on their feet, thunderously applauding the costumed men as they curtseyed their way behind the heavy velvet drapes. Laurel chattered excitedly in his ear as they were carried along by the crowd, back outside into the fresh night air. Ron smiled and nodded, his body strolling between booths alongside her, his fractured mind drifting away on the wind to another time and place that no longer existed.

"I think this is it," Laurel said as she came to a halt by a rickety old trailer with peeling sides. It was tucked away in the shadows, low-hanging branches tracking along the mildewed roof like skeletal fingers in the moonlight. A lamp hung by the door, its weak glow straining to illuminate the handful of metal steps that led to the doorway. Etched in the greying paint by the door was a haphazard clown face, something that would look at home in a child's drawing pad but took on a sinister appearance beneath the flickering light cast by the lamp. "Do you want me to go in with you?"

Ron shook his head and climbed the steps as though in a trance. He rapped on the door and was greeted by a gravelled voice. "Come in!" it bellowed. Ron stepped inside and shut the door behind him.

The interior of the trailer belied its outward appearance. The main area was warm and cosy, an overstuffed couch resting along one wall, and a couple of comfortable looking chairs placed in the corners. Soft pillows and throws adorned each one, and a large rug lay beneath a small white coffee table in the centre of the room, an array of books stacked upon it. A dainty floral cup sat on a coaster, steam rising from within, beside it a tray of cake, one slice removed, and a knife still covered in frosting resting on the edge. Tasteful art decorated the walls, and the air smelled of lavender. On the couch sat two clowns, a third appearing from behind a door further back in the trailer. He greeted Ron cheerfully.

"You must be Ron!" he said gaily.

Ron's left eye twitched, his gaze never leaving the face of the clown seated nearest to him. The green-haired clown smiled at him before lifting the slice of cake back to his mouth, crumbs falling in his brightly coloured lap as he nibbled.

"Pete, you're getting crumbs on the rug again," the other

couch-clown scolded the green-haired man beside him. The three laughed, as though Pete and his crumb-dropping ways were a constant source of amusement. Ron's mouth twitched before pulling upwards in a smile, invisible fishhooks lodged in his skin forcing his features into place. In one fluid motion, he stepped forward and lifted the cake-covered knife from the tray, his arm slashing in an outward arc. Pete dropped his slice of cake to the rug, his two white-gloved hands fluttering to his neck where the skin had opened. Blood gushed from the gaping wound, and the clown gasped and choked as his comrades rushed to stem the crimson flow.

Ron stepped quickly behind the standing clown. One arm forced its head back as the other pulled the blade across its throat, an open wound appearing to mirror that of the shuddering heap on the sofa. The body twitched and jerked forward, landing across the last remaining clown, whose panicked eyes spoke the truth he knew. Death's shadow had draped across him, and he was about to feel its cold embrace.

As he opened his mouth to scream for help, Ron rushed at him, jabbing the blade into his face, his neck, his chest. Over and over, he thrust the knife, the coppery scent of blood overpowering the gentle lavender fragrance. The only sound in the trailer was the wet, sucking sound of steel against meat. Thwack.

A gentle knocking on the door pulled Ron's attention away from the lifeless form before him. His heart beat furiously in his chest and he panted heavily, his eyes wild as they darted around the gore spattered space. The door swung open, and ice crawled up his spine as another clown entered the trailer.

Cracked white paint covered its face, bright red lipstick smeared across its mouth like blood. Its eyes were black and soulless, and it shrieked at him as it approached.

"Come to Daddy, Ronnie!"

Tears fell from his eyes, and with a roar of anger, Ron rushed the demonic-looking clown. He slammed into it, his knife burying deep into its chest, both of them tumbling to the ground hard. Ron scrambled away from the creature, afraid that his blow wasn't enough, but too scared to get close and retrieve the weapon.

"Ron," the clown croaked, a hand pawing weakly at the air around it. "Babe. . ."

Pulling himself to his feet, Ron stumbled past the bloodied

figure, ignoring its mewling pleas and the scarlet-tinged blonde hair with the daisy barrette as he bolted from the trailer, the door slamming shut behind him.

Everywhere he looked, he was surrounded by clowns. Tall ones, fat ones, child-sized ones; a sea of cracked porcelain faces and soulless painted eyes that seemed to follow him as he staggered through the maze of tents and wagons.

His heart rate steadied as his car came into view. Behind him a scream cut through the night air. It reminded him of a nightmare he might have had once before. Everything would be okay soon. He knew his gun was in the trunk of his car. He fumbled with the keys, his hands shaking as he lifted the trunk and flipped open the shiny metal case.

No more clowns.

No more nightmares.

*Born and raised in the garden county of Wicklow, Ireland, **Leigh Kenny** lives by the Irish Sea with the all her favourite people. She has released two standalone books,* Cursed *and* Hush, My Darling. *Leigh's novellas* Knock on Wood *and* Tiny Dancer *have appeared in the Crystal Lake Publishing series* Dark Tide 20: Urban Legends *and* Hurt People Hurt People *respectively. She has also appeared in a multitude of anthologies.*

You can find out more about Leigh's work here: https://linktr.ee/leighkenny

DINNER WITH THE SCHIMBĂTOR

JASPER BARK

THE COACH HAD no driver.

Mina nudged Jonathan as they climbed from the carriage. Nodding to the empty box seat. They hadn't heard him climb down and there was nowhere to hide in the courtyard.

When had he gotten off? When they passed under the castle's portcullis or before they entered? Had the horses driven themselves? Mina had paid it no mind when they embarked. She'd been too enchanted by the Tihuţa Pass and the looming Călimani Mountains.

The horses were uneasy. They whinnied, shook their heads and stamped. Hooves echoing across the vast courtyard. Night was drawing in, the only illumination the full moon and the pitch-soaked torches.

Jonathan shrugged, affecting diffidence. He fingered his high stiff collar, uncomfortable in his double-breasted frock coat with its silk faced collars. He'd fumbled his cravat. Mina had tied and pinned it for him. Mina herself found it hard to breathe in the fitted bodice of her bottle green dress, its lace and crinolines made disembarking a gymnastic feat.

Lucy managed it with elegance and grace, like everything she did. Mina noted, with envy, the boned bodice and tight sleeves of her brocade dress did nothing to restrict her movements, nor did the high collar or the bustle at the back.

She stepped daintily from the carriage. Arthur, in an uncharacteristic show of gallantry offered his hand. Nearly a head taller than Jonathan, he cut a dashing figure in his checked, double-breasted frock coat. The bowtie around his stiff collar caused him none of the discomfort Jonathan was suffering.

Arthur glanced with jaded indifference at the four towers of the castle. He was no more impressed by the picturesque stone balcony that sat above the entrance.

"So, this is Castle De Sange. Seen better days, hasn't it?"

Jonathan ignored him. "We're expected inside. We mustn't keep our host waiting."

Arthur slapped him on the back, making him take an involuntary step forward. "Perish the thought, old boy."

They passed through a dark, oak clad vestibule and into the central hall. Moonlight streamed through the twenty foot, leaded-glass windows in the south wall, spilling onto the worn flagstones. In the high arches of the timbered ceiling it picked out the many cobwebs and their inhabitants who favored the shadows. Mina tried not to think of them or the hapless insects they fed on.

At the end of the hall a wide mahogany staircase curved upward to a broad landing supported by a colonnade. Mina saw seven pricks of light at the top of the staircase. As they drew closer, the tiny pricks grew to become candle flames.

A tall, thin figure was carrying a candelabrum in his left hand. His hair was jet black, his features aquiline and his skin too pale to be human. He was dressed for dinner in a tail jacket and black tie. He stopped at the top of the staircase and gazed down at the party of four.

"I am Lord Fiara De Sange. I bid you welcome to my home."

Mina felt less emotion than she'd imagined. Their host was unrecognizable.

Outside, in the foothills, a pack of wolves bayed. A plaintive, yearning cry that spoke of hunger, kinship and territorial claims . His lordship smiled indulgently, gazing out the windows.

"A nocturnal choir, such a fitting accompaniment, wouldn't you agree?"

A loud ping rang out, like the striking of a tiny silver bell.

Everyone looked at Arthur.

He smiled sheepishly, reached into his frock coat and produced his cellphone.

"Sorry, should've had it on silent."

Jonathan rounded on him. "You should have left it in the hotel, like you were supposed to."

"Oh come on, who leaves their phone behind in this day and age?."

"Someone who's been told to leave it behind because it will compromise the integrity of the experience. Someone who's jumped a ten year waiting list to come on this unique and exclusive experience. Someone who's friend spent millions of dollars so he could have this one-of-a-kind experience."

Arthur drew himself up and took a step toward Jonathan, to emphasize the height disparity.

"You didn't spend anything. You bought into the company like you buy everything, including your friends."

The two glowered at each other.

Arthur threw his hands up. "Okay, fine, I'll hand it in. I just need to answer this text." He skulked into the shadows, thumbs moving across his screen.

Lucy leaned into Mina. "It's that bitch he keeps in an uptown apartment. Thinks I don't know about her, but I do."

Lucy put her shoulders back, tossed her hair and took Jonathan's arm. "Didn't you say we mustn't keep our host waiting?"

2

The dining table could have seated twenty. The banquet hall was the size of a small auditorium.

Lord Fiara De Sange sat at the head of the table, Jonathan and Mina to his right, Lucy and Arthur to his left. Waiting staff, in period costume, served them dishes from a tasting menu prepared by a chef with three Michelin stars. All the staff avoided their host.

They ate off the finest porcelain with sparkling silver cutlery. There were antique sideboards and drinks cabinets along both walls, along with suits of armor and shields with crossed swords. But most of the wall space was taken up with portraits of the De Sange family.

De Sange ate nothing, preferring to sip from a golden goblet filled with red liquid. Lucy, hand on chin, considered the Lord through hooded lids.

"Aren't you going to dine with us, your lordship?"

"No, excuse me, but I have dined already."

Arthur sucked a piece of lobster tail from his fork and gestured at the paintings with his knife. "Tell me about these paintings?"

De Sange glanced up at the portraits. "They are my ancestors."

"All of them?"

"The Fiara and the De Sange families have a long and distinguished history going back to the middle ages."

Arthur narrowed his eyes, pointing at De Sange with his fork. "But they're not really *your* ancestors, are they?"

"I'm not sure I follow you?"

Arthur sat back in his chair and pushed his plate away. Satisfaction crept over his face.

"You see, I work in finance. I look after high-net individuals, managing their wealth. I manage Jonathan's as it happens."

Jonathan put down his cutlery. "A small portion of my wealth."

Arthur batted his comment aside. "Anyway, in my business information is key. I did a lot of digging on you, before we came and you're not really a lord, are you?"

"I am the last of my line. I inherited the title."

"Only by default. I mean, it was given to you, along with this castle and everything else. You're not the real Lord Fiara De Sange, are you? The fearsome Schimbător of legend, that was someone else, someone dead."

De Sange set down his goblet with a sharp clang. "I am the oldest male heir, therefore the title is mine."

"But not legitimately. You only have the title because the Fraternitas Aquae Sanctae gave it to you, you were born out of wedlock to the wrong side of your family. They made you a lord just like they made you a Schimbător and look how that turned out. Heard you caused them quite the problem when you escaped."

Mina felt a stab of anguish. She studied De Sange's face for a hint of remorse. His expression remained stoic but his grip on the goblet tightened. Jonathan interceded.

"Let it go, Arthur, you're being a bore. Let's just enjoy his lordship's hospitality."

Arthur snorted. "That's right, *his lordship's* hospitality."

Lucy stroked her neck and put her other hand lightly on De Sange's wrist. "Please excuse Arthur, your lordship. I think he's a little intimidated by the size of your. . .castle."

De Sange said nothing.

Lucy tucked a strand of hair behind her ear. "I, for one, find your ancestry fascinating. I don't care what Arthur says, the family resemblance continues from generation to generation. Must be where you get your good looks."

De Sange turned to regard Lucy for the first time, a dark intensity in his gaze. Lucy put a hand over her mouth.

"Oh, what you do to a girl with that look."

She tapped his goblet with a perfectly manicured fingernail. "Is that what I think it is?"

De Sang stared pityingly at its contents. "It's artificial plasma."

"Don't they let you have the real stuff?"

"Occasionally I get pig's blood, when they are happy with me."

He sounded crestfallen, and Mina wondered if it was possible to pity De Sange.

Lucy licked her lips and moved a little closer. "Why don't we add something a little stronger to your meal."

She picked up her steak knife and drove it into the pad of her middle finger, drawing blood. Then she held the digit over his goblet and let the blood drip into it, licking the last of drops from the blade.

This did not have the effect she expected.

De Sange's neck began to bulge. He reminded Mina of a bullfrog about to croak. Then his jaw dislocated and his mouth fell open much further than it should.

An impossibly large tongue slithered out. The root of the tongue was like a long, pink snake. The midsection was thicker and flatter. Mina caught a glimpse of its underside, it reminded her of a giant leach with a series of cavities containing teeth. The end was forked like a serpent's tongue.

The huge, prehensile organ darted toward Lucy's bloody finger. She made a fist and pulled it to her chest, mesmerized by the movements of De Sange's tongue.

An alarm sounded. De Sange's chest began to glow with a strange orange color.

The tongue shot back into his mouth and his jaw clamped shut. He grabbed at his chest and his body went into spasms. Doors in each corner of the hall burst open and six men marched in. They wore sackcloth robes, body armor, and visored helmets, and carried semi-automatic rifles.

The tallest approached the dinner table. His manner was calm and polite. "No need to worry, folks, the situation is now contained. If you don't mind, dessert will be served in the suites we've provided. And, if you'll allow me a polite word of advice, it's best never to expose a Schimbător to human blood."

3

You found the devil, Archimandrite Di Segni knew, lying in the detail. Lying through his teeth. Lying in wait for the unwary.

To control the details was to control everything. There was no detail in the control room that he missed. He saw the way Brother Moretti sat forward as he monitored the surveillance screens, unwilling to let his back touch the chair, or the sackcloth of his robe. Brother Moretti had been self-flagellating, therefore he had a guilty conscience and must be watched.

Brother Lombardi was silently mouthing prayers, counting them off on his rosary, as he monitored the Schimbător's organism. He did this when he was fighting to stay awake, he didn't sleep when he was troubled. Di Segni would look into whatever was troubling him.

He approached the bank of surveillance screens. "Are the guests in their suites?"

Moretti nodded, beads of sweat breaking out across his shaven scalp.

"Yes, Reverend Father, they've been served the remaining courses. Should I lock them in for the night."

"No. Continue their access to public areas, keep a careful eye on them. What of the Schimbător?"

"It has been contained and neutralized, Reverend Father. Should we immobilize it?"

"We need the creature conscious and active so it can interact with our guests. It's our most valuable asset. Have it duly castigated and sent to the east parapet."

"Right away, Reverend Father."

Di Segni took a moment to stand in the middle of the command room and scan everything. Even the monitors seemed to flinch beneath his gaze. When he was done, he left, nodding to the monks on the door who saluted.

At the end of a short corridor, in what had once been the servant's quarter, Di Segni entered his office. It was almost as small as the cell in which he slept. Privations such as these kept Di Segni and his brothers closer to God. He knelt and prayed before the wooden cross on the wall, the only decoration in the otherwise spartan workspace.

He prayed for the strength to carry the burden God had seen fit to grant, to continue the legacy of the Fraternitas Aquae Sanctae. Di Segni had joined the Fraternitas soon after his days as a novice. He'd taken holy orders at his family's prompting. They'd all but given up on him after he was expelled from three exclusive private schools.

At first, he'd fought the strictures of monastic life, but he came to see it as the antidote to everything he hated about modern life. The permissive culture of tolerance and promiscuity had always disgusted him and the liberal values of the West were sapping its energy and vitality, making it vulnerable to foreign rivals. The Fraternitas offered a life of devotion to a tradition that had protected Christendom for millennia.

It was founded in 1209 by Pope Clement III, during the time of the Albigensian Crusade, a period when the Church was beset by enemies from within and without. The worst of those enemies were the Schimbător—an ancient, parasitical race of shape-changers who fed upon the blood of the innocent. Who claimed to have walked this earth before man was created. Who skulked in the shadows, preyed on the unwary, and gave birth to countless myths and folklore.

The Church had long known of the Schimbător, but they weren't mentioned in holy scripture, so belief in their existence couldn't be sanctioned by the Church. Pope Clement III's answer was to found a secret order of monks trained in martial prowess and esoteric arts. Thus the Fraternitas Aquae Sanctae were born. Crusaders, inquisitors, and holy instruments of God's will in the fight against the menace of the Schimbător.

Sadly Clement III's successors did not appreciate the threat of these monsters. The order had been sidelined and underfunded since the Second Vatican Council. Few in the Church believed in the existence of the Schimbător, and the Fraternitas was seen as an anachronism and embarrassment.

Di Segni had risen quickly through the ranks of the Fraternitas but, by the time he assumed the mantle of Archimandrite, the Fraternitas was close to collapse, a ghost of its former self. It was incumbent upon him to save the crusade against the Schimbător and continue the order's nearly nine hundred year legacy. His first order of business was to restore its funds. This would take a bold initiative, and so he'd launched, 'Operation Shark-Tank.'

Di Segni finished his prayers and opened his laptop. He had a zoom call scheduled with Seneschal De Molay, his second in command.

De Molay was a tall man, with broad shoulders and pleasing, non-descript features. Though ten years Di Segni's junior, he was held in high esteem by the brotherhood who looked to his competence and pragmatism. Di Segni had learned to watch him closely.

"Allow me to pay my humblest respects, Reverend Father."

Was that the ghost of a smirk playing about De Molay's lips, or was Di Segni being too sensitive?

"I'm going to need you to assign more men. I'll expect them in the morning."

"I heard there was a minor incident, Reverend Father. I trust you're unharmed."

"I'm in no danger, Seneschal, there was never any threat to my person or position. You should not put too much stock in the wagging of our brothers' tongues."

A micro-frown crossed De Molay's face and he regained himself.

"What of our potential investors?'

"They are safe and well."

"The, um, incident hasn't affected their interest?"

"The funds are as safe as our guests."

"Very good, Reverend Father. She's *your* niece, no one knows your family better than you."

Was that a subtle rebuke, a reference to nepotism? Or was De Molay aware of the deeper web of relationships at play here? Di Segni would file it away for consideration.

"You see to the extra security, I will see to the success of Operation Shark Tank."

"And what of our Schimbător, Reverend Father?"

"It's still unharmed and fully operational. I'm surprised by your interest in its welfare."

"We need a shark for our tank, Reverend Father, otherwise there's no operation. It's a near priceless asset, the only one in captivity. They're next to impossible to capture."

"Quite. See to the extra security and we'll speak again in the morning."

"Goodbye, Reverend Father."

Di Segni closed his laptop without signing off. How dare De Molay remind him how rare the Schimbător was. No one knew better than him. He'd discovered the phial in the Vatican archives, packed in ice, preserved for over a century. He had confirmed it contained the blood of Lord Fiara De Sange. The original De Sange, perhaps the most infamous Schimbător in history.

He had hatched the scheme to resurrect De Sange, to keep him in captivity and use him to raise the funds to save the Fraternitas. The Schimbător propagated by sharing their blood with a host organism, taking over the physiognomy of the host and converting them into one of their own. Di Segni decided to use De Sange's blood to create a Schimbător rather than capture one. But, because De Sange had once been human, they would need a member of his family. Otherwise the blood would not bond with the host DNA.

After much research, Di Segni discovered there were three surviving members of De Sange's bloodline. Two of them shocked him, the third was perfect. Di Segni had the man abducted and forcibly converted to a Schimbător.

To keep his monster on a leash, Di Segni had a container of Aqua Benedicta, placed in its chest along with an explosive device that would shatter the container when a specific code was transmitted. Aqua Benedicta, the most powerful form of holy water, was the only substance that could kill the Schimbător. And Di Segni was the only one with the code for the device. He had full control of the creature.

He had tested its abilities once only, letting it think it had escaped. Di Segni knew it needed to feed for the conversion to take effect. He had selected its victim very carefully, someone who served Di Segni's purposes and extended his influence in other areas. Once the Schimbător had fed and its transition was complete, he tugged on its leash, took it back into custody, and set it up in this castle in the Călimani mountains.

With the creature in place, he could raise the funds needed to save the Fraternitas. Charge the super-rich millions of dollars to have dinner with a real Schimbător, a unique experience with a waiting list a decade long. All he needed was the seed money to fund the operation, an investor with the vision to see its potential.

That's where his niece had come in, bringing her tech-billionaire husband to the table, because she knew what she owed

Di Segni. Granted, she had objected to his interventions in her life, but in time she had come to see their wisdom. Her participation tonight was proof of that.

She had come to learn that purity was everything. Purity of mind, purity of family. Purity in God.

Tonight was the test run. The maiden voyage of Operation Shark Tank. A way to stress test the whole system from the guests' arrival until their departure. It had gone perfectly until one of the guests had cut herself.

Di Segni would write a memo to his guests, explaining that this evening's drama was an added thrill. A demonstration of the creature's terrible abilities. As they could see, the situation was entirely under control and they were never in any peril.

The rest of their stay would go without a hitch.

4

"Never in any peril! Entirely under control! What kind of an idiot do they take me for?" Jonathan had read her uncle's memo and was building up to one of his rants. If he'd had Wi-Fi he would have taken to social media.

"They don't take you for any kind of an idiot. Without you they can't make any of this happen. They're afraid of you, afraid you'll pull the plug on their whole venture and they're trying to reassure you."

Mina knew the best way to mollify Jonathan was to play to his ego.

"Well, they're not doing a very good job."

"That's why they need your expertise. Why you have to see the whole system in operation so you can tell them where to improve it."

"They could start with better décor. What is it with all this antique furniture?"

Mina sighed. "It's part of the period detail, recreating the gothic past for the clients that come here. Giving them the most authentic experience."

"If you say so."

"I quite like it. Some of these pieces are over three hundred years old. The four poster bed's quite comfy. Maybe we can give it a spin later."

Jonathan scowled and then shuddered at the thought. "Not gonna happen."

Did he always have to treat her like that? Did she repulse him that much, or was he just intimidated?

"Maybe you could get Lucy to warm it for you."

"What's that supposed to mean?'

"I didn't see you objecting when she hung off your arm at dinner."

"I couldn't help that."

"You were enjoying it."

"No I wasn't. She's got a nice rack, but that's about it. I don't want Arthur's cast offs. I can afford better. And what was that crap she pulled, slicing her finger open in front of that creature?"

"I think she was flirting with him."

"Flirting?!"

"Yes, she was sore at Arthur over the woman he was texting."

"It was a woman was it?"

"She thought so, and when she couldn't make him jealous with you, she moved onto De Sange."

"De Sange now, is it?"

Mina took a deep breath, calmed herself. She didn't want to provoke Jonathan. "Yes, De Sange, our host."

"You act as though you've known that thing for years."

Mina folded her hands in her lap, not wanting to give anything away. Jonathan poured himself another scotch. The hundred year old single malt was the only thing he liked in their suite.

He knocked back his drink and threw his cravat and collar on the floor. "I'm not wearing those things anymore. I'm sick of them, I'm sick of this whole place."

"And what does that mean?"

"I'm not sure about this whole deal. I think I should pull out."

"You've already transferred the funds."

"Not all of them. Maybe I should cut my losses."

"It's a sound investment. The figures are good. Actually they're great and you know it."

"You're only saying that because of your damned uncle."

"This has nothing to do with my uncle."

"Then why are you trying to talk me into this. You saw what that thing did, what it's capable of. It's too risky."

"It's not as risky as your Bitcoin holdings."

Jonathan stood dead still in the middle of the room, grinding his teeth, his hands bunched into fists. He looked as though Mina had just slapped him. Maybe she'd been too blunt. She needed him to stop spiraling, and it was the best lever she had.

Bitcoin was the magic word. Bitcoin had won Mina one of the world's richest men.

She'd never been popular at school, never been good with people. But she was good with computers. She understood code and, by the time she was a teenager, there was no system she couldn't hack.

It hadn't been hard to get the goods on Jonathan. Her family had pulled strings to land her the job at his start up. She was the only woman in her department, and her colleagues had underestimated what she could do. She'd bided her time until she had access to all their financial records. They were sloppy, overconfident and amateur. Not one was legitimate, and this suited her purpose.

By the time Mina had compiled the full dossier on Jonathan's cryptocurrency, she had enough to put everyone in his company away for the rest of their lives. That's when she made her play.

Jonathan was furious. He threatened her with everything from financial ruin to murder. She held her ground. They needed her alive or the files would fall into the wrong hands. She had them dead to rights, and if anything happened to her, they were all done. Unlike their woeful cybersecurity, her files were un-hackable.

She made her case. There was only one way to ensure her silence. To make sure she could never testify against him. And that was to marry her. Tie the knot and waive all prenups. He raged, he ranted, he refused. But he couldn't escape the inevitable.

Within a month she was one of the richest people in the world. And one of the least happily married.

Jonathan knocked back another scotch. "I'm going to go find Arthur."

"Are you sure that's wise?"

"Stop trying to manage me."

"You can't stand Arthur. I don't even know why you invited him."

"What else should I do, stay in this room with you?"

"Would that be such a bad thing? Such a terrible way to pass the time?"

"I'd rather pass it with your sister."

Mina closed her mouth and swallowed hard. Jonathan smiled, pleased at her reaction. Having scored that point, he stalked from the room.

Mina blinked rapidly. She could hold back the tears, but not the memories of Marya. The way her body had looked on the stretcher, under the sheet, crumpled, misshapen, one hand hanging over the side.

And Marya's hand made her think of Quincey's hands. The most beautiful part of a once beautiful man. The way he'd touched her, like no man ever had. Why hadn't she recognized his hands?

She checked her sleeve to see if the syringe was still there. It was, and Arthur's phone was still in her pocket. She'd taken it from him before they'd gone into dinner. Promised to pass it on to her uncle's men. But she hadn't passed it on.

She had a much better use for it.

5

De Sange was alone on the parapet when it happened. The subtle hum in his chest got weaker, as if powering down, and then it stopped.

Was he free? Had it really worked?

He'd changed in so many ways since the Fraternitas Aquae Sanctae had lured him to that hotel room. He hadn't seen the needle until it was too late, and after that he'd been unconscious. They'd flown him half way around the world and done unspeakable things to him.

To make sure he played along they'd put the explosive device in his chest. That wasn't the worst of it. He would very likely survive the explosion. His body could regenerate, recover from the internal damage, no matter how severe. What he wouldn't survive was the release of a substance that was harmless to any human—Aqua Benedicta, water blessed by a minister of the faith. What kind of a creature had he become, if that could kill him? What sort of an existence did he have to look forward to?

Imprisoned in this castle, like a fly trapped in amber. Moving forever through a period drama enacted for the amusement of the excessively rich and incredibly cruel. His eternal torment made into entertainment, for those who have so much they can only gain

149

pleasure by taking something away from others. And what better privation for them to witness, than to see his soul, his only chance at salvation, snatched away by a holy order. By men who claim to serve God.

Every second of every day De Sange had spent in this castle, he'd been searching for a means of escape. Every detail he observed, every action his captors took, all of it was examined and assessed for an opportunity to break out.

Nothing he'd seen brought hope. There were no cracks in their prison, no weak points in their security. Nothing to suggest he might ever walk out of this place. And if he did evade them, he still had the device in his chest. They could trigger it at any time. All they had to do was punch one code into a keyboard.

A part of De Sange understood why they kept him on a tight rein. There was a savage force growing in him. It was a bestial, lustful hunger that threatened to subsume every aspect of his existence. A need to feed and take and deprive everyone of everything. To drain the world of its juices and, when he was done, to drain himself.

This was what the super-rich had come to see. They recognized its raw magnificence in themselves. It was the drive that brought *them* such wealth. They were excited to see it coursing through a living organism with such intensity and focus. They yearned to incite just a little more in themselves. To take pleasure, by more than human means, in the things they had done to succeed.

De Sange had carried over a vestige of his former life. Scraps of memory and personality, tiny moments of continuity from his time as a human. They were the most precious things he possessed and he guarded them zealously. But his hunger threatened to turn on him, to consume those tiny scraps of humanity. He had to keep it at bay, had to feed and confine it within himself, a jailor to the worst parts of his new nature. That's why he understood his captors so well.

They feared the very thing he did. They had seen it in action and it terrified them as much as him, and they were trained to deal with his kind. They had sent him to that woman. They pretended it was an escape, but they may as well have driven him to that remote lake house and pushed him through its doors.

They'd filled the air with a mist of her blood, knowing what effect it would have on him. They must have drawn it when they sedated her, then sprayed it into the room before he entered. Every one of his senses was maddened. Every molecule in his body was animated by hunger, howling, undeniable hunger.

He'd taken the woman they'd left for him. He'd never felt such pleasure, nothing in his life had prepared him. Because it wasn't a human pleasure and that was terrifying. When he'd come to his senses and his hunger was abated, when the last of his humanity saw what he'd done, he'd wept for the state of the woman.

Wept more when he realized who she was.

They'd swept in and recaptured him. It was easy for them with the device in his chest. They needed him to feed so the change would take full effect. But they also needed to demonstrate how hopeless and ineffectual his plans for escape truly were.

He'd believed them. Until she had gotten in touch.

De Sange still couldn't bear to say, or even think, her name. She was part of his former life, back when he was human, and he couldn't bear the pain it brought him to recall. He was too ashamed of what he'd become to allow it.

She'd contacted him through a guard, one of the armed monks. De Sange didn't know what she had on the monk, but he was more afraid of her than De Sange or the Fraternitas. The monk had opened a line of communication between De Sange and his benefactor.

He'd smuggled a burner phone into the castle. When he wasn't being watched, he would show De Sange the phone screen, with a message on it. Always too far away and too briefly for a human to have read it. But the guard knew De Sange had the senses of a Schimbător and it would be easy for him.

In this way, she was able to outline her plan. Slowly, piece by piece, she mapped out how she would disable the device in his chest and lead him from the castle on the night when her party arrived.

How it had pained him for her to see him this way. Paraded in front of her rich friends, forced to parlay his suffering into a third rate performance for their pleasure. Had they enjoyed his reaction to the blood. It was so unexpected. He'd lost all control, shamed himself in front of them.

He'd expected her to renege after that, to go back on everything she'd promised. He'd slunk off to the parapet as she'd instructed him, stuck to the plan with little hope of it coming to fruition. He'd stood at the very edge, without moving a muscle for a very long time.

His senses were sharp enough to hear the cameras stop functioning. Then the device in his chest had disarmed itself. She'd come through for him. After everything she'd seen, she'd come through.

The tiny echo of his humanity questioned why she'd done this? The rising tide of Schimbător answered through its understanding of the world. The woman desired him. That's why she continued to help him. His Schimbător side knew and understood all kinds of lust, even those unavailable to humanity. What other explanation was there for the woman's assistance?

"Thought I'd find you out here," said a voice from the doorway.

<h1 style="text-align:center">6</h1>

De Sange turned. Lucy walked toward him. There was a loose and sensuous rhythm to her movements, well-practiced, calculated to gain his attention.

This might complicate things.

"You do like to brood don't you?"

De Sange didn't answer. He watched as Lucy sidled up next to him and rested her elbows on the crenelated wall that enclosed the parapet. She gazed out into the night, knowing he was watching, enjoying it.

"Don't get me wrong, it's a trait I find attractive in a man. But I find all the wrong things attractive in a man."

De Sange's manner was gracious but revealed nothing.

"I didn't expect you to join me here."

"Men never expect the things I do. That's why I do them."

"And what *do* these men expect you to do?"

"To hang off their arms like a debutante. To put myself on display, so they can prove how wealthy they are. I'm no different than the Rolex on their wrist or the Rolls Royce in their driveway."

"How does that make you feel?"

Lucy shrugged. "It's a living. Don't think I don't see what you're doing."

"What am I doing?"

"Diverting the conversation, by asking about things that don't interest you."

"Things that don't interest me?"

"Like how I feel and what men think of me. I graduated Harvard Law and I speak four languages, but when does that ever matter to a man?"

"What makes you think it wouldn't matter to me?"

Lucy bowed her head, blinked slowly, then looked up at him. "Because you're male and the male of any species is interested in one thing.

"And what might that be?"

"Proving their potency, exercising their power. Whether they fuck you in the bedroom or the boardroom, that's what they're really doing. That's the first rule of the game."

"Do you like to play games?"

"It's my principle source of delight. It's what I get out of this. Call it an intellectual pleasure. I set the rules, choose the prize, and if the man plays along he wins what he's after."

"And what do you think I'm after."

Lucy swallowed and moistened her lips. "I thought we'd never get to that."

She brought her middle finger up to her mouth and fastened her teeth on the Band-Aid. She peeled it away and bit down on the wound, encouraging the blood to flow.

When she had a tiny trickle, Lucy let it hover by De Sange's lips, nearly brushing them.

The scent of the blood reached his brain and overrode all other functions. A dark new instinct gripped him. Ancient, yet alien muscle memory kicked in.

De Sange felt his throat bulge. It was involuntary. As was the dislocation of his jaw and the appearance of his tongue.

It moved of its own accord, with a consciousness all its own. One that fought to subdue and control De Sange's mind.

Lucy caught her breath at the sight of the tongue. She put her hand to her chest, rising and falling with short, shallow breaths. Her cheeks reddened.

His tongue darted toward the blood dripping from her finger. Lucy stepped back, holding her finger just out of its reach. Moving it slowly side to side like the end of a snake charmer's pipe. His tongue swayed in time with the movement.

Holding her bloody right finger behind her, Lucy wagged her left index finger at the tongue. "Nuh, uh, uh. Let's see what we have here first."

She ran her fingers under the broad midsection of his tongue, shaped like a leech. Brushing lightly over the needle fine teeth in their oral cavities. "Prickly."

Lucy stroked the pharynx just above the oral cavities, then she leaned close to the tip of his tongue and put her own out. She licked first one fork, then the other.

"Do you like that? I bet you do."

Her lips parted and she took both forks of his tongue into her mouth.

That was her undoing.

De Sange's mind closed down. He was all hunger. His tongue forced its way into her mouth and down her throat.

Lucy put her hands to his chest and tried to push him away. His tongue continued down her throat, blocking her windpipe. She moved her hands to the red, serpentine base of his tongue, but it slipped through them and into her esophagus.

The tongue reached its full extended length and as it thrust further and further it pulled Lucy to him, until her lips were pressed up against his.

The pharynx on his tongue's underside attached itself to her stomach wall. The oral cavities sought out her hepatic arteries and buried their teeth into them. The tongue's muscles began to expand and contract, pumping the blood from Lucy's body into his.

Venom shot from the needle fine teeth into her stomach wall, flooding her body. First numbing, then paralyzing it.

The release of poison was like a mini orgasm. But it was nothing compared to the feeling of her blood pouring into his body. That was a physical elation no human body could possibly comprehend.

Lucy went limp. Her body collapsed in on itself.

De Sange's tongue detached itself, slithered out of Lucy and back into his mouth. Lucy's body fell at his feet.

The tiny part of him that was still human woke from its stupor and looked, out of eyes that were entirely inhuman, at the broken form before him. He was irredeemable.

His last trace of humanity wasn't imprisoning the Schimbător. It was imprisoned by it. And very soon the humanity, that he prized so dearly, would be consumed by the Schimbător as brutally as Lucy was consumed.

There was nothing he could do about it. He could flee the castle, but he could never outrun what he was becoming.

He heard footsteps approach the door to the parapet. His senses were not only sharper, they were more discerning. He recognized the way this individual walked. It was the one they called Arthur.

7

De Sange lifted the empty shell of Lucy's body and carried it to the shadows of the parapet.

Now that he had fed, and the device was no longer active, there were other abilities available to De Sange. The Archimandrite had told him, during the long ordeal of the change, that Schimbător was Romanian for *Changeable*. It was at once a noun, a collective noun, and an adjective. Unique in the Romanian language for a very good reason, there was nothing else like the Schimbător.

They were named for their species' special ability—they could shift their shape. The talent manifested differently in ever Schimbător, but in De Sange's case it meant he could take on the physical likeness of any person on whom he'd just fed.

Until now, the device had inhibited that. It monitored his vital signs and would be triggered by any deviation, such as changing shape. But the device wasn't working and he was free to use every weapon in his arsenal.

De Sange's flesh began to ripple and liquify, reforming itself. His skeletal form shrunk. The cells of his epidermis rearranged themselves into a perfect replica of Lucy's skin. The follicles of his scalp released more hair, growing it longer and changing its color.

De Sange shed his clothes like a snake sloughing off skin. He wriggled out of them and removed Lucy's dress, slipping it on as quickly as he could.

Arthur strode out, shoulders back, chest puffed. Certain of his physical dominance, never doubting the protection his social status brought.

"What's going on out here?"

He thrust out his chin and scanned the parapet, eyes adjusting to the gloom. He hadn't seen De Sange or Lucy.

"Don't think I don't see you."

Arthur marched up to him. De Sange stepped out of the shadows, adjusting his vocal chords to replicate Lucy's voice.

"Arthur, it's you."

"What the devil are you playing at?"

"What do you mean?"

Arthur jabbed a finger. "Your hair's a mess and your dress is all awry. I know what you've been up to. You think Jonathan's going to dump Mina and take you on? Don't count on it."

De Sange tossed his hair, adjusting every strand so they fell perfectly back into place. At the same time he shifted his skin so the garments he was wearing looked perfectly tailored to his feminine form.

"It's not like that. Look again. See, I'm perfectly composed."

"How the devil did you do that?"

"Do what?"

"Change like that. I just saw you."

"Don't be silly. I didn't do a thing. It's dark out here and you were mistaken."

De Sange moved close to Arthur, placed an expensively manicured hand on his chest.

"Oh Arthur, I was so scared. I'm so pleased to see you."

"I'll just bet you are."

Arthur's top lip curled, but anything he might have said was cut short by the loud "*Oof*" that escaped his lips as if he'd been struck in the stomach.

De Sange had pushed first one finger then another into Arthur's abdominal wall, just below his sternum. Arthur put his hands on De Sange's shoulders, a desperate attempt to repel him.

De Sange ignored the gesture and reached inside Arthur, sliding his hand between the man's liver and his stomach. Finally, when he was nearly up to his dainty shoulder, De Sange took hold of Arthur's vertebrae.

One squeeze was all it took. The vertebrae crumbled like chalk. Arthur's spine collapsed and his upper half listed backward, widening the tear in his midriff and exposing the underside of his ribcage.

De Sange reached up and grasped Arthur's frantically beating heart. He tugged hard and tore it away from its aorta and pulmonary arteries.

Arthur's body plummeted back against the stone floor. De Sange held the heart above his open mouth and squeezed. It's thick, red fluid ran down his throat.

It didn't bring the same elation as Lucy's blood. He was too glutted. But now he had Arthur's DNA.

More footsteps approached. It was Jonathan and, a little way off, Mina. He had to get off this parapet.

Jonathan appeared in the doorway. His eyes wide with shock and incomprehension. He saw the blood that covered De Sange's arm and the human organ he still held.

"Lucy, what. . .what in God's name have you done?"

De Sange smiled, coy and coquettish. "I haven't done anything in *God's* name."

8

Mina was busy activating the viral software she'd secreted in the castle's mainframes. It was criminal how easy she found it and she'd done it from a cellphone. She would have to overhaul the whole system when this was done. She was appalled by how amateur their defenses were.

She'd just finished locking all the security doors when she heard Jonathan's footsteps on the stairs. She had to be quick. She didn't want to miss this. She checked to make sure she still had the syringe, then she went to join him.

Jonathan was on the landing that led to the east parapet. He was backing away from the outside door. Lucy was standing in the doorway, covered in blood.

No, it wasn't Lucy. It was. . .she cut the thought short. She couldn't identify him by that name. He was De Sange now, that's how she must think of him.

Jonathan's head spun round as she approached. "Mina, get out of here, fetch the guards. Why the hell aren't they here already?"

"Because I blocked their access to this part of the castle."

"You did what?"

"I hacked the system and locked all the security doors."

Jonathan was incredulous. "Why? What on earth would you do that for?"

Mina held up Arthur's cellphone. "There's something I want to play you. I didn't want any interruptions."

Jonathan's head snapped back and forth between De Sange in the doorway and Mina behind him. Mina pulled up the edited audio file she'd downloaded and pressed play.

". . . and this won't be traced back to me?"

"My men are professionals. They don't leave a trace."

"It'll look like an accident?"

"No one will ever guess and she won't know what hit her."

Mina clicked off the file. Jonathan puckered his lips and lifted his nose haughtily.

"What did you expect, after the position you put me in?"

"A little gratitude for how rich I was about to make you."

Jonathan scowled. "I have my own money."

"And you thought to keep my hands off it, being your sole beneficiary."

"I had to find some way to cut you out of the will."

"No, you didn't, and that was your biggest mistake."

"So, I underestimated you, is that what this is about?"

Mina looked to De Sange. "You know what to do."

De Sange stalked across the landing toward Jonathan. His form altered with every step he took. He grew in height and his shoulders broadened as he took on Arthur's physique. The dress he was wearing tore down the front and burst all the stitching in its seams.

Jonathan bolted for the staircase, pushing Mina out of his way.

De Sange intercepted him, moving faster than any human could. He placed a thick, meaty hand on the top of Jonathan's skull and began to squeeze. Jonathan's hands shot to De Sange's wrist, trying to push the hand from his head, his legs strained trying to pull away. De Sange's grip tightened, and Jonathan's arms went limp, his legs giving way under him.

There was an audible crack as Jonathan's skull broke open. His left eyeball popped out of its socket. Ruptured brain tissue chased the eyeball down his cheek.

De Sange released his grip and Jonathan's lifeless body dropped to the landing. He turned to Mina, a few scraps of Lucy's dress still clung to his near naked body.

"What now?"

Mina looked at Jonathan's broken form, his disheveled costume soaking up the blood. She glanced toward the door to the parapet. She didn't want to think about the corpses out there.

Mina realized she was glad De Sange had taken on Arthur's likeness. It made everything she was about to do that much easier.

She forced a smile. "Now, we both get what we *really* want."

9

Di Segni's phone and laptop were back online. And about time. The tech team would know his displeasure.

Communications had been down for over twenty minutes. He'd been unable to access security footage or contact any of the team. If there'd been another incident, he would feed some of the brothers to the Schimbător.

His phone rang. It was Moretti.

"Reverend Father, are you by your laptop?"

"I am, for all the good it did me. Did you know I've been offline for-"

Moretti cut in. "Our digital security is under attack from a hostile outside force. I've only just got our comms back online. I'm going to send some security footage to your laptop. You have to see this."

Di Segni brought the footage up. He could clearly see the dismembered corpses of two guests lying sprawled on the east parapet. His office listed, like the cabin of a ship. Bile burned the back of his throat. Two of his guests were dead. What in the name of our Heavenly Father?

"How did this happen?"

"It's not just our digital security."

"What do you mean?"

"I'm sorry, Reverend Father, someone has also overridden the device in the Schimbător's chest. We have no control over it."

"How many men have you dispatched?"

"None, Reverend Father."

A vein throbbed in Di Segni's temple. "I beg your pardon?"

"All the security doors have been locked. None of our men can get into the castle. They're trying to break down the doors as we speak."

"And this was done by the same outside force?"

"Yes."

"Are you sure it was an outside force?"

"What do you mean, Reverend Father?"

"Never mind. Alert Seneschal De Molay and have him helicopter in reinforcements. We need heavy arms and Aqua Benedicta. Do you understand?"

"Yes, Reverend Father."

Di Segni tried the door of his office. It was unlocked and, as there were no security doors in the servants' passage, he could still get to the front hall and the castle's main door.

There were very few people with the cyber skills necessary to hack into a system as well guarded as theirs. It was too much of a coincidence that one of them was in the building right now.

What Di Segni couldn't understand was why she'd done it? He'd shown her the error of her ways and brought her to heel. Put an end to her youthful rebellion and her dalliance with that half breed. It was bad enough that mongrel had sullied the Di Segni bloodline in the first place, but for her to take up with it. That was unconscionable.

His methods might have been tough. He'd be the first to admit they involved sacrifice, but the end had justified his means, or so he'd believed. He was a man of power and influence. He couldn't have family members defying him. Their actions affected his standing in the Church.

As he'd told Mina, we all fight the things we're born to become, but in the end we submit. She had submitted, accepted his authority. She married a billionaire, a match he'd approved, and then she'd brought the man and his fortune to assist the Fraternitas. Unless. . .no, that didn't bear thinking about.

Or did it?

Di Segni set his shoulders. He straightened the front of his robe and retied the belt around his waist. He was full of God's purpose. He went to his wall safe and punched in the combination.

There was a pressurized cannister of Aqua Benedicta inside. He had been saving it for just such an occasion. He attached the nozzle and closed the safe. Then he left his office.

He was going to slay the bloodsucking creature. And he was going to make his conniving niece pay for what she had done.

And she was going to tell him why she'd done it, God help her.

10

Mina descended the staircase with De Sange. The vestibule that led to the main door was in sight.

But her uncle wasn't.

He should be here by now. She'd left the way clear. There was a side door to the left of the vestibule. That's where she expected him to appear.

They reached the bottom of the stairs. He still wasn't there. She'd have to stall for time.

"Hold on!"

De Sange turned to her and cocked his head quizzically.

"There, uh, might be guards waiting for us—an ambush."

He raised his nose, sniffed, and then listened. Damn, Mina had forgotten about his Schimbător senses.

"One set of footsteps approaches. And your heartrate has increased."

He sniffed again.

"The sweat on your forehead and upper lip is giving off a particular pheromone. What aren't you telling me?"

"Nothing, we just need to be cautious. There's too much at stake."

Then Mina heard the footsteps racing toward them. Her uncle appeared from the side door.

De Sange smiled. "But of course. Your revenge is not yet over."

Mina hated to be so transparent. But, in his overconfidence, De Sange had taken his eyes off Di Segni. He didn't see Di Segni's right hand come out from behind his back, or the cannister he was holding until it was too late.

"No!" Mina leaped between them, and the stream of Aqua Benedicta hit her in the face. It would have been comical, like a scene from the *Three Stooges*, if the few drops of holy water that splashed off her hadn't caused De Sange to scream and cower as they burned his flesh.

"Damn you!" Di Segni cried, most of the cannister now spent.

De Sange backed away into the shadows, hissing in pain. Mina blinked and wiped her face with the back of her hand.

Di Segni fumed. "What do you think you're playing at?"

"I'm not playing, I would have thought that was obvious by now."

"Nothing about your actions is obvious. Do you realize what that monster could do if it got loose, if it had nothing to control it?"

"What about the other monsters, right here in this castle."

"There are only men of God here. Men of God who've devoted their lives to fighting those creatures."

Mina shook her head. "You've spent so long fighting them, you've become worse."

"We've done what we had to in order to survive, to continue our legacy. If we have to create a monster to do that, then that's what we'll do. I believe it was the French philosopher Diderot who said: *What is a monster? A being whose survival is incompatible with the existing order.*"

Mina pointed to De Sange, crouched in the shadows, careful to keep herself between him and Di Segni.

"He wasn't always a monster. He was the man I loved. The only man I've ever loved."

Di Segni's eyes widened with fury. "He was a half caste, his dirty, foreign genes corrupting our family, the purity of our bloodline. His mother. . ."

"Your sister."

Di Segni pursed his lips and took a breath. "His mother slept with a man from another race. That's why she was exiled and cut off. You chose to ignore that. Chose to ignore he was your cousin."

"I loved him."

"You were committing incest and miscegenation. You're nearly as bad as your sister, the child murdering whore."

"She worked in planned parenthood."

"She was beyond salvation, but you weren't. It's like I told you, we all fight the things we were born to become, but in the end we submit. You needed to be shown the error of your ways, to be brought back into the fold. To recognize my authority in all things!"

Mina threw up her hands. "Is that what you were doing? Showing me the error of my ways by kidnapping the man I loved and turning him into a Schimbător?"

Di Segni drew himself up. "It worked. You gave up your foolish ways, did what I told you and married a man worthy of our family."

"I married a coward, a bully and a criminal."

"You make it sound like polygamy."

"No, they were all the same man. But one insult alone doesn't do him justice."

Di Segni and Mina glowered at one another. Locked in a death stare stand-off. Neither noticed De Sange until it was too late.

He leaped from the shadows and hit Mina between the shoulder blades. The blow nearly lifted her off her feet. She went sprawling into her uncle.

Her left shoulder struck the cannister and knocked it from Di Segni's hand. She hit the floor, cracked her chin on the flagstones.

Her teeth snapped together and she nearly bit through her tongue.

De Sange fell on Di Segni, knocking him onto his back.

Mina propped herself up on her elbow, rubbing at her chin. There would be a dark bruise by morning.

She watched as De Sange held Di Segni down by his throat. He pushed the fingers of his left hand into Di Segni's abdomen, tearing and parting the muscles of his stomach wall.

Di Segni shrieked. De Sange tightened his grip about the Archimandrite's throat and the scream choked off.

De Sange pulled his hand back out. A wet loop of Di Segni's lower colon gripped in his fist.

"I believe Diderot also said: *Men will never be free until the last king is strangled with entrails of the last priest*! What say we go find us a king?"

Mina clambered unsteadily to her feet.

"Stop! You're killing him."

De Sange looked up from his labors. "I believe that was the general idea."

"It's not my idea. I need him alive."

"I don't like your idea. I prefer mine."

"I'm telling you to stop!"

De Sange let go of Di Segni's innards and rose to his feet, his face twisted with venomous anger. "You're telling me to stop? Who are *you* to tell *me* what to do?!"

Mina pulled the phone from her dress pocket. The screen was cracked in the bottom corner, but it still worked. She pulled up the app she'd created specially and punched in a code.

There was a muffled *beep* from De Sange's chest. He put a hand to it. The rage and arrogance drained from his face as fear replaced them.

Mina held up the phone. "I'm the person with the code to your device."

"But you disarmed it."

"No, I disabled it, there's a difference. Because now *I* get to use it."

De Sange held out his hands to her, imploring. But also measuring the distance between them.

"Wait, don't. Why are you doing this?"

"Because of Marya."

"It wasn't my fault."

De Sange pointed to Di Segni, still writhing on the floor.

"It was him. He tricked me, activated the hunger. I couldn't help myself. He forced me to do it. He needed me to feed so I would change into this."

"She was my sister. I loved her and I saw what *you* did to her."

"What *he* did to her, not me. I didn't know it was her until it was too late."

"It's always been too late."

De Sange was desperate. His skin began to ripple. He was changing shape, even though it might activate the device. He shrank several inches, his frame becoming slighter, his skin darker. He held out his hands to her. The beautiful hands of. . .

Quincey, the human De Sange had once been.

For a moment, Mina couldn't breathe. The sight of her former lover hit her on a molecular level, twisted the particles of her body into frantic, yearning knots. She had not anticipated the depth of her feelings.

It almost gave him enough time. He crouched, ready to spring.

Mina held her finger over the screen. "I wouldn't!"

"But you promised. You said we'd both get what we really want."

"Quincey, this *is* what you really want."

Mina touched the screen and activated the device.

There was a muffled *WHOOMP!* The inside of De Sange's chest was lit from within by a burst of orange flame.

His mouth fell open in silent panic. The phial in his chest cracked and his flesh and bone began to melt, slipping to the floor in fat, sizzling gobbets.

Mina pulled the syringe from her sleeve and raced to De Sange. She sank the needle into his carotid artery and pulled back the plunger, drawing his blood into the barrel while he still had any left.

Most of his midriff had melted away as he reached up and placed those gorgeous hands on her shoulders. She looked into his eyes and, like a prospector who lifts up their pan from the stream and finds a nugget, she saw the last traces of Quincey staring back at her. Saw his love and gratitude, still burning, until their last spark was extinguished by the death of the monster he'd become.

Mina heard bolts and levers turning in a lock. Hinges creaked and the huge double doors at the front of the castle swung open.

A squadron of armed monks swarmed through the vestibule and into the main hall. The rustle of body armor, clank of weapons and slap of boots on flagstones echoed round the hall.

They surrounded Mina, training their weapons on her. A tall, broad shouldered man in an abbot's garb and body armor strode in. They parted so he could address Mina.

"Make no sudden or unexpected moves or my men will shoot you where you stand."

II

Mina kept her arms at her side, the syringe in her hand, De Sange's remains lay steaming at her feet.

Mina looked the commander in the eye. "Seneschal De Molay, I presume."

"And you are?"

"Mina Feldman, your principle shareholder."

"I thought Jonathan Feldman was our principle shareholder."

"I'm afraid my husband is no longer with us and, as his sole beneficiary, I hold all his shares. A search of the premises will verify that. Tell your men to lower their weapons."

"I will do no such thing. And I can't guarantee you'll leave this place alive."

"And why wouldn't I leave alive?"

"There's a little matter of your complicity in the deaths of your husband and his guests."

"Isn't that a matter for the courts?"

"Nothing that happens in this castle is a matter for the courts. There are too many powerful people who would be compromised."

Mina took a deep breath and folded her arms, wary of the armed monks around her.

"I thought you might take that approach, which is why I instructed my lawyers to contact you with the plans for my estate on the occasion of my sudden and unexpected death. You should have received it by now."

De Molay scowled. "Why would I be interested in your financial arrangements?"

"Because, as my lawyers will confirm, all my holdings, including the majority of the shares in this enterprise, will go to the Immortalis Foundation."

De Molay's scowl deepened. "The Immortalis Foundation is a front for. . ."

"The High Convocation, the most powerful Schimbător organization in the world. It would be more than embarrassing, in fact I would go so far as to say disastrous, for the Fraternitas Aquae Sanctae, not to mention the Vatican, to be in debt to an outfit like that."

De Molay turned on his heel, stalked into the vestibule and made a call on his cell.

It took him less than a minute to return. "It seems you *do* have us at a disadvantage."

"Tell your men to lower their weapons."

De Molay nodded and the monks lowered their semi-automatics. Di Segni, who'd been unconscious until now, groaned in pain.

One of the monks pointed to him. "Sir, the Archimandrite."

De Molay snapped his fingers. "Get a medic in here, on the double."

Mina stepped up to his body. "Cancel that, we'll need a surgeon, the same one you used on De Sange."

De Molay bristled. "You don't give the orders here."

"Except, we've just established that I do. I'm the principle shareholder in this enterprise."

"What enterprise? We don't have any enterprise without our principle asset, namely the Schimbător, which *you* just killed."

"And you don't think I have a contingency?"

Mina bent and stabbed the needle of the syringe into Di Segni's carotid artery, injecting De Sange's blood into him.

De Molay moved closer. "Is that the Schimbător's blood?"

"Yes."

He sneered. "It won't work. It only bonds with the DNA of a blood relative and you've just killed the last of those."

Mina stood and dropped the syringe. "That's right, he didn't tell you. It's a guilty family secret. Quincey was his cousin, once removed. So, as soon as your surgeon plants a device in him, we'll have another valuable asset, and the revenue will continue uninterrupted."

"Do you think I'll let you do this to the Archimandrite?"

"He's no Archimandrite. He's not even human now. And, as the former Seneschal, that would make you Archimandrite, unless I'm wrong about succession within your order."

De Molay looked at Mina with a growing mixture of wariness and admiration. "Your assumption is accurate."

He turned to one of his men. "Have this thing flown to our field base and made ready for surgery."

The monk nodded. "Yes, sir."

De Molay bristled.

The monk realized his mistake. "Forgive me. Yes, Reverend Father."

As the monks ran for a stretcher, Mina knelt next to Di Segni's body. The wound in his abdomen was already beginning to heal, the lower colon crawling back into his midriff. Very soon he would take on the likeness of his distant ancestor, just as Quincey had.

Mina put her lips up to his ear and whispered. "And now you submit to my authority, uncle. How fitting, don't you think, that your need for purity, your love of family tradition, has led you to uphold the darkest of our family's traditions. What was it you told me? '*We all fight the thing we were born to become.*' Well, you've become the thing you were born to fight."

*Multiple award-winning author, **Jasper Bark** is infectious—and there's no known cure. If you're reading this you're already contaminated. The symptoms will manifest any time soon. There's nothing you can do about it. There's no itching or unfortunate rashes, but you'll become obsessed with his mind-bending books. From the acclaimed Draw You In trilogy and the ground breaking Bark Bites Horror series, to graphic novels like* Bloodfellas *and* Beyond Lovecraft.

Then you'll want to tell everyone else about his visionary horror fiction. About its originality, its wild imagination and how it takes you to the edge of your sanity. We're afraid there's no way to avoid this. These words contain a power you're hopeless to resist. You're already in their thrall, you know you are. You're itching to read all of Jasper's bloodstained books. Don't fight this urge, embrace it. You've been bitten by the Bark bug and you love it!

WINDCHIMES

JAY BECHTOL

MORE STUPID BOATS this morning. Sixty-three now with the two that drifted in last night. They think I don't notice but I can add, yes indeedy. I can add those numbers right up.

The boats came three years ago, maybe five. Very, very hard to keep track of when anymore. Doesn't matter. Boats float in and I count them and stand guard with my pile of rocks. I wonder if they are real or not. Real. Maybe I'm the only one that sees them. But there's no one to ask. No one no one no one. Just me.

So I keep my rocks, and once a day, to show them I know what they're up to, I chunk one of the rocks at a boat. The closest one today looks like one of those lifeboats from the old movies.

Clunk goes my rock, right off the wooden side. Clunk then plink. That sound means those boats are real, yes indeedy. If it only went plink, then that would mean there's no boat, just a rock falling into the water. Plinkity plink.

Sometimes the wind will blow, and the boats will all push against each other. The sides of them clack together and sound like something I remember. Something at my mom's house when I was a kid. When the ocean was a lot farther away. When my mom and other people still walked around.

I think it was a windchime by the front door. It had tubes of bamboo that clacked together. Dull sounds. That's what the boats sound like when they bump into each other. Clack clack. The worst music ever.

I have to keep watch during the day with my pile of rocks.

Now there's seventy-one boats. I'm tired. My rockpile is getting smaller and this is no job for one man. Person. Human. Somedays I'm sad that all those people left. Somedays I'm angry.

I'm about to throw a rock toward the nearest boat, when I see one of the creatures stumbling down the shore toward me. It's still far away, but I can see it coming. It waves its arms, but I don't fall for that. No indeedy. I pick two rocks from my pile, smooth and round. They'll go straight and far. I'm very good with rocks now.

I wait. Like my mom taught me. On the water the boats clack together.

The thing is close enough now, so I give my first rock a toss. High in the air, like a rainbow, just without all the colors. The creature sees it and dodges. But that's all part of the plan. Because while it's watching that first rock, all pretty in the air, I'm lining up the second rock.

Smack-a-whack, it slams right into the monster's chest. It screams out loud and falls down.

Weird. The rock didn't go sploosh and splash straight through.

"Jesus Christ," the creature screams, "what the hell is wrong with you?"

I pick up another rock and the thing raises its hands.

"Wait! Stop!" It hollers. "I'm a friend."

I rub my thumb on the edge of the rock. All the people are gone, yes indeedy, but maybe not. "Are you a person?" I holler back at him.

"Of course," he calls. "Jesus, what do you think?"

I decide that it's time to close my mouth. Quiet quiet quiet.

He keeps his hands up and gets on his feet and walks toward me. Slow, like a butterfly with one wing. When he gets close to my rock pile, I can see he is telling the truth. He's a person with skin and hair. Long, like a girl's. He has a backpack.

"You're not going to throw another rock at me, are you?"

I shake my head but keep the rock in my hand. Just in case.

"My name is Charles," he says. It sounds strange to hear another human voice. "What is yours?"

Quiet, I remind myself.

"Is there anyone else? Here with you? Do you know what happened? Where everyone went?"

I shake my head again. My mom used to say she could hear the pebbles rattling around in there when I did that. I hope Charles doesn't hear them, too.

He glances out toward the water. "Holy shit," he says. "Was this a resort, some sort of marina? Where'd all those boats come from? There's gotta be a hundred out there."

"Seventy-one," I tell him.

"Is there food on them? Weapons, first aid kits? Anything? Holy crap, they could be like a gold mine. No people on any of them?"

Stay quiet, I tell my mouth. Quiet. It ignores me. "No people," I answer.

He looks at me, my pile of rocks, the boats, and then back at me. Like he's trying to put a puzzle together but one piece fell on the floor and he can't find it.

"Where'd they come from?"

I shrug.

"Jesus, man, let's take a look."

He drops his backpack and pulls off his shirt. There's a huge red mark in the middle of his chest and he catches me staring at it. Right at it.

"You're a pretty good shot with those rocks. Is that what you hunt with?"

But he doesn't want an answer, he's too busy stripping his pants off. Not a good idea. I squeeze the rock in my hand, like it can tell me what to do. Like my mom used to. Used to. "Don't go out there," I say.

"What?"

"You shouldn't go out there. To the boats. Bad. Clack clack," I tell him.

He smiles at me then. I'd forgotten how nice it is when another human being smiles at you. "You can wait here," he says, "but I'm going to check one of them out."

"Don't," I tell him, but he doesn't hear me because he's already running into the water.

He swims toward one of the bigger boats. It has a ladder off the back, like maybe a rich person used to have it. He puts his hand on the ladder and pulls himself up. "See," he yells back at me. "Nothing to it." He looks into the boat and then back at me. "Whooee, it stinks out here," he calls across the ocean. "Like a foot of standing water inside this. . ."

WINDCHIMES

The thing that lives on the boats rises up then, splashity splash. Like it had been waiting there just for him. The thing looks like a person, but it's made of water. Seaweed and other stuff floats in its body. I think I can see eyes bobbing around where the head should be. One of the eyes looks down at Charles. The other eye looks past the other boats, over the water, to me and my pile of rocks. And it gurgles with hungry excitement.

Charles doesn't even have time to scream. Another creature pops up and the two things suck him right up. Slurpity slurp, like he wasn't a person at all. Like he was some kind of food or something for these monsters.

Then the things slide over the side of the boat. I can see Charles' arms in one of the things, his legs in the other one. His long hair swishes inside both of them. They ripple through the water, coming to the shore. I pick up a handful of rocks. I don't bother to pick out the good ones. No time for that now.

When the ripples get to the edge of the water, they stand up, like they want to be people. But they are not. No indeedy. Charles' face floats in the middle part of one of the creatures. He isn't smiling anymore. The thing with my friend inside takes a couple of steps out of the water onto the shore. Bad idea, they aren't very strong once they are on dry land. I spin my first rock, a perfect shot, right to the head of the thing. At least what I think is the head. It splurshes into a jillion little drops and splashes back into the ocean. The other one keeps a foot in the water, stronger that way, and it takes five good shots with the rocks to really make that one turn around.

I watch the things ripple back toward the boat with the ladder, slide up and over, and plop into whatever stinky water is on the inside of all those boats. I keep the extra rocks in my hand until the sun goes down.

⚷

I'm so tired. There are one hundred and nine boats now. Every day the creatures get a little braver. Sometimes five or six of them come at once. One of them looks like the person that smiled at me. I throw the rocks so hard and fast.

I remember that when the boats bump together, they sound like the windchimes outside my mom's door. Clack clack. And I wonder when everyone will come back and I can go home.

JAY BECHTOL

Jay Bechtol *likes to write, so he does. Recent short stories may be read at Penumbric, Crystal Lake, and Sirens Call. His debut novel,* The Great American Coward, *is available from Golden Storyline Books. He can be found on-line at www.JayBechtol.com or on Twitter @BechtolJay. He can be found in person in Homer, Alaska.*

THE EMPEROR OF ROAD KILL

KYLE TOUCHER

THE **NIGHT GRASS** feels familiar, wet under her feet, every drop of dew the sweat the sky leaves behind. Each blade folds and succumbs like an inferior army overrun by marauders. Her breath boils pressurized and acrid, spiked with hormones so ancient their name escapes the written word.

Run, Run. The end is here somewhere.

A sound, familiar in her day-life, reaches her ears. The wide hiss of a huge river. Her neck straightens, leaning right toward the sound. Nose raised and mouth open, she tastes the night air. The smell of complacency and plenty, the fat, greasy aroma of hubris. Want canceled from the daily struggle. She cannot articulate it in this state, but Luby knows those feelings, has lived them for decades.

But tonight those decades hang weary on her frame, like the strands of endlessly pulled taffy in those spooky machines at the carnival, the ones decorated with smiling maniacal jesters laboring forever, molding it into a miles-long tendon of her aches and trials; insignificant victories over small prey in the open spaces outside of town, failures in the filthy ponds shat from factories, and bloody, howling successes in the shadows behind truck stops. She knows them all, speaks the language.

Luby sprints toward the river. It flows loud and long, wide and busy. There is a cadence to it, artificial but a cadence nonetheless, the machinations of men in their harried ways, bustling and urgent with trivialities and terrors.

Run. Run. Toward the sound. The end is there, at the river.

She leaps, a mighty specimen of glory and power, guile and ferocity. And when Luby's feet hit the gravel, a tremendous shockwave rolls through her hide.

Luby recognizes Interstate 10, but cannot speak its name. Trucks the size of whales overtake schools of speeding cars. The road roars immense, a whitewater rapids of stimuli. Luby remains hidden in the tall brush, near the empty beer cans that smell of headaches and bad dreams, a reeking fast food bag crawling with thousands of ants, and a discarded maxi pad that for a moment, fuels her need for the squeal of horrified prey.

She nestles down to her belly, and for close to an hour she watches the road. There are breaks in the current, ebbs and flows. Before long she recognizes patterns, a sense of order in the chaos. Though thoughts tumble through Luby's mind in an odd combination of remembered words and ineffable instinct, she knows that now, in the late hours as the moon begins to set, the time to make her move has arrived.

It approaches from the left, a gargantuan, roaring Freightliner. Glaring lights and road noise, the rumble of its diesel heart and the glimmer of its chrome pipes beneath the sodium-vapor lamps. It rolls alone in the middle lane, its flatbed stacked with two giant shipping containers.

Luby rears back on her sprinter's legs, and before she can think of hunger, a nose buried in entrails, or the daughter she leaves behind, Luby Barlleaux bounds onto Interstate 10.

Run. Run. The end is here, at the river.

She cannot count steps or strides, and it is irrelevant. The timing, the *rhythm* is all that matters. Luby crosses into the middle lane, the snarling Freightliner only yards away. The thrill, the adrenaline, far beyond that of the hunt, lights her blood with fire not seen since prehistory. To live in this state of ferocity, to stalk the world as an apex predator with the knowledge of men and the cunning of the oldest memories, the world has become a maelstrom of—

The Freightliner smashes Luby's hind quarters. The sound is like no other, a hideous bone-surrender crack blended with the terrible collapse of muscle and tearing skin.

The immense wolf running at top speed upends and spins, limbs splayed, magnificent maw hinged open, tongue loose and flopping like a discarded pink ribbon. Luby Barlleaux slams into the concrete center divider with unimaginable force. The nexus of skull and spine suffer the brunt of impact.

The driver in the wolf-spattered Freightliner, no stranger to animals braving the road, rolls hard and fast, staying on schedule. In its wake, chaos erupts on this sliver of west Texas highway. The pod of follow-up traffic launches into a fractal pattern of locked-up brakes and fishtailing. The drivers gawk, stunned at not only the trucker's indifference, but the brutality of this colossal canine's unfortunate end.

Only Luby knows this is suicide.

Luby, now with a spine crushed in three places, skull opened and leaking like a slashed waterskin, watches in an odd underwater silence as wheels occupy her field of view. Scarlet fills her one remaining eye, turning the nightworld red.

The scent of the final hunt is her own spilled blood.

The end is here, at the river.

There is memory and awareness.

Glee on the schoolyard swings. The thrill of independence behind the wheel of her father's 1967 Cougar for the very first time. A high school heartbreak, bereavement a ballad written for her alone. The sight of the first moon rise witnessed through a new, unobfuscated lens. Heartless cruelty in a dim alley, the taste of flesh seasoned by fear. The river.

Open your eyes, a voice murmurs.

Male. A confident baritone rumble supplanting the grating, white noise rush of the interstate and shrieking tires.

Breathe for me.

A sensation of speed overwhelms Luby, a nauseous whirlwind of corkscrew motion as if gaffed by a whaling hook and pulled through a long, twisting pipe. She emerges frigid and trembling, her body a swarm of unimaginable aches and brutal bone-deep pain. Her toes curl like young ferns. A feeling of being *here* instead of *there* sizzles beneath every follicle.

"Open your eyes and breathe, I said."

Luby gasps, choking on a fist of winter. Her lungs fill, and what little blood remains greedily hordes the gift of fresh air and restarts her heart. She feels fingers on her neck—her human neck—void of warmth and subtlety, a forgery sent to beguile the foolish.

Luby's eyes flutter open. The light is sour and ugly in this cinder block alcove crammed with pipes and road tools. Shovels, spades, pickaxes, and wheelbarrows. Caution lights and hazard markers. Though the cement floor is like frozen sandpaper on her nude body, she raises a hand to swat that counterfeit grip away, but there is no strength. It falls back to the floor with a fleshy thud.

"See me, Luby Barlleaux."

He squats on his haunches like a forty-niner panning for gold, but there comparisons to humanity end. His legs are almost laughably short, a dwarf's dimensions on a frame suited for heroic deeds and feats of daring. Three toes claw the concrete, tipped in long, jaundiced nails the size of kitchen shears. His bulbous knees boast coarse tufts that appear silver in this hopeless basement light. At the nexus where his deformed legs meet his mighty torso, the work of a master silversmith forms a wicked codpiece. It features scenes of Hell in sharp, unrelenting relief, yet regal in its brutality: skewered men in poses of ultimate agony, women lanced mouth to rectum, entire populations chained and dangling over pits of unimaginable cruelty.

"My eyes, Luby. Look into my eyes."

Luby cranes her neck, and the vertebrae howl. Reset into their human positions, this comes as a grim surprise for a suicidal werewolf. She mewls like a child scared of the dark, and for now that is precisely her role—a babe in an unfamiliar landscape, torn from the glory of a hunter's death to the pitiful writhings of a meat-girl in a garden shed. And now, jolted from a nightmare spiked with adrenaline, skidding tires, and shattered bones, Luby meets the gaze of her resurrector.

The Emperor of Road Kill. His eyes shine in this neglected murk, irises bloody gold rings, the pupils black as every demon's promise. No nose to speak of, a whistling vacant hole resides in the acre between eyes and mouth. His lips open like a Venus fly trap, lined with soft bristles and hard, jagged barbs. Flesh and spirit have met equally miserable ends there.

"Daughter of the Wolf. Rise."

"The truck . . .the road . . ." Luby's voice is threadbare and wanting, a syrup of confusion and disappointment.

"A shameful end," The Emperor says. He drapes his wrists over his knees and opens his legs. More damned languish in his hideous silver armor. "Shame earns suffering. A circuit of guilt and regret, beyond the misery of unrequited love. Is that not a superior torture, to deny exit from a maze one cannot endure? The torn flesh of those foolish enough to brave a night when your cyclops moon shines are but luxuries compared to my Imperial Decree. Rise. I will repeat myself not another time."

Luby pushes upward through a series of groans, her pose now that of a Renaissance painter's muse. Bruises and acres of road rash. Swollen lips and missing hair. If this is the afterlife it is cold and unwelcoming, but preferable, she hopes, to the decades of duality and the undeniable fact her daughter knows that she has a monster for a mother.

"Your body has been unceremoniously peeled from the road by a work crew," The Emperor says. He takes Luby's hands and stands. Luby yelps as her bones straighten. "Brought here until their Animal Control tragedy retrieves you. Alas, they will find this alcove barren. When your eye filled red and the last breath wheezed from your muzzle, I heard you."

"Oh God. Why?" Luby's face runs like molasses. Her features collapse in grief.

"Contrition. The shame of purpose. It belies the master you were summoned to be. Luby Barlleaux, your lyncanthropy is a gift bestowed by your betters."

"Twyla. I ruined her."

"Twyla, even your daughter's name shows your commitment to your enhanced life, the frontier where day surrenders to night. The blood shed at her birth brought wolves, and to them you owe allegiance. What drove you to such desperate measures, to forget the hand that feeds?"

Luby's mind tumbles back to that wondrous yet terrifying night at Garland Memorial. Despite the epidural, pain churned insurmountable, a bulldozer destruction derby—pelvis versus cervix obeying the ancient law as they opened a door from one world to another. A warm flood came, gravy-smooth though riding on a bolt of immense agony. In that instant, Luby locked eyes with a nurse struggling to maintain her composure, and she knew. The nurse abruptly turned to Doctor Hildebrand, forehead sweating, glasses steamed. *She's hemorrhaging, Doctor. Baby is crowning, and she's hemorrhaging.*

Far away, audible nonetheless through concrete walls and city noise, the call. Not the squealing, gibbering mania of coyotes, but the resonant sustained howl of wolves. A summoning. It thrummed in her skull, wormed down her spine. As Luby pushed and screamed, her pulse pumped in tandem with a pack only she alone could hear, and her daughter slipped into the world wreathed in sanguine glory.

At Twyla's first cry, Luby lost consciousness.

In her mind's eye, a brutish, vulpine thing the size of a bison emerged from a leaning shack, a windowless, dilapidated wreck whose door had been snatched from its hinges. The beast sneered canine and predatory, bits of bloody meat and tattered clothing dangling like sleeping bats. Overturned cars and burning telephone poles lined the ruined street, and Luby knew this dirt speck of a town had been vanquished in one bloody night. At this creature's rear, at least a dozen smaller wolves escaped the shadows, lit by flames and the searing Cyclops moon.

The massive beast reared on hind legs like pistons and sniffed the night air. Intelligent yellow eyes scanned the ruins with cunning and resolve, satisfied that every living thing had been humiliated and devoured. It hinged its great mouth open like an old-style steam shovel, drew breath, and unleashed its voice against the enormous Texas sky.

"They chose you," The Emperor says, palm on Luby's forehead. Eyes shut, he recalls her memories as his own. "Selected for greatness."

"Twyla was barely three years old. . ." Luby stands slack-jawed, limp, and naked as a rock. In the presence of The Emperor she is little more than a malleable dupe in a carnival hypnotist's show. "They surrounded us in a parking lot. Christmas shopping. Twyla loved all the pretty lights."

Luby breaks into staccato sobs as she recounts the ultimate dread not only of being eaten alive, but the inability to protect her daughter. The monster from her birth-vision, stinking, huge, and panting, pinned her to the asphalt like a television wrestler. Paws the size of baseball gloves, eyes like liquid glass, it filled its huffing wet nostrils with Luby's scent, then lapped at her sweating neck with a tongue the size of a kitchen knife. With a single claw, extended like a man's index finger, the wolf penetrated her sweater and slashed her sternum. The speed incredible, yet skillful as a master chef. The wolf kissed the leaking wound in the gentle way loyal dogs do, then leaped atop the hood of Luby's car. It cocked its massive, regal head. Watching.

THE EMPEROR OF ROADKILL

"The others surrounded Twyla, but not like hunters. They *protected* her."

"And suicide is how you repay them," The Emperor says, releasing Luby from their shared vision.

That first Cyclops moon after the parking lot, Luby met a new horror: shifting and fusing bone, yawning tendons, and incisors shedding their enamel to allow razor fangs passage. The family dog Buttons met a shrieking end when a newly relentless Luby snatched him from his hiding place beneath the sofa. She thrashed little Buttons in her jaws until his neck snapped, then gobbled the poor thing down like a deviled egg at a July Fourth barbecue. With a throat slippery with terrified blood and a heart enlarged to twice its normal size, Luby stalked past shrieking Twyla and set her eyes on Gerald—poor, stupefied Gerald—wielding a baseball bat with the ferocity of a chubby kid on his first day of little league. A swipe of her claw unzipped his flesh to the scapula. He bumbled from the house bloody and dumbfounded, never to be seen again. Three months later, Luby filed for divorce on grounds of abandonment.

Livestock followed, opened and steaming along miles of rolling fences. Within six months, Luby moved on to transients in the train yards near Lubbock. Prostitutes in Midland, followed for hours for the sheer thrill of stalking unwitting prey before taking it down. Fort Stockton cab drivers outside dive bars and strip joints. The nightman at a fleabag hotel outside of Leapersville. A grade school kid on a pre-dawn paper route. The Interstate bursting with truck stops flush with meat proved a lure too ripe to refuse.

With new instincts and cunning, Luby's wealth and prestige blossomed. Business investments took profitable turns as adversaries capitulated in even the most tame negotiations. She maintained her human facade with elegance and authority, paying the balance due when the animal asserted its dominance every twenty-eight days. Should lunar and menstrual cycles merge, Luby's trophies bled savage and numerous. Bodies split like summer fruit, she rolled in entrails until nothing but cartilage and sinew remained. Rampant promiscuity followed. Only the moon determined whether her lover was canine or human.

By the time a nineteen-year-old, pregnant Twyla ran off with a guy she'd met at an AC/DC show in Dallas, Luby had ended so many human lives she'd stopped counting.

Still, a sliver of her Evangelical upbringing survived. *Even if these irredeemable sins ensure my place in Hell, at least suicide will hasten the trip.* In her Wolfmind, the solution lay in the rush of a river, a dive into shallow waters filled with stones. In her human mind, Interstate 10 and an unstoppable force. *Twyla inherits everything but my bloody legacy. I'll pay damnation's price.*

Now in this mausoleum of cinder block and filthy things, the resurrected Luby Barlleaux lowers her eyes from The Emperor's stare.

"All fortune brought by the Wolf, and you tempt its ire with the showmanship of suicide. Unbecoming of royalty."

"It seemed the only way," she says.

"Do you know the True Death? It is accepted with honor and has but one, solitary avenue."

Luby nods. She'd seen it in the old corny movies, heard it from a Swiss Master Wolf in a Geneva ski lodge yet feared it purely myth, a lie to keep the hunt alive. Perpetuation of species safe in a border most were not willing to cross, too absurd to be real. What parent would eagerly confront their child with such a task?

Kill me, if not for love, then greed.

"A Wolf may only die at the hand of the one that loves him most."

The Emperor taps his silver codpiece. The sound is hollow as a church bell in thick winter fog. "These eternal tortures you seek, do you hope to find absolution there?"

"I don't know," Luby responds. "My daughter knows what I am, and I can no longer live with that."

"Nor will you. Now that I have found you, *restored* you, know that your hunting nights are over. Your damnation lies not in the Undervoid, but *here.*"

Luby shakes her head. "I. . ."

The Emperor of Road Kill raises a massive hand to silence her. Where fingerprints commonly swirl writhe the faces of countless creatures, human and animal alike, warped with suffering, squirming over one another like beetles clearing meat from a bone. Centuries of lives scraped from trail, street, and highway.

"Each moon summons the old urges, but now it will bring only frailty. You will lie as I found you, broken and panting, one eye soaking in your own blood. Insatiable, yet unable to satisfy. Maimed; an invalid within sight of death's door. Did not I mention a superior torture? A maze with no escape?"

THE EMPEROR OF ROADKILL

Luby drops onto a pallet of concrete mix. As shock wanes, reality blooms. She thinks of Twyla in her shitty house, a single mother with an even shittier job, unwilling to accept even the slightest bit of help or charity from her raging carnivore of a mother. She's fantasized about Twyla decapitating her with an axe, envisioned scenarios where Twyla abides by legend and minces her mother into hamburger in a hail of silver bullets. Still, every time the prospect crosses Luby's mind it brings dishonor's slap, a rebuke of her cowardice. After amassing such power and superiority, who would envy a lummox like Lon Chaney Jr. in those old melodramas, winging and blubbering, pacing in a hotel room, eager to die?

And yet, Luby aches to tell Twyla she is the only one who can sever the curse and inherit her mother's fortune, one gained from the instincts of killers as old as the Texas plains. Twyla barely entertains her mother's phone calls, let alone a terse, tension-filled yearly visit. She resents the luxury clothes and immaculate cars, the offers of money, the promise of only the best for her son. All required of Twyla is she perform her duties bound by the Old Rules, and Luby knows in her heart that if Twyla is presented with the choice, she'll refuse purely in spite of it.

Private schools and a nice place to live, Twyla, honey. Wherever you like; Texas, Maine, Italy. It does not matter as long as you two are happy. I beg you skewer my heart and slay the stinking savage I've become. It's all I ask, then everything I have is yours.

"And what of the True Death?" she asks The Emperor. "It is looked upon without shame and judgment?"

Luby takes the incredible hands of her resurrector and looks again into irises stained golden-blood. He is the deliverer of cruel justice, governed by a set of laws unknown to mortals. Ah, but to be immortal in the grip of shame is her only avenue toward sympathy. *I never asked for any of it. I was marked like a dog's piss-stop, used over and over again.*

"A hunter's end," The Emperor says.

"Will you help me?"

Summer in Texas stews painful. In the town of Hollis the heat

KYLE TOUCHER

holds sway at the first inkling of sunrise, a maniac oven, full-bore from June to October. On a sweltering September afternoon, the barren landscape a brown carpet of discarded roof shingles, Luby Barlleaux sits in the passenger seat of her Lexus. Her man of the month, Heinrich, helms the wheel.

Two traffic lights preside over Hollis. One hangs from a cable like a fly in a spider web, gawking with one yellow flashing eye, the other lashed to a wooden pole at the intersection of Grand Avenue and Bemis, and it is there Luby instructs Heinrich to turn right.

Twyla's rental house tilts to the left like a hut in a storybook, slipping from a foundation poured so ineptly a town with a code enforcement division would have condemned it. A pale green bike leans against a porch populated with mismatched outdoor furniture. A hopeful splash of color sits on the glass-top table, a handful of perennials in a clay pot. The Texas sun breathes spite upon their petals.

Heinrich pulls into the driveway behind Twyla's old F150, a faceless early 1990s model with peeling paint and dented tailgate. An air freshener hangs from the rear view mirror, and inside this luxurious sedan with closed windows and air conditioning, Luby recognizes the fake, acrid pine scent.

She reaches into the glove compartment and removes a black velvet bag. She tilts the bag into her other hand and out slides an ingot the length of a soda pop bottle. At its apex snarls the work of a master silversmith.

A gift from the Emperor of Road Kill.

Kyle Toucher is the author of the novel Live Wire *and the* collection The Medusa Psalms: Welcome to Walpurgis County, *both from Crystal Lake Publishing. Other works include the* novella Life Returns *and appearances in the anthologies* Dead Letters: Episodes of Epistolary Horror, To Hell and Back, *and* Halloween Horror Volume 3. *He is a two-time Emmy Award-winning visual effects artist, a musician with old school punk rock street cred, and also writes under the name Mason Chaine.*

X and Instagram: @kyletoucher

DEEP CUTS

MIKE DEADY

A PLAIN BROWN MAILER, the kind with the padded bubble interior, was waiting for Reinier and his wife Nora when they got home from work. It was on the porch, propped against the front door of their Colonial. There was no return address.

Reinier scooped it up and brought it into the house. "I wonder what this is," he said.

"I think you have to open it to find out," Nora said.

"Funny." Reinier wrestled with the top of the mailer and peeled off the self-seal flap. He reached in and felt a flat disc-shaped object. At first, he thought it was an old-fashioned CD. But when he slid it out, he saw it was an even older-fashioned 45 RPM vinyl record. At least, he assumed it was 45 RPM. There was no label on the record, just a white sticker with "Play this side" written on it.

He stroked his perfectly maintained five-day growth of stubble. "Why would somebody send us an old single? Nobody has record players anymore." He moved across the open living area to the kitchen and stepped on the trash barrel's foot pedal.

"Wait a minute," Nora said. "What if it's some rare old record that's worth money?"

Reinier's eyes lit up. "How can we find out?"

She sighed deeply, a sound he was becoming all too familiar with. "Doesn't your buddy Spencer still have a turntable?" she asked. "And that antique stereo system from the twentieth century?"

"That's right!" He pulled out his phone. "Let me text him and see if he's home."

"I'm surprised that hipster doofus even *has* a cell phone," Nora said.

The response came within seconds. "He's home," Reinier said. "Let's go."

Spencer's place was less than a mile from theirs. There were a couple of cars in the driveway in addition to Spencer's van when they got there. Reinier pulled his BMW in behind them.

"Looks like Spence might be having a little party," he said.

"His whole life is a party," Nora said.

"It's a good spot for them. Dead end street. Conservation land behind the house. No neighbors close enough to be bothered."

They got out of the BMW.

"Adam's here," Reinier said, pointing at a nondescript beige Toyota.

Nora smirked. "He's such a sad sack."

"What's wrong with Adam?"

"He's always moping around about how he can't find a girlfriend. 'I'm an Adam without an Eve.' It's pathetic. Women can sense his desperation, and it just pushes them away."

She was probably right, but Reinier didn't want to give her the satisfaction of admitting it. He gestured to the other car in the driveway instead, a new red Mustang. "That's Fitness Frank's car."

Nora frowned.

"What? You have a problem with him, too?" Reinier asked. "Jesus, don't you like any of my friends?"

They had only been married for less than a year, but he was already wondering if he had made a big mistake. She was always complaining about something.

"Even *you*—" she poked him in the chest "—have to admit that's a ridiculous nickname for a grown-ass man."

"It's not his fault. You know he's a trainer at the gym. They gave all the employees silly nicknames. And he's only doing it until his music career takes off." *If it ever does,* Reinier thought. He had heard some of Frank's attempts at songwriting and he was not impressed.

They approached the front door and knocked. The door opened, letting out a cloud of sweet-smelling marijuana smoke. Behind it stood Spencer, holding a can of IPA from a local craft brewery.

"Reinier, the human palindrome!" he said. "And his lady love. . .umm. . ."

"Nora." Spencer never seemed to remember her name. Reinier wondered if he did it on purpose to irritate him.

"Right! Well, come on in. The game's on."

The living room was just off the entrance foyer. Frank and Adam were engrossed in a soccer match on the huge flat screen television that took up nearly one whole wall. Frank was as outgoing and physically fit as anyone Reinier had ever known, while Adam was just the opposite: timid and bland.

Spencer's longtime girlfriend Celeste was there, too. She waved. Reinier always wondered how Spencer had managed to bag such a hot number.

"Grab yourselves an IPA," Spencer said.

"Don't you have any real beer?" Reinier asked.

"And you know I hate beer. I'll have a glass of white wine," Nora added.

"I'll grab them," Frank said. "I need a refill anyway."

Reinier and Nora settled themselves on the loveseat.

Spencer sat down next to Celeste. A fanatical soccer fan, Spencer even slightly resembled his boyhood idol, Alexi Lalas, with his long red hair and ludicrous goatee. He nodded at the TV. "The Revolution has the home field advantage," he said.

"So did the Alamo," Reinier said. He hated soccer himself, but it was almost halftime or whatever they called it, so he endured it. Finally, the whistle blew.

Reinier cleared his throat and put down his beer. "Could you turn off the game during halftime? I want you to play a record for me."

Spencer clutched at his heart. "*You* want to play a *record*? Have you finally seen the error of your ways and embraced the glory of analog, unprocessed music?"

"Yeah, I just love listening to pops and scratches," Reinier said. He held up the record and explained to the group how he and Nora had found it on their stoop with no explanation or return address.

"Wait a minute," Frank said. "Somebody at the gym was telling me about this. I think it's some kind of social media challenge that's been going around lately."

"That's right!" Celeste said. "I've heard about it, too." Spencer and Adam bobbed their heads in agreement.

"A social media challenge?" Reinier asked. "How does it work?"

"The record comes anonymously, usually dropped off at the

door like yours was," Celeste replied. "But sometimes, if the house has a security system like a doorbell camera, it comes in the mail instead. Almost like it has intelligence. Anyway, the challenge is to start and finish listening to it."

"That's it?" Reinier said. "Listen to a song? That's not much of a challenge." He snapped his fingers. "Wait a minute. Let me guess. The song is supposed to be cursed. After you listen to it, something bad happens, like in that horror movie where they watch an old VHS tape."

"Not exactly," Celeste answered. "There's a twist. If you listen to it all the way through, you're fine. But if you start listening to it, and don't finish, *that's* when the bad things happen to you."

Reinier snorted. "Sounds foolish. But even if someone really believed this nonsense, what would prevent them from listening to the whole song so they're not 'cursed?'"

"The song is supposed to be really hard to listen to," Celeste said.

"It must be a country song," Spencer said.

Everyone laughed.

"Or a Grateful Dead song," Reinier said.

Spencer stopped laughing.

If Spencer loved anything more than soccer, it was the Dead. Reinier cranked the flame a little higher. "I didn't think it was possible for them to suck any worse, but then they added John Mayer to their lineup."

Spencer's face turned red. He looked like he was ready to lunge at Reinier, but Celeste put her hand on his thigh.

Reinier chuckled. Spencer was so easy.

"I don't think the song is supposed to be bad, necessarily, just hard to listen to in an emotional way," Celeste said.

"What a load of crap," Reinier said. "It's all an elaborate internet hoax. An attempt to create a new urban legend."

"Oh, and one more thing," Celeste said. "The song is supposed to be exactly seven minutes and six seconds long. Get it? Six minutes and sixty-six seconds! Cool, huh?"

"Ooh, spooky," Reinier said. "This is getting dumber and dumber. No sense even playing the damn thing now."

"Oh, come on," Nora said. "We didn't come all the way over here for nothing. We're listening to this record."

"Yeah," Spencer said. He snatched the record from Reinier's

hand. "Since you don't want to hear it anymore, I'm going to make sure you do."

He stormed over to the stereo system in the corner. He powered up the receiver and turned the dial to the turntable input. He lifted the hinged plastic dust cover on the turntable, placed the 45 adapter on the center spindle, dropped the record on, and moved the speed selector from 33 to 45. He lifted the tone arm.

"Wait," Celeste said. "This is where anyone who doesn't want to risk listening to the song should leave."

Frank got up. "I'm going outside for a smoke."

Reinier taunted Frank as he left the room. "Frank the musician afraid of a song? And Fitness Frank the trainer smoking? What would they say at the gym?"

"Anyone else?" Spencer asked, glaring at Reinier. "No?" He dropped the tone arm. The song began.

Adam was the first to tap out. He barely made it a minute into the song before he lurched off the couch, tears in his eyes, and ran down the hall into the kitchen.

I'm so alone, he thought. Something about the dissonant music, and the words he thought he could hear underneath it, had exacerbated the loneliness, ratcheting it up to an unbearable level. Why couldn't he find someone who wanted him? What was wrong with him? Reinier had Nora, even though the greedy prick didn't deserve her. Fitness Frank had his pick of women from the gym. Even Spencer, the burned-out hippie wannabe, had a beautiful girlfriend.

He knew what he had to do. The song had told him.

He pulled out the carving knife from the block on top of the kitchen's center island. He lowered himself to the floor and sat with his back leaning against the island's base cabinet. He unbuttoned his shirt and felt along his rib cage, looking for a soft place to cut. Being right-handed, he figured he'd have better leverage on his left side.

He slid the knife in and started cutting below the bottom left rib. He ignored the pain. With a few quick slices, he outlined a large rectangular swath of flesh. He put down the knife. He dug the fingers of both hands into the edges on either side of the cut, gripped the chunk of meat, ripped it out, and tossed it aside, exposing his lower rib cage.

Panting and sweating profusely, he wiped his blood-soaked

hands on his pants. He took a deep breath, reached in, gripped the bottom rib, and pulled as hard as he could.

The rib snapped off with a *crack*. His vision blurred for a moment. When it cleared, a beautiful woman was standing over him.

It worked, he thought with a surge of joy. *My very own Eve!*

Celeste made it halfway through the song before covering her ears and running from the room. It wasn't even a song, just the most discordant noise she had ever heard, although some of it was strangely familiar. And underneath the noise, voices. Mocking her. Telling her she was ugly. Overweight. Stupid. That Spencer would never put a ring on her finger. That she would never be able to hang onto any man. Everything she had always feared about herself, confirmed.

She could still hear the voices, even outside the room with her hands covering her ears. She had to do something about them.

She ran into the kitchen and stopped short. Her hands dropped away from her ears in surprise. Adam was sitting on the floor, back propped against the center island, with an enormous hole in his side. Blood was pooling underneath him. There was a carving knife lying next to him. And what looked like a huge piece of uncooked steak.

He was cradling something against his bare chest. *Is that a bone? A rib?*

Adam's eyes fluttered open, and he looked up at her with a beatific smile. "Eve," she thought he said. But it was hard to hear him over the voices.

She picked up the carving knife from the floor. *No,* she thought. *Too big.* She dropped it.

She moved to the block of knives on the island's countertop. She pulled them out one by one, tossing each onto the floor until she found the one she was looking for: a narrow-bladed boning knife. She sat on the floor near Adam, avoiding the pool of blood. She giggled. *Why am I worried about that?* She thrust the knife into her left ear, withdrew it, and plunged it all the way into her right ear.

The voices stopped. All noise stopped. It was blissfully quiet.

She listened to the silence until she couldn't hear it anymore.

Spencer snapped to attention. The record had just warned him that Reinier was going to kill him. He looked across the room and saw Reinier stirring, giving Spencer a look of pure hatred.

I need a weapon. I can't take Reinier in a fair fight.

He shot out of his seat and ran down the hallway into the kitchen.

Celeste and Adam were both sitting on the floor against the center island in pools of blood. Neither was breathing. Knives were strewn all over the floor.

Spencer dropped to his knees and skidded to a halt at Celeste's side. A knife was protruding from her right ear.

"Oh, Celeste. . ."

That sonofabitch Reinier had to have done this. The corporate stooge had never liked Spencer or Celeste, detesting their carefree lifestyle. His hand closed around one of the discarded knives lying on the floor as he heard a sound behind him.

Reinier felt eyes on him. He glanced across the living room and saw Spencer staring at him, studying him. He knew exactly what Spencer was planning. The song had told him.

Spencer bolted out of the room. Reinier got up and followed, a few steps behind. When he got to the kitchen, Spencer was on his knees, bent over Celeste's body. A knife was sticking out of her ear. Adam's mutilated body was next to Celeste's.

Jesus fucking Christ. What had that stoned-out hippie bastard done?

His foot kicked something on the floor. He looked down. A knife. They were everywhere. He picked it up and advanced on Spencer. He raised the knife and brought it down toward Spencer's back, just as Spencer rolled away waving a knife of his own at Reinier.

Spencer sprang to his feet, which slipped on the blood-slicked floor and went out from under him. His head hit the corner of the center island, and he crashed to the floor, his neck at an unnatural angle.

Well, that was easy. Hippies can't fight for shit. His fury was nowhere near abated, though. He bent down and started sawing. He detached Spencer's head quickly, aided in no small part by the already broken spine. He lifted the head by its long red hair and placed it on the center island.

There, he thought with satisfaction. *Now you're a true Deadhead.*

Reinier was surprised to find himself out of breath from the brief exertion. His skin was clammy. He didn't feel well at all.

What the hell is wrong with me? He looked down at himself. A knife was sticking out from his side. That bastard Spencer had managed to luck out when he blindly took a swipe at him. He kicked Spencer's headless body in a rage, making himself dizzy.

He gripped the knife in his side and yanked it out. Gouts of blood followed.

That may have been a mistake.

Frank came back in just after the song ended. He could hear the static of the stylus traveling over the runout grooves. The tone arm lifted, auto returned to its cradle, and the platter stopped turning. Then the living room was quiet.

And empty except for himself and Nora.

"Hey," he said, "where is everyone?"

"What?" Nora looked around in confusion. "I don't know. I didn't even notice them leaving."

She stood up a little unsteadily. They both listened for the others, but the house was silent. They stepped into the hallway. Nobody there. They continued down the hall into the kitchen.

The first thing Frank saw was Spencer's head on the center island's countertop. "Holy shit," he said.

Nora wasn't looking at the head. She was looking down at her husband. "Reinier's dead," she said, no emotion in her voice.

"I think they're *all* pretty dead."

"Reinier's dead," she repeated. "He's really dead." She threw herself into Frank's arms. She pulled his head down and kissed him hard.

"It worked," she said. "You did it, babe."

Nora had started coming to his gym months ago. Her marriage to his buddy Reinier was an unhappy one. What had started off as the innocent comforting of a friend's wife turned into a torrid secret affair. He had had his share of lonely housewives before, but Nora was different. She didn't treat him like a piece of meat. They were in love.

He wasn't sure which of them had first broached the idea of getting rid of Reinier. But it had been his unorthodox plan they had agreed to try first. If it didn't work, no harm no foul. They would just do it in a more conventional way.

But it had worked spectacularly. Better than he could have imagined. Reinier was out of the way, and now Nora was all his. And his other asshole friends were out of the picture, too. They had all thought he was a stereotypical dumb jock. They had ridiculed his modest home recording studio and his dream of a musical career. But he had shown them. And used music to do so.

That reminded him. . .

Frank ended the embrace. He turned and walked back into the living room, stopping at the stereo system.

"What are you doing?" Nora asked.

"Taking the record."

"Why? The whole point of the plan was to take advantage of that idiotic social media challenge going around. Leaving the record creates that smokescreen."

"Yeah, but what if they analyze it and trace it back to me somehow?"

"Hell of a time to worry about that. Explain to me again exactly what's on the record."

"A bunch of the angriest and most depressing songs ever recorded layered on top of each other. Songs that have actually caused murder and suicide like 'Helter Skelter,' 'The Hungarian Suicide Song,' Ozzy's 'Suicide Solution,' and more. Some sound effects like screams and crying thrown in. It's a cacophony of rage and sorrow.

"But the real kicker? What pushed them over the edge? Hidden voice commands, like subliminal messages but even better. A trick I picked up on the dark web. I've known my asshole friends for a long time, so I knew what buttons to push. Add weed, and booze, and a little something I spiked their booze with. . .well, you saw the results."

"Did I ever," Nora said. "And no one saw you drop the record off at my house?"

"No, I was careful. And I used gloves to handle the record and the envelope."

"And you deleted all the digital music files at your home studio once you cut the record?"

"Of course."

"Then there's nothing to worry about," Nora said. She shook her head. "Would you believe Reinier was going to throw it out after all that work and planning? I had to practically put a ring in his nose and lead him here."

Frank smiled at the image but stopped when he saw Nora shiver. "What's wrong, babe?" he asked.

"Even though I had some idea what to expect, the record was still very hard to listen to," she replied, rubbing her arms.

He chuckled. "Yeah. That's the main reason I went outside. I had to listen to the damned thing over and over while I was making it. Plus, like I said, I wanted a smoke. My cigarettes were in my car. And I checked my messages while I was out there. I had to kill six minutes and sixty-six seconds."

She gazed out the living room's picture window, and Frank thought she suddenly looked a little sad. Was that a tear? Likely a delayed reaction to all the deaths.

"Leave the record," she said. "Let's just go back to the kitchen. I want to have one last look to make sure we didn't miss anything."

They walked back down the hall. Frank stepped into the kitchen. He shook his head. All that carnage in a little over seven minutes. And his record had been the cause of it all. As proud as he was of his accomplishment, he was surprised to feel a sharp pang of regret.

And an even sharper pain in his back.

Nora twisted the knife, pulled it out, and stepped back so no blood would get on her. *I just broke his heart,* she thought hysterically. *And mine.*

Frank reached behind him, brought his hand back and looked at it. It was covered in blood. He looked at her in surprise, took a couple wobbly steps, and sank to the floor.

"Why?" he gasped.

"I'm sorry, babe," she said. Tears ran down her face. "I really loved you. But you fucked up."

"How. . ."

"You were supposed to walk over here through the woods. Or have Adam pick you up. Someone could have seen your car. I noticed it when I first got here, but I forgot about it until you mentioned it a minute ago."

Frank was shaking his head slowly. "No. . .one. . .saw. . ."

Jesus, she thought. It was like explaining things to a child. "Even if nobody saw the car, the GPS would have shown it was here, should it be examined later."

Frank opened his mouth to speak, but no words came out. Only blood.

"And you brought your phone, too," she continued, shaking her head at his stupidity. "They can be tracked. We went over this! Why do men never listen?"

Frank wasn't listening now, either.

Or breathing.

Nora tossed the knife to the floor with the rest and tucked the handkerchief she had used to handle it back into her pocket. Spencer's, or possibly Celeste's, fingerprints would still be on it. She went back to the living room and retrieved her purse and her wine glass. She returned to the kitchen and washed and dried the glass and put it away, careful not to leave any prints.

She took one last look around. What a mess. Forensics would be hard-pressed to figure out what the holy hell had happened here. The record left on the turntable would muddy the waters and add to the urban legend of the social media challenge. And even if they could somehow trace it back to Frank, it didn't matter anymore. Hell, they might even think Frank had been behind the whole social media challenge from the start.

She sighed deeply. If Frank had stuck to the plan, he would be beside her now, ready to exit the house via the back door. They would have crossed the back yard together and entered the conservation land behind the house until they reached the walking trail that cut through the woods. Frank's car and phone would be at his house where they were supposed to be. She and Frank would both have been back in their respective homes before any alarm was raised and the police came knocking at her door to tell her about her husband. When questioned, she would say she stayed home tonight while her husband went out to Spencer's to watch the soccer game, and her phone's GPS would bear that out. And after an appropriate period of mourning, she and Frank would have gotten together for real.

But he had doomed that perfect plan and himself with his blunders.

She sighed again and walked toward the back door. As she reached for the knob, a voice behind her said, "Leaving so soon?"

She froze. She could have sworn they were all dead. One of them was still alive somehow? She would have to remedy that. She turned around.

All five bodies were still on the floor. All were still dead.

But someone was standing in the entranceway from the hall.

Nora gasped. It was a man, and *what* a man. He was the hottest guy she had ever seen. Was he some friend of Spencer's she had never met, arriving late to Spencer's soccer viewing party?

He stepped fully into the kitchen, stopped, and looked at all the bloodied bodies on the floor. He closed his eyes and inhaled deeply. When his eyes opened, they were glazed. Orgasmic.

Nora glanced down at the floor, looking for one of the discarded knives. She had to take him by surprise and strike while he was distracted. She could not risk leaving a witness. But none were close enough.

The man turned to her. "That worked out well," he said. "I see my record was a big hit."

"What do you mean, your record? It's Frank's record that did this," she said indignantly.

He chuckled. "Do you really think your buffoon of a boyfriend, who was totally clueless about basic car and phone technology, could have had the ability to create a record that would drive people to violence with a few minutes of music and some voice commands? Oh, you sweet, naïve child."

Now that she thought about it, she had to concede he was right. She had been blinded by her love for Frank and her desperation to be rid of Reinier. Frank couldn't have made a record that would do that. No one could.

It wasn't humanly possible.

"Who are you?" she asked.

"I think you already know the answer to that."

"But. . .Frank *did* make the record and leave it on my doorstep," she said.

"A simple enough thing to replace it with mine," he said. "You popped up on my radar back when you started planning to kill your husband, and I've been monitoring you two ever since. When you came up with the plan to use my records as a smokescreen for your murders, I decided to pull the old switcheroo. It struck my funny bone."

"You mean all that social media challenge stuff was really true?"

"For the most part."

Cold slipped between her ribs like a knife. "I listened to an actual cursed record? That would have killed me if I had stopped listening?"

He grinned.

"Why?" she asked. "Why would you do something like this?"

He shrugged. "I was bored."

"Bored?"

"With the rise of the internet and social media, it became too easy for me to manipulate the truth and sway people to do whatever I wanted. I realized I was getting stale. Complacent. I worried that my skills were atrophying. I decided to challenge myself. So I went old school."

"By making *records*?"

"Vinyl is making a comeback. And one of the few things your bonehead of a beau got right is that music is a powerful emotional tool. It can drive some people to murder and suicide under the right circumstances. Of course, he had absolutely no clue how to harness that power. But I do."

Killing him was probably impossible, Nora realized, but it didn't matter. He would never turn her in, would he?

"This has been so very fascinating," she said, "but I think I'll be leaving now. I survived the challenge, after all. You have to let me go."

He laughed. "I think not."

She turned and grabbed the back door knob. It didn't turn. She fumbled to find the latch.

"Your screams will grace my next record," he said.

"But I listened to the record all the way through!" Nora wailed. "I'm supposed to be fine!"

"Where did you get that idea?" he asked as he closed in. "The internet?"

He roared with laughter, but her shrieks drowned out the sound.

Mike Deady's work has appeared in The Rack II, Wicked Sick, Reader Beware, Totally Tubular Terrors, *and other publications. He is a member of the Horror Writers Association, the New England Horror Writers, and the Boston Horror Society. He is a lifelong resident of Massachusetts. After retiring from a forty-two-year career in engineering, he started writing horror fiction at the urging of his brother, Bram Stoker Award-winning author Tom Deady.*

THE BURIAL SHOE
OR A TRUE AND FAITHFUL ACCOUNT OF CINDERELLA

ALISON LITTLEWOOD

I.

You know this story, or you think you do.
A fairy tale, you call it, and you should;
for the maid, in faith, never comes to any good—
any fool could tell you the opposite is true.

A tale as old as 'Once Upon A Time'.
'Cinders' he called her—it wasn't her name
but remembering her was not his game
and housemaids look the same beneath the grime.

He had his way, and cast her out
for her silken slipper (so he called it) fit.
Beyond that, he had no use for it
this thing of glares and tears and pout
(and soon she would be growing stout
        oh: soon she would be growing stout!)

. . .Why should he? She chose to dance the dance.
To hope for more was surely treason
nothing more than blind unreason.
To be cast aside? Her own mischance.

THE BURIAL SHOE

Even if she pleaded her belly since,
hers was never a marriage bed.
The cold, hard world must do instead
for the Prince cannot always be a prince.

But the cold, hard world was too much blame.
Two mouths to feed? Too much strife.
She bared her wrists, took up a knife
so Cinders sliced; died of her shame.

Still, happy, happy, happy news!
The Prince is ready for a wife
a pretty, wealthy, healthy wife
a princess wife! But who to choose?

All will love her—yes, surely all
for he'll only choose from those most worthy.
The lovely, golden, fair and curvy
Are invited to a splendid ball.
(No need for princes to fawn or trawl.
              He'd simply pick one at the ball!)

And so we close here our Part One
the Prince all set to be ignited
by one true love, the hordes excited
princesses primping, and Cinders gone.

II.

Nothing filthy, nothing flawed.
The face is washed, the best possible finery
picked out. One fair mother prepares her girl for venery.
Another dresses her child for God.

The God-mother weeps, the other smiles.
The time is nigh! The ball, the ball!
She doesn't doubt she'll take it all,
this child of hers. But first: pause for a while.

ALISON LITTLEWOOD

There's something you should know about Death.
It doesn't do much for the looks:
the limbs grow stiff, the skin turns pale
the cheeks grow hollow, the blood turns stale
there is no breath, there is no light
the eyes film over purest white
as grim as 'Always', as cold as 'Never'
the scent is sweet and vile together
nothing is ever the same, you know
from head and hair down to the toe.
        Ah yes—

The toes, for even lovely feet
are touched, deformed by Death's despair.
The toes pulled down, the flesh will swell
no dancing shoes could fit this belle
        (glass slippers would only show the hell
        awaiting for us there as well—)

No: her dance is done. A burial shoe's the thing
suited to this poor dead maid.
Slit up the back and laced instead
one size fits all—like his wedding ring
(one purchased e'en before the ball.
Oh yes! E'en before the ball.)

This shoe fits all—but only ever belongs to one.
Wrapped in a clean and shining shroud
quite still, dressed to make her mother proud
here's Cinderella, dead and gone.

Aye, pretty Cinderella in her coffin.
(Also not her name: you'll never know it.
Who would ever feel the need to know it?
They now just call her 'Sin'.)

But whirl, whirl, whirl the dancers
ring, ring, ring the bells
presaging the wedding knells.
She's banished all the other chancers

this girl of ours. For all agree
that she's the fairest and the best
her steps are fleeter than the rest
she's fit for princely matrimony.

The crowd is rapt, the Prince is chipper.
They dance and dance right up to midnight.
They're ever in each other's sight.
To seal the deal—she leaves her slipper.

An age-old, ancient game, is this.
The girl goes home, but leaves behind
this sign and signal of the bind
between them. Just like true love's kiss.

The prince must keep it, till he may
replace it on her foot, so slender.
It proves this girl is no pretender;
that moment is their wedding day.

III.

He wakes upon the splendrous morn
a day of gleaming bridal white.
Snow has fallen in the night
come in blessing—ne'er to mourn.

He goes, excited, to fetch the shoe
to try on her sweet toes;
the slipper he'll slip her, neat as it goes
then: a wedding that none will rue.

But what is this? The slipper he'll base
his wedding upon's no longer there.
The Prince can only stand and stare
at what's found waiting in its place.
(The crowds gathering already apace
jostling to see the pair embrace!)

A burial shoe in gravedirt grimed
slit up the back and instead laced
is sitting here before his face
with damp malformed, with frost berimed.

Aye, the Prince may stand and stare
a moment more; then he decides, this is some
jest; a nasty trick. But he need not bow to custom.
It's not like he won't know her there

not like he doesn't know her face, her hair
her shape, her form, her cheek, her nose.
She has a name—of course she does!
He'd know his Princess anywhere.

He needs no shoe—
and so he weds her.
Kisses, touches, licks her, beds her.
They get to start their life anew.

IV.

And after the marriage
the honeymoon.
They're leaving soon—
a silver carriage

awaits them. He smiles and hands his bride inside
cloaked and furred. She's warm against the weather.
The two of them will cling together;
they'll heat the blood and more beside.

For snow is whirling, whirling, whirling
and is there something else, within it?
Who could say what lies within it?
But they're off: the pipes are skirling

THE BURIAL SHOE

heralding departure. The carriage leaves.
The crowd now cheers and cries and tattles
horses heave and harness rattles
until they're deep within the trees.

All's quiet. In the forest, the snow lies deep
and darkness moves apace.
Daylight's driven from this place
as the lovers softly sleep.

Then all is tumbling, all is turning
north is south and south is north;
the Prince is thrown and driven forth
as the carriage keeps on turning, turning.

Then: only silence. The Prince, thrown clear
strokes his head, inspects his bones.
Hearing then some distant moans
he turns to see what he held dear.

The horses are felled, still kicking, dying.
The coachmen are dead, broken simply as mice.
And there, lying sidelong amid the ice
the carriage, crushed as if t'were a pumpkin.

On shaking steps, he goes o'er the snow
and just once, looks within.
He thought he'd recognise her grin
but this? Her own mother wouldn't know

Her face.
Her face.
Her face.
Her face.

He turns now from the sorry scene
and sees instead what scared the horses;
what turned them from their natural courses:
the thing that they had seen.

ALISON LITTLEWOOD

There: nought but footprints in the snow
though oddly formed and oddly placed
as of one shoe split up the back and laced
and there: the other, left for him, to show

some sign. An ancient game, is this.
A girl, who's gone, but left behind
this sign and signal of the bind
between them. Just like true love's kiss.

He stoops, takes up the burial shoe.
A thing begrimed, befouled, rejected
like her. And at the edge of sight, detected
he: the thing he suddenly knew

he'd see. She stretches out her toes
towards him. Waits for he, her prince
to give it back, this evidence
that she is his, he hers, despite their woes.

There is no breath, there is no light.
Her limbs are stiff, the skin turned pale.
Her cheeks are hollow, her blood turned stale.
There'll be no joy for him tonight

only this. He slips onto her foot the shoe,
his poor dead Cinderella.
As grim as 'Always', as cold as 'Never'
a wedding vow is made anew.

Her white eyes gleam, she gasps hoarse laughter.
He feels a cold, cold hand in his;
oh, that it should come to this—
this life in death; unhappily ever after.

Alison Littlewood's latest novels, published as A. J. Elwood, are The Other Lives of Miss Emily White *and* The Cottingley Cuckoo. *Her first book,* A Cold Season, *was selected for the Richard and Judy Book Club and described as 'perfect reading for a dark winter's night.' Other titles include* Mistletoe, The Hidden People, The Crow Garden, The Unquiet House *and* Path of Needles. *Her short stories have been selected for several Best Of anthologies and published in her collections,* Quieter Paths, The Flowering *and* A Curious Cartography. *She has won the Shirley Jackson Award for short fiction. Alison lives in a house of creaking doors and crooked walls in deepest darkest Yorkshire, England.*

UNCONDITIONAL

John Durgin

I **WAKE UP** clinging to the edge of our bed, as I do most nights. Our daughter, Liv, has been coming into our room in the middle of the night to sleep with us since she was two years old. She's now six. No matter what we tried, she would always tell us that when she woke up, there would be someone standing in the room, watching her. We'd let her sleep with the lights on, leave the door open to both her room and our own, but it didn't matter. My wife, Julia, used to get frustrated with her, trying to force her to sleep in her room like a big girl. But then I reminded her that our little girl won't do this forever. She'd eventually grow up to resent us and want nothing to do with us. I said we should enjoy these moments, because someday we would reminisce about it as empty nesters and that we should be honored a little human being felt so safe around us that we would protect her from anything, big or small. Julia realized I was right. It's our job to protect our daughter. *My* job.

The air feels a bit stale this morning, but I don't think much of it. A mix of Julia's perfume, Liv's favorite vanilla lotion, and something else. Something I can't quite place.

Liv has always been a bed hog, and for a body that isn't even 46 inches long, she finds a way to take up more space than both my wife and I. She loves to sprawl out, extending her limbs like a flying squirrel gliding through the air. So, being on the edge of the bed is nothing new to me. And quite frankly, I could sleep anywhere. Give me a pillow and a place to lay, and I'll pass out within ten minutes if I'm tired enough.

UNCONDITIONAL

I roll over to face my daughter, whose eyes remain shut. She's perfect. I often think about how lucky we are. To create a human being so full of love, beauty, humor. Liv is the perfect blend of our personalities, with her mother's good looks and my strong desire to always make everything right.

It has become my morning ritual to lay in bed and stare at my wife and daughter, wondering what I did to deserve all this. The love I feel for them is unconditional. This is a snapshot in time that I could hold onto forever. Even through my darkest times, I know I can always come back to these moments to center myself. Nobody can take that from me.

As I stare at Liv, I think of how much she's changed over the last few years. Hell, the last few weeks. She's almost unrecognizable to me. She has shed that new baby smell, but she's still as sweet and innocent as when she was crawling across our floor, reaching for us with that desperation only a small child can possess. Now, she's looking more and more like her mother every day. Her skin tone has changed to mirror Julia's, as well as her shifting face and thin blonde hair. I remind myself that kids grow up fast, and that features change before you realize it.

I remember last year, on her fifth birthday, how I started to see the crack in her perfect personality. That innocent youth that we had grown to love, began to transition to tantrums and disobedience. Don't get me wrong, she was still our lovely Liv, but the signs were there that maybe we were growing out of our honeymoon phase. We'd had a party with some of her friends from kindergarten, which had started off perfectly. Julia and I went through extra measures to make it the most memorable party possible. We hired a clown, rented a two-room bouncy house, and ordered a special cake from the most popular bakery in the state. Most people might look at how extravagant it all was and say we went overboard, but they don't get it. Liv is our world, and we want her to know that.

When Liv saw the cake, and that it wasn't the design she had in her mind, she flipped out. Causing a scene in front of her friends and their parents. She shoved the cake off the table, screaming that it wasn't right, and then even screamed that the clown was stupid and sucked at doing his tricks. We were mortified. After ending the party early and apologizing to all the parents who had taken the time to buy gifts and drive their children to our home, we had a long, serious talk with Liv about how wrong it all was. She eventually apologized and we moved past it. That was the first time I saw the shift in her happy-go-lucky personality. She wasn't my little girl anymore—not entirely. The sweetness, the innocence—it was slipping through my fingers, and I wasn't ready to lose it. But I wouldn't let that happen. I would *never* let that happen.

For the first time in my parental life, I wanted to freeze time. I wanted to keep her that age forever before we lost her for good to the teenage resentment years. Over the following months, she had a few more of those outbursts mixed in with all the good times. Julia and I explored therapy as a way to get out in front of it before it was too late. After talking with a few therapists, nothing seemed to click. We would have to take matters into our own hands and just hope that we could curb these episodes before they escalated into something far worse.

And that's just what we did. What *I* did. Julia wasn't in full agreement with my ideas of discipline, but she came around eventually. So, here I am, admiring the product of all that hard work and sacrifice. I've earned the right to admire my work. Liv takes up as much space as she always does, and I think I'll risk moving her a bit so I can shift in bed to get more comfortable. She'll forgive me.

"Darling, I need a bit more space. Can you move closer to your mother so I can get more comfortable, please?"

Liv doesn't budge, dead to the world. I'm going to have to adjust her myself. I move a strand of her blonde hair from her face, taking note of the coldness of her skin from the cool morning air. I gently place one hand beneath her neck, and the other beneath her knees, and lift her a few inches off the bed. Carefully, I set her a few feet over and then shimmy on the bed to get more comfortable. The moment I lift her, a putrid stench uncoils from beneath the sheets, thick and cloying. It fills my lungs before I even realize I'm gasping. The smell of rot. Decay. It's getting worse.

As her body settles into the new spot, the stench releases from her and consumes my nostrils. The smell is getting bad. I realize I need to clean her soon, or else our entire home will stink of death. She's laid in this spot for three weeks now, and the odor of her demise has erased any last hope that I'd get that fresh baby smell back ever again. Applying her lotion only masked the smell for so long. I also noticed that when I lifted her, it felt as if her skin was peeling from the bones, sagging like a set of baggy clothes.

UNCONDITIONAL

Like I said, I don't even recognize her anymore. Her eyes stay closed, but the eyelids are sunken, as if the eyeballs beneath have retreated deeper in her skull. I don't dare open her eyelids to check. Her lips are dried and cracked as the flies continue to try and take her away from me. I've done everything I can to keep them away, but they are getting worse each day.

All of these sacrifices are worth it, though. My little girl will stay this size forever. While one might think it would be difficult to go through with such a plan, it really wasn't. After poisoning their food, all I had to do was sit back and wait for it to happen. Of course, seeing the fear in her eyes as her throat tightened, the breath trying to force its way out, that wasn't easy to watch. But I assured her it would all be okay. That it was all worth it. I said the same to Julia as she clawed at her own face, attempting to get beneath the flesh and tear out what ate her from the inside. I promised my wife that I'd look after them. I promised her that we'd never argue or disagree again, and that our little angel would stay this way forever.

As I stare at their rotting corpses, my mind is taken back to the love I feel for them. It's an unconditional love that I will never let go of.

John Durgin is an award nominated author. Growing up in New Hampshire, he discovered Stephen King much younger than most probably should have, reading IT before he reached high school—and knew from that moment on he wanted to write horror. His debut novel, The Cursed Among Us released June 3, 2022, and went on to become an Amazon bestseller. Next up, his sophomore novel titled Inside The Devil's Nest, released in January of 2023, followed by his debut collection, Sleeping In The Fire in June of 2023. In 2024 he released two more novels, starting with Kosa which released to stellar reviews, and Consumed by Evil through Crystal Lake Publishing in November 2024. His most recent novels are The Devil's In The Next Room and The Envelope.

Twitter/X- @jdurgin1084   Facebook- John Durgin author
Website- www.johndurginauthor.com TikTok- @johndurgin_author
Instagram- @durginpencildrawings
Big Cartel (signed books) https://johndurginauthor.bigcartel.com/

THE SKIN TAX

JOHN WARD

THE TWO-HOUR FLIGHT from Cleveland to Atlanta had been a double-edge sword for Chris. Excitement and anticipation coursed through his veins leading up to the trip. A little over a year prior, he had booked an appointment with one of the most world-renowned tattoo artists in America—Scott Cole—for the Big South Tattoo Festival being held at the Waycraft Hotel. On the flip side of the blade—Chris was terrified of flying.

Under normal circumstance, he would down several cocktails before finally boarding the aircraft in an attempt to calm his nerves. But drinking alcohol the day before a tattoo appointment would've led to his blood thinning and running the risk of excessive bleeding—diluting the ink and thus the quality of the artwork. So, Chris begrudgingly flew stone cold sober, clutching at his pant pockets with white knuckles for the duration of the flight. Chris had been dying to get a tattoo from Scott ever since he saw his photos and videos going viral on social media. Scott was a genius when it came to black and grey work—particularly with his horror pieces. Chris opted to get a full sleeve on his left arm of his favorite horror movie monsters and killers from Scott. His right arm was covered in colorful Halloween holiday-themed artwork. Horror had always played an integral role in Chris' life. He stayed up late reading horror books and watching horror films whenever he could, which led him to becoming the special FX artist that he was today—building monstrous creations for haunted house attractions and movie studios. His tattoos served as a tribute to an industry he had put blood, sweat, and tears in for.

"Chris!" Scott said with elation, extending a welcoming hand out for a shake. "Happy to meet you and to finally get to work on this!"

Chris grabbed his hand firmly, meeting Scott's warm smile with one of his own. "It's great to meet you, as well! I am so excited. You have no idea!"

The Waycraft Hotel had been transformed from a commercial lodge to a space filled to the brim with eager patrons excited to get tattooed, watch artists work, or buy merch. Vendors were packed like sardines into the grand ballroom. The sound of tattoo guns buzzing permeated the air like a power line after a heavy rain.

Scott had the stencil laid out on the table next to him. It looked even better than Chris ever could've dreamed. They made small talk while Scott took a Bic razor and shaved the hair off Chris' arm. He then applied a soapy lotion and applied the stencil, carefully wrapping it around his arm. When he peeled the paper away, Chris could begin to visualize what the tattoo would look like once finished. Scott pulled out a sharpie and began marking up different areas around the sleeve that did not fit in on his stencil. Chris was enamored with his process.

"Are you a smoker?" he asked with the sharpie lid still in his mouth.

"I am, yes."

"Awesome. Why don't you go grab yourself a smoke. We gotta give this stencil about ten minutes to dry before we can start."

Chris zigged through the mob of people and headed outside to the smoking section in front of the hotel. He promptly lit the cigarette fixed between his lips, knowing this would likely be the only cigarette break he was going to get the rest of the day. Chris took a long draw and flicked an ash into the nearby receptacle, being careful not to rub or smudge the stencil when he heard a faint woman's voice call out from behind him.

"Excuse me, sir."

Chris turned to face the frail voice that'd called out to him and found himself staring down at a woman clad in a floral pantsuit and a beige derby hat. She appeared to be in her sixties. Her skin was beginning to show signs of aging—slight wrinkles on her sun kissed skin and liver spots beginning to line her arms. Her gaze held a warm smile and large doe eyes.

"Hi! Uh, yes! How can I help you?" Chris asked, taken aback.

Her eyes shifted down to Chris's arms before focusing back up at him, her soft expression never leaving her face.

"I'm Linda. Linda Shaw," she said, her voice oozing with that southern charm Chris had heard so much about.

Chris smiled. "Chris. Chris Tillman."

The two shook hands, but Linda kept a firm, unrelenting grasp as she eyed up the stencil on his arm.

"Are you here for the tattoo festival?" she asked candidly.

Chris found her demeanor and her tight grip around his hand to be rather unsettling. He didn't want to yank his arm away out of fear that he may hurt the older woman. He could feel her artic blue eyes peering daggers into him.

"I am, yes," he replied with a forced uncomfortable chuckle.

"You know, the human body is a temple. You're desecratin' God's creation."

Her words were cold, like ice picks puncturing his insides. Chris began to realize the stories about being down in the bible belt might actually be true. This lady was crazy. He hastily yanked his hand free from her grasp. The move seemed to take Linda aback— an audible gasp escaping her lips.

Chris stifled a laughter—something he would frequently do in uncomfortable situations.

"I appreciate your concern, Linda," he said, finally breaking the tension.

Her eyes bore into his with a smoldering intensity—a look that betrayed the smile that slowly stretched across her face.

"I'm so sorry. I meant no harm," she said, throwing up cautionary hands with an unwavering grin. "But here, let me give you somethin'."

"No. Really, it's fine," Chris reasoned.

"Oh, bless your heart," she said as she rummaged through her purse.

Chris impatiently stubbed his cigarette out and waited. He half-expected her to pull out an old butterscotch candy with lint stuck to it.

"Here." She held out her hand and placed what felt like a playing card into his hand. "I will pray for you, honey."

Chris glanced down at the thing she placed in his hand. It was a prayer card. It had the name, *St. Bartholomew* on it, along with a prayer. Chris eyed it up pensively before peering over his shoulder to see Linda walking briskly toward the parking lot.

"What a fuckin' looney tune." He felt a wave of anger and promptly crinkled the prayer card up and tossed it into the receptacle next to him.

He looked back and saw her staring at him next to her car in the parking lot. He forced a fake smile and a half-hearted wave. She remained stone faced and still, her eyes never leaving him. Chris hurried back inside the hotel, trying to shake off the icy sensation soaring up his spine.

2

Back inside, Chris told Scott about his encounter with the lunatic outside.

"Are you serious?" Scott asked, pausing from tattooing with laughter erupting from deep inside him.

"Yeah, I was just as caught off guard as you are!" Chris laughed in return.

Scott was from Chicago and also traveled to be here for this event. He shook his head. "Man, I fuckin love it."

Scott was really getting a kick out of this story. He apologized after a moment and fired up his tattoo gun again, the buzzing sending a rush of excitement coursing through Chris' veins. To first-time tattoo recipients, the sound can send a flare of anxiety and fear, but for Chris—it was serene. A sound that told him he would soon be sporting some new artwork on his body.

The needle dug in as Scott began to work away. The fiery hot sensation of the needle dragging across Chris's arm as Scott worked on the outline kept him alert. He shook his head at the thought of Linda and her thinking he needed someone to pray for him, just because he was getting tattoo work done. The visage of her cold stare from across the parking lot still left his insides feeling rattled. He worked in the horror industry, but dare he say the glare of an elderly zealot creeped him out more than any book or movie he had borne witness to.

3

Time ceases to exist when you're getting a tattoo done. Depending on your pain tolerance, a few hours can feel like a dozen—or—the polar opposite if you were used to it.

When Scott finally finished the sleeve, nearly eight hours had passed. He sprayed the green soap solution on Chris' arm, carefully wiping away the blood and excess ink. Something about the smell of that solution always brought Chris comfort.

"Hop up and let me know what you think!" Scott said.

Chris eagerly hopped up from the chair and walked over to the mirror he had set up next to his station. He carefully twirled his arm around to look at the work Scott had put in. Chris' mind was blown. The amount of intricate details Scott had managed to squeeze in between all the faces and scenes from Chris' favorite horror films was staggering. It nearly rendered Chris speechless.

"My God!" was all Chris could say.

"You like?" Scott asked with a chuckle.

"Dude. You are an absolute rockstar!" Chris beamed, glancing over at Scott who was smiling from ear to ear.

"I'm glad. That was such a fun piece," Scott said, standing up to shake Chris's hand.

Normally a full sleeve would take two or three sessions. Scott's ability to work so fast with so much detail was one of the reasons he had become one of the biggest names in the industry. Now Chris could proudly wear Scott's art for the rest of his life.

They made small talk a little while longer before Chris handed Scott the large sum of money—with a hefty tip included. Scott thanked him and took photos and videos to share on his social media pages.

Chris couldn't believe it, he was going to be featured. That was such an honor. Scott then placed a clear adhesive called Tegaderm around his tattoo and explained the aftercare he recommended to keep his tattoos looking fresh long after they healed.

Chris was smitten. He couldn't help but to continually glance down at the artwork now covering his left arm. He shook Scott's hand once again.

"Thank you so much, Scott. I love it, man. Seriously!"

"It was my pleasure, Chris. Thank you for traveling all the way out here to get tattoo work done," he said.

Scott began sanitizing his work station. He said he had another appointment scheduled for tomorrow, as well. Chris wished him luck and darted off, ready to have his first cigarette since earlier. Hopefully without the crazy woman outside waiting for him.

4

After the long day, Chris had finally gotten checked into his hotel room for the night. He went upstairs, tested out his plush queen-sized mattress and took a shower—careful to not dredge his new tattoo under the running water for too long as he washed off with his soap.

Chris' stomach grumbled and he realized he hadn't eaten all day. He checked the time. It was a little after nine. He looked at the complimentary menus the hotel staff had left in the room. He didn't really want to drive anywhere.

After careful consideration, he pulled up the hotel restaurant's menu. It didn't have a ton of options, but an old-fashioned with some chicken wings would surely hit the spot. Chris closed the menu and threw on a loose-fitting Hawaiian style button-down shirt with skulls and roses adorning it, along with khaki shorts and a pair of white Hey Dude shoes.

The restaurant inside Waycraft was small and doubled as its pub. Every barstool around the horseshoe-shaped bar was filled, so Chris wandered to a nearby booth and took a seat. A cute waitress came over and introduced herself as Emily. She looked like the poster child of a southern belle. Her southern twang and sweet smile drew Chris in like a honeybee to a flower.

"I already know what I want," he said with a smirk. "I'll take an old-fashioned and a dozen of your spicy garlic wings, please."

"Comin' right up!" she replied warmly before whisking away out of sight.

Chris opened his phone and thumbed through his social media feed when he stumbled upon Scott's post from *Day One at the Great South Tattoo Festival*. Excitement thrummed around his insides seeing the photos and video of the artwork that was now attached to his body. Thousands of likes and comments piled into the post, and Chris couldn't help but to eagerly scour through them.

"Here you go, darlin'." Emily sat the glass of amber liquid in front of Chris.

Chris eyed the drink, impressed by the presentation. An orange peel lay neatly placed in the center of the glass, with a maraschino cherry resting atop the glass on a garnish pick.

"This looks wonderful. Thanks, Emily."

Chris plucked the cherry from its little metal skewer and popped it into his mouth with delight. He continued to scroll through the comment section of Scott's post while sipping on his drink. He was elated to see all the positive comments coming in about his tattoos.

Without missing a beat, Emily brought over Chris' wings and a second old-fashioned. He was taken aback by her service. He hadn't even realized he was nearly empty on his first drink, but she had been on top of it.

Chris dug into his wings. He was sure he was making a mess—but he was so hungry, and the sauce was so good that he didn't care. After he finished eating, he told Emily he would be right back and headed out to the restroom.

He hated to admit it, but those hotel chicken wings might just be some of the best he'd ever had. This had to be one of the best days Chris had had in a while. New tattoo work, delicious wings. He sighed as he pissed into the urinal. He felt warm. He felt happy. He felt at peace. The old-fashioned was doing its job.

When Chris got back to his booth, he sat down and realized he still had about half of his second drink left. He lifted the glass and downed the remains of the cocktail. Emily peered over at him from across the aisle and motioned to him, asking if he'd like another and he smiled and nodded. She returned a friendly smile and darted over toward the bar. Chris' eyes couldn't help but stare at her from afar. The way her hips swayed put him in a trance-like state until he noticed her.

Staring at him from a table on the opposite side of the room was Linda. Her eyes were glued on him, her face expressionless. Chris' blood ran cold. He could feel his insides tightening.

This was a staring contest he was okay with losing. He quickly pulled his phone out, attempting to ignore the ghastly stare of the old bag.

"Here you go, hon," Emily said as she slid Chris his third drink of the night.

Chris looked up with a weak smile and attempted to look around Emily to see if Linda was still there, but she was gone. He shook his head, attempting to loosen the cobwebs.

"Th-Thank you," Chris muttered.

"You're very welcome, darlin'. Nice tattoos by the way!"

Was she flirting? Or just being nice? Chris couldn't be sure. And to be completely honest, his entire equilibrium was beginning to feel *off*.

Chris lifted the glass to his lips with a shaky hand. It felt like the room was spinning. He couldn't possibly be *that* drunk already, could he?

He tilted the glass back, taking in a swig of the sweet cocktail and nearly dropped the glass on the table. He couldn't think straight. He dropped both of his arms to his sides, surveying the area in a state of confusion when he noticed a woman in a floral pantsuit walking toward him and sliding into the booth on the opposite side of him.

"Fancy meetin' you here!" she said sweetly.

Chris shook his head vigorously in a state of utter confusion.

"Y-You. . .you. . ." he stammered.

"You know," Linda said, shaking an orange pill bottle like a rattle. "You really should be more careful about leavin' your drinks unattended."

Chris wanted to yell. He wanted to call out to someone. The only thing able to leave his mouth was garbled gibberish. Linda got up from her seat and slid in next to him, placing an arm around his shoulders.

"Is. . .everything alright?" Emily asked as she walked up to the table.

"Oh, yes sweetie. I think my son had one too many drinks tonight. Can you bring me his tab? I will pay it for him."

"Sure thing," Emily replied in a friendly voice, ignoring Chris' slurred attempts at trying to ask for help.

"God bless you, darlin'," Linda replied.

As Emily walked away, Linda placed a hand under Chris' chin and forced him to look at her. "Now you just quit your belly achin'."

The last thing he remembered was her smiling face dancing around in his stupor before his eyes cemented shut.

5

When Chris finally stirred awake, he made the horrifying discovery that he couldn't see. Disoriented and his head throbbing, he attempted to move but couldn't. His limbs were stretched out and strapped down like he was standing in the shape of a cross. He sluggishly shook his head, realizing some sort of black bag had been slipped over his head. He wanted to yell, but felt a cloth tightly wound around his mouth.

Only grunts and groans of anguish could escape him. Chris yanked feverishly at his arms. They had been splayed out from his sides, shackled to some sort of plank. His ankles had been bound together and strapped to a wood plank, as well. The sudden realization that he was completely nude and bound in the form of a crucifix wasn't lost on him, considering the last thing he remembered was that nut job Linda spiking his drink at the bar.

"Well, Well, Well. Look who finally woke up," her voice said softly.

Chris grunted angrily into his gag. If only she could hear the venom behind the words he was trying to yell. Abruptly, the bag covering his head was torn away. He looked first at Linda, who was wearing a pure white gown, before his eyes averted to his surroundings. It took a moment for his vision to adjust in the dim lighting, but once it did, Chris' eyes grew wide with terror.

The small room was canvassed by the soft citrusy glow of white candles scattered around the room. What appeared to be animal skins plastered to the walls were anything but. A chilling realization that sent his heart and stomach into a spastic fit was that the surrounding walls were covered with human flesh, preserved and nailed to the walls. Every single piece had tattoos on it. Every single one. But something was off. Chris squinted at the preserved skin stretched across the walls. The style of the tattoos looked familiar. He was sure of it. Chris screamed into his gag as loud as he could—frustration and fear setting in. His words hung helplessly inside his mouth like a mumbled undertone.

Directly before Chris sat a shrine with a wax figure of what appeared to be one of Jesus' apostles. Rosaries, chains, and other religious artifacts lined the display. What troubled Chris the most was the flaying knife that lay front and center before an oval mirror. Chris tugged at his bonds, frantically glancing to and fro at the leather straps encasing his wrists.

"You know, I tried givin' you a chance. A chance at salvation. A chance to see the light. A chance at becoming closer with God. I gave you the opportunity to right your wrongs and it ended up in the trash can," Linda said coldly as she made her way to the shrine.

She stood in front of the shrine with her back turned to Chris.

He tugged fiercely at his shackles, his body tensing at the thought that this psychotic woman was going to kill him.

"Did you know?" she asked, slowly turning to face Chris, the long blade grasped between both hands, "that St. Bartholomew was so strong in his faith, that in the face of unrelenting anguish—he never wavered."

Linda took a slow, lurching step toward Chris.

"He was flayed alive for refusin' to renounce his faith. So, when I see a young man such as yourself—tarnishin' the sacrifice of one of the great apostles. It makes me a little angry." She took another agonizing step toward Chris.

The chill behind Linda's voice was absolutely haunting. This was the end of the road. Chris was hundreds of miles from home, and no one would even realize he was missing until it was too late.

"With your blatant blasphemous behavior, I must work as God's soldier, and a tax must be paid to right the wrongs of the sinners. Tonight, I will make an offering to Him. And well, sugar, tonight is not your night."

Linda lunged forward with a surprising quickness. She placed a hand on Chris's bicep and held it steady. Chris did everything he could to struggle and scream. He was completely and utterly helpless as he watched the gleaming blade make its way up to his arm. The pain was instant as the blade poked into his flesh. Chris screamed and howled in agony as Linda sliced the blade from the top of his shoulder down underneath his armpit. Chris could instantly feel warm blood pouring down his back and rib cage.

Linda aggressively grabbed him from behind his shoulder and yanked forward as far as his socket would allow before digging the blade in from the bottom near the base of his armpit and dragging the blade toward his shoulder in a swift slicing motion.

The pain was excruciating. Chris watched in horror as Linda repeated the process around his other shoulder. She then took the blade and sliced around his arms near the base of the leather cuffs.

"Almost done, hon. Soon enough, you'll be able to ask God for his forgiveness yourself."

The words sat in Chris' stomach like a rock. He felt like he was going to hyperventilate. His heart beating so rapidly, and sweat beginning to slick across his body, he was afraid he was going to pass out.

Linda sauntered across the room back toward the shrine. She

knelt down in front of the wax statue that Chris now attributed to being St. Bartholomew and began muttering a prayer. When she clambered back to her feet, she turned to face Chris. She was holding what looked like wire between her hands that were now encased in white gloves.

The visual of the cold, dead eyes of Linda, her gown covered with splatters of blood, and her vacuous stare and emotionless expression as she silently marched back toward Chris, sent him into another frenzied attempt at breaking free.

How could this be happening? Was this real life? Surely, he was still at the Waycraft Hotel having a nightmare in his room after his shower. The searing pain emanating from his arms was a stark reminder of the present situation. Chris knew fanatic zealots existed, but not like this. She needed to be locked away in a psych ward.

"Now," Linda said with a brief pause, "let's get the rest of that blasphemous skin off."

Without another word, she stalked forward and wrapped the wire around Chris's arm, tightening it with extreme force that caused Chris to yelp in pain and bite down on his gag. Tighter and tighter, she pulled the wire. Chris could feel millimeter by millimeter as the thin metal wire dug deeper and deeper into the skin around his new tattoos. Blinding white light lined his vision as Linda walked away from him, wire still in hand as she dragged it down his arm.

Chris vomited in his mouth, the gag keeping it locked in place and forcing him to swallow it. Blood began to pour out of him as she snaked the wire farther and farther down his arm. The last thing Chris saw before he passed out from the shock was the way his skin raised as the wire passed beneath it like a hot knife through butter.

6

Linda noticed that Chris was no longer conscious. It didn't bother her. This wasn't about pain or torture. She was doing God's work. She was making an offering to forgive the human race for their sins. She slid the wire down the remainder of Chris' other arm cleanly before pulling the wire free.

With a surgeon-like precision, she took a scalpel and sliced down the now loose flesh and peeled it away from Chris' hungry muscle fibers. She placed the carved pelt on a nearby table and walked back over to Chris. She placed two fingers up to his jugular and felt no pulse.

She knew she had a lot of work to do to dispose of the body and clean up the mess that was made, but she had one last thing to do.

She grabbed a handful of old rusted square nails and picked up the loose fillets from Chris' arms. She walked over to the opposite wall, where she promptly nailed them into the macabre shrine, and stood back to admire her offering. She sighed, feeling much better.

Linda slipped her gloves off, casually tossing them aside as she walked to the mirror and knelt before it. Her face, neck, arms and gown were covered in Chris' crimson gore.

Creeeak.

The door behind her opened. Moments later, she felt a hand grip lightly on her shoulder. She glanced up knowingly at her son, Scott, who smiled fondly down upon her. By the grace of God, he'd created another offering.

She smiled meekly at her boy and motioned for him to kneel beside her. Scott obliged.

They closed their eyes, bowed their heads, and prayed to God in unison.

"Dear Heavenly Father, please forgive us all for our sins. . ."

*John Ward is a horror author from Northeast Ohio. He lives in Canton with his dog, Bo, who is his best friend. In 2023, John decided to break into the horror industry by writing his very own middle grade horror series, Scareville! He wanted to bring back fun, exciting, yet spooky stories for young readers of the modern age, while also serving up nostalgia for the adult readers as well. Over the past few years, John has been busy typing away on the keyboard—completing nine stories for his Scareville series—with more on the way! He has also had three short story acceptances in anthologies so far—*Be Careful Who You Kill, The Skin Tax, *and* Keep Smut Out of Horror. *He just completed his debut adult horror novel—*A Blackened Heart, A Blackened Soul—*which will be released in January of 2026 through Crystal Lake Publishing.*

ONE ANIMAL DIVIDED BY HOPE

Jamal Hodge

Here, my love,
our world of tourniquets,
and lies.

Where storms never leave.
They tutor the torturer I buried
in the back of my skull.

Exhumed, cruelest decency:
It was never meant to be
by my heart, by my hand.

Time only sharpens some blades.
Torn apart, one kiss at a cry,

a single night together,
a final misuse,

turning wine into water,
left sober.

These civilities I extend,
a coat I lend only
when the weather's warm.

"I've missed you."

ONE ANIMAL DIVIDED BY HOPE

You opened your mouth,
and let the facts walk out,

Drooling wet slimy birth,
a banquet of our bones,

Chewed to pieces
within the curated patchwork
of memories, holding together
this Frankenstein all our own.

When I bare my fangs, yours grow.
Whose mirror flinches first?

We end as we began,
beautiful, tragic.

One animal,
divided by hope,

in each other's teeth.

Jamal Hodge *is a native New Yorker and an award-winning filmmaker, writer, and poet. A member of the HWA and SFPA, he's a Bram Stoker Award finalist, a two-time Rhysling nominee, a 2nd place Dwarf Stars winner, and a 3rd place Elgin award winner, and the author of* The Dark Between the Twilight *and* Everything Endless *(with Linda D. Addison) and editor of* Bestiary of Blood: Modern Fables & Dark Tales.

Jamal loves the broken things that want to be understood and the secret things that never bothered to hide. Through his writing, he aims to explore the paradox between suffering and meaning, using darkness to show light.

MINUTES LATER, ON THE ROOF...
AT LAST, SOME REAL HORROR! FLAMING DEATH BY METEORITE!
ARE YOU SURE THIS IS A GOOD IDEA?
I'M HOPING FARLES-CHORT'S LUCKY STARS WILL SHIELD US FROM THIS METEORITE!
"FORCING IT TO ALTER ITS COURSE IN ORDER TO SAVE HIM AND LAND HARMLESSLY IN THE BOG NEARBY..."
"...WHICH JUST HAPPENS TO BE OVERRUN WITH NEWTS!"
NO FLAMING DEATH BY METEORITE, AND NOW IT'S RAINING NEWTS, NOT FROGS, BUT NEWTS! I'M LEAVING AND I'M NEVER COMING BACK!
GUESS HE DIDN'T LIKE GETTING A NO STAR REVIEW FROM AN ACTUAL SHOOTING STAR.
HE FROGMARCHED HIMSELF OUT.
AND AFTER WE GAVE HIM FREE RAIN OF THE PLACE.
HOPE YOUR STAY AT HOTEL MACABRE WAS A FIVE STAR EXPERIENCE, READERS.

"To read without reflecting is like eating without digesting."

—Edmund Burke

THE END?

Not if you want to dive into more of Crystal Lake Publishing's Tales from the Darkest Depths!

Check out our amazing website and online store
or download our latest catalog here.
https://geni.us/CLPCatalog

We always have great new projects and content on the website to dive into, as well as a newsletter, behind the scenes options, social media platforms, our own dark fiction shared-world series and our very own webstore. Our webstore even has categories specifically for KU books, non-fiction, anthologies, and of course more novels and novellas.

Readers . . .

Thank you for reading *Hotel Macabre Vol. 2*. We hope you enjoyed this anthology.

If you have a moment, please review *Hotel Macabre Vol. 2* at the store where you bought it.

Help other readers by telling them why you enjoyed this book. No need to write an in-depth discussion. Even a single sentence will be greatly appreciated. Reviews go a long way to helping a book sell, and is great for an author's career. It'll also help us to continue publishing quality books.

Thank you again for taking the time to journey with Crystal Lake Publishing.

Visit our Linktree page for a list of our social media platforms. https://linktr.ee/CrystalLakePublishing

Follow us on Amazon:

MISSION STATEMENT:

Since its founding in August 2012, Crystal Lake has quickly become one of the world's leading publishers of Dark Fiction and Horror books. In 2023, Crystal Lake officially transitioned into an entertainment company, joining several other divisions, genres, and imprints, including Torrid Waters, Sinister Smile Press, Crystal Lake Comics, Crystal Lake Games, Crystal Cove Press, Crystal Lake Kids, Memento Mori Ink, and The House of Shadows & Ink on YouTube.

While we strive to present only the highest quality fiction and entertainment, we also endeavor to support authors along their writing journey. We offer our time and experience in non-fiction projects, as well as author mentoring and services, at competitive prices.

With several Bram Stoker Award wins and many other wins and nominations (including the HWA's Specialty Press Award), Crystal Lake puts integrity, honor, and respect at the forefront of our publishing operations.

We strive for each book and outreach program we spearhead to not only entertain and touch or comment on issues that affect our readers, but also to strengthen and support the Dark Fiction field and its authors.

Not only do we find and publish authors we believe are destined for greatness, but we strive to work with men and women who endeavor to be decent human beings who care more for others than themselves, while still being hard-working, driven, and passionate artists and storytellers.

Crystal Lake is and will always be a beacon of what passion and dedication, combined with overwhelming teamwork and respect, can accomplish. We endeavor to know each and every one of our readers, while building personal relationships with our authors, reviewers, bloggers, podcasters, bookstores, and libraries.

We will be as trustworthy, forthright, and transparent as any business can be, while also keeping most of the headaches away from our authors, since it's our job to solve the problems so they can stay in a creative mind. Which of course also means paying our authors.

We do not just publish books, we present to you worlds within your world, doors within your mind, from talented authors who sacrifice so much for a moment of your time.

There are some amazing small presses out there, and through collaboration and open forums we will continue to support other presses in the goal of helping authors and showing the world what quality small presses are capable of accomplishing. No one wins when a small press goes down, so we will always be there to support hardworking, legitimate presses and their authors. We don't see Crystal Lake as the best press out there, but we will always strive to be the best, strive to be the most interactive and grateful, and even blessed press around. No matter what happens over time, we will also take our mission very seriously while appreciating where we are and enjoying the journey.

What do we offer our authors that they can't do for themselves through self-publishing?

We are big supporters of self-publishing (especially hybrid publishing), if done with care, patience, and planning. However, not every author has the time or inclination to do market research, advertise, and set up book launch strategies. Although a lot of authors are successful in doing it all, strong small presses will always be there for the authors who just want to do what they do best: write.

What we offer is experience, industry knowledge, contacts and trust built up over years. And due to our strong brand and trusting fanbase, every Crystal Lake book comes with weight of respect. In time our fans begin to trust our judgment and will try a new author purely based on our support of said author.

To date we've published around 300 books, and with each launch we strive to fine-tune our approach, learn from our mistakes, and increase our reach. We continue to assure our authors that we're here for them and that we'll carry the weight of the launch and deal with third parties while they focus on their strengths—be it writing, interviews, blogs, signings, etc.

We also offer several mentoring packages to authors that include knowledge and skills they can use in both traditional and self-publishing endeavors. This includes Shadows & Ink Creators on our The House of Shadows & Ink YouTube channel and our Crystal Lake Academy.

We look forward to launching many new careers.

This is what we believe in. What we stand for. This will be our legacy.

Welcome to Crystal Lake Publishing—
Where Stories Come Alive!